CHINA CODE

Jeffrey E. Seay

To Don

Regards,

Jeffrey E. Seay

To the Men and Women of the
Naval Criminal Investigative Service
May they always be vigilant

CHAPTER ONE

February 20, 2005

"Control." A two-syllable declaration was delivered in monotone.

"This is tech support." The voice was wavering; an anxious comeback. For some reason Ryan Henderson expected an immediate explanation for his dilemma.

"Tech support, this is an unscheduled call on an open line. Are you compromised?" The tone was again flat, but direct.

"I don't know...maybe. The delivery was not made." His voice rose half an octave.

"Calm yourself, tech support, and explain." Quiet but commanding, it was clear that Control didn't have any answers.

"The guy didn't show. I was there ready to take delivery, but the dude did not come on board." Taking a breath, he wondered if he should include the other stuff as well.

"Is that all?" Control asked, as if sensing the indecision.

"Heightened security...more than I've ever seen for a place like this." Revealing additional details on an open line made Ryan even more nervous.

"Go on."

"The place was crawling with Feds and auxiliary security. I don't know if it had anything to do with me, but they were definitely cops and they weren't there for the free food."

"You're safe. Go back and resume your duties. We won't initiate contact again until you're reassigned."

"Huh? Reassigned?"

"Control out."

That's just fucking great.

Back on board, standing in his stateroom, he contemplated jumping ship. He believed any minute the Navy cops, NCIS, would come knocking at his door. Evaluating what that meant, he sat down, face in hands, resolved to wait it out.

He said I was safe.

Reflecting on the shit he was steeped in, he mentally retraced the events leading to the call. He'd waited over an hour that evening to be contacted by a man known only as Mr. Smith, before he walked off the ship. Certain the meet was a bust, and fretting he was somehow at fault, he had no choice but to report the mission fail status.

A civilian computer support technician, Ryan Henderson had been embedded aboard the USS Blue Ridge, the U.S. Navy's Seventh Fleet command and control vessel, for the past six months. An employee of the government contractor supplying and installing system upgrades for navigation and communication, he served as a technical consultant, trainer, and systems handyman.

A Mr. Fix-it, who through some considerable effort, made himself an indispensable member of the crew. He not only solved problems related to upgrade integration, but lent his considerable computer and network savvy to iron out bugs in unrelated—and often highly classified—system applications. This included occasional assists with issues concerning Seventh Fleet components. In his brief stint, Henderson gained access to all critical system hardware and most of the associated software.

Ryan had a genius-level IQ, maintained a rigorous physical fitness regime, and exhibited a work ethic second to none. Viewed by most as a truly a great guy, he was friendly, helpful, and unassuming. He was also a traitor, bound inexorably to a group that had him by the balls. Like an indentured servant, Ryan did their bidding without question.

An organization called The Board was Ryan's benefactor. They found him sitting in a federal penitentiary doing hard time for some playful hacking involving a few multi-national financial institutions.

As a grad student at MIT, he found scholarship money didn't touch his numerous social demands. A couple of fraudulent wire transfers helped augment those needs. His rationale during interrogation: "Hey, the money's insured. Besides, they shouldn't have made those types of withdrawals so easy."

The Board made him an offer he couldn't refuse. To get his record expunged, obtain a high paying job and his PhD status reinstated, all he had to do was run an errand once in a while for the enigmatic organization. He learned too late he'd sold his soul.

The original port-of-call for the Blue Ridge was Port Klang in Malaysia, but the Blue Ridge rerouted to Singapore because of a security threat specifically targeting the Seventh Fleet. The scuttlebutt floating around the ship was about Al Qaeda-planned attacks. Henderson got the straight poop later from a techie working in the same space as the on board NCIS Special Agent—referred to as the Staff Counterintelligence Officer. Apparently, three or four NCIS agents had been killed while conducting a routine advance for the ship's visit in Kuala Lumpur. Whether it was terrorist related, no information came out, but orders from PACOM shit-canned Malaysia from the schedule.

It didn't take a genius to realize his real mission objectives were in a holding pattern. His only instruction from Control was to sit tight; a new plan was being developed. Twelve hours before the ship pulled pier side, Control contacted him with a bullshit cloak and dagger scheme featuring some dude named Smith. They scheduled the meet for 19:00 on Sunday the 20th during the Blue Ridge big top reception. With a cockamamie code to confirm authentication, Ryan was supposed to ask Smith how he spelled his name. *I guess it could be with a "y".*

As Henderson thought back, he considered Smith's no-show a lucky break. The heat he spotted wasn't there to thwart terrorism. If he accepted the package—a wristwatch with a thumb drive—his next port-of-call would have certainly been Leavenworth. After a sleepless night, he went to work still apprehensive the jig was up, until he learned of a shootout between NCIS and local thugs in an inner city park. That action was somehow related to the capture of two U.S. Embassy employees in Kuala Lumpur suspected of espionage. The target of their evil plot being the USS Blue Ridge.

He was indeed safe for the time being. The next port was Zhanjiang, in southern China—the location of the South China Sea Fleet for the People's Liberation Army Navy. The Blue Ridge was underway by 08:00 and Ryan heard nothing more about the incident in Singapore. In fact for the three days they cruised north into the South China Sea, he heard nothing at all. Everyone was friendly and the job orders kept coming, but something had been said—a directive given changing the environment. Ship security had tightened, and areas on the vessel he used to have free access to, particularly on decks occupied by Seventh Fleet personnel, now required escort.

Mid-day on the 24th, the ship pulled into port at the commercial docks in Zhanjiang. The PLA Navy, in a demonstration of cooperation with NCIS port security requests, locked the berthing area down. Guard posts were set with armed sentries, and access to and from the ship required appropriate ID and attire. Bus transportation into the city for Navy personnel was provided by the husbanding agent, and taxis roamed the area to pick up stragglers.

Ryan sat through yet another NCIS port security briefing before disembarking, not sure where he should go. Control hadn't contacted him yet. He had no idea when he would receive a new assignment, either in this port or the next, but he needed to be ready. He packed his gear. Once he had it sitting on the deck in the middle of his stateroom he realized he couldn't carry it off the ship. There was too much. To avoid any suspicion, he limited the carry to what could reasonably be viewed as a three-day bag. Even that was pushing it.

Most of the Blue Ridge crew knew his routine. It rarely varied at any of the ports along the southern swing, and he never used hotels. Any sightseeing or nightclubbing he did rarely went past midnight. If he missed the last bus, a taxi got him to the ship before the first bell on midwatch. There wasn't an officer of the deck who didn't consider the him a role model for compliance to curfew.

While authorization for overnighters did not present a problem for Ryan as a civilian, breaking the routine was noticed. The people he worked with would know if he had a hotel reservation. That's why it was a notable surprise to the OOD on the quarterdeck when Ryan Henderson asked him for a hotel recommendation.

The second stop for the squid bus was the Crowne Plaza—a bona fide Southeast Asia five-star—running special rates for the honored Blue Ridge guests. The hotel staff spoke English, and the manager, a loquacious Brit, always took the time to greet the first few busloads of the boys in blue. When Ryan presented his passport at check-in, he discovered a room already booked in his name and a message waiting for him: a note with a phone number and a Chinese prepaid calling card.

The room had a good view of the hotel's fifty-meter pool and the harbor channel a few kilometers in the distance, but he barely noticed. As soon as he walked in he closed the curtains and picked up the phone on the desk. The call took several seconds to connect, being routed through several switchboards.

"Control." Again the single pitch.

"I'm in the room at Crowne Plaza." *He ought to know my voice by now.*

"In one hour the front desk will notify you of a mail delivery. In it you'll find your instructions."

"Where am I going?" Control rarely provided details, but now that he was alone, Ryan needed a sense of assurance.

"You'll find your instructions in the envelope. You have the rest of the day to relax and enjoy yourself." The line went dead.

An hour. Instead of hanging up he pushed the disconnect lever until he got a dial tone, then hit a single button on the cradle.

"Health Spa," a young, perky female voice answered in English, but with a heavy Chinese accent.

"I'd like a massage."

"Certainly, sir. We'll send a masseuse immediately.

How will you be paying, sir?"

"Charge it to the room."

Ninety minutes later, he held a large manila envelope containing a Canadian passport in the name of Randall Ian Hodges, and ten thousand renminbe—Chinese currency also known as yuan. Along with the cash and new identity, he found a train ticket. He was going to Shanghai, via Guangzhou, leaving at ten that night.

The passport had been stamped for exit and entry more than a dozen times. While the Z visa had expired, he found a permanent residency card for Shanghai tucked between the center pages. The note said all the residency certificates were current and waiting for him in his apartment in Pudong. His new Control would also be there upon arrival.

In China permanently. Fuck...

CHAPTER TWO

June 1, 2005

Ruben Carver's gaze slowly shifted from the document he was reading to the man in the doorway. Ray Benson, the Supervisory Special Agent for counterintelligence, stood looking at him as he leaned back in the only chair in the room, feet propped on the desk. Until the interruption, which he knew was going to be unpleasant, Carver had been examining the contents of a red paper file marked SECRET NOFORN.

"Hey, Ruben, welcome back." Benson wasn't exactly the jovial type, and rarely outgoing to Carver. Case in point: Carver came off administrative leave two days prior and Benson was only now acknowledging his return.

"Hey, Ray, what's up?" In Ruben's mind, when Benson came around it was to complain about him or one of his team. It was either that, or Benson had been told to use him for some task. Since he was being nice, Ruben figured it must be a real shit detail. *You got to be kidding.*

Ruben Carver, a journeyman Special Agent with the Naval Criminal Investigative Service, spent three months "on the beach" waiting for the results of a 2B—an internal affairs investigation by the Inspector General's

Office. Three and a half months earlier, Ruben lead a small team from Yokosuka, Japan, to Singapore, to investigate the deaths of three special agents, and the disappearance of another.

A particularly bloody week, those responsible for the murders were identified, and—in a few minds—dealt with injudiciously. In doing so, the team uncovered an espionage ring involving two U.S. Embassy employees, a now-deceased husbanding agent, and the suspected collusion of one of NCIS' own. The final piece of upside being collaboration with the Singapore police in dismantling an organized crime syndicate.

The downside to all the hard work and stubborn determination was Carver's suspected tally during those seven days—he'd been credited with eight dead gang-bangers, and the disappearance of seven bent Royal Malaysian Police Officers. There was also the little matter of the Legal Attaché in Kuala Lumpur being beaten and held captive.

The final IG report capped its findings with a comment about the impropriety of placing a number of special agents and local law enforcement officers at risk, both physically and professionally. In the end, Ruben received a letter of appreciation from the Director of the FBI for the rescue of his man in Malaysia, and a letter of caution from the Director of NCIS for being a pain in the ass.

"I can see you're settling back in okay." Benson's sneer was the closest semblance to a smile he could muster.

"Whaddya want, Ray?"

"What, I can't come around for a little social call?"

"You and I both know the only time you give me a reach around is when you've already got my pants down. So, what's this about?"

Benson dropped the friendly face and stared back at

Carver, then stated in a neutral tone, "We've got a lead from headquarters that has something to do with Chinese hacking, and Ed wants you on it."

"Well, my man, the cyber crime specialist is across the hall. Why aren't you talkin' to him?" Ruben referred to Frank Rogers, a former procurement fraud agent who moved over to cyber in the late nineties. A guy with demonstrated talent in tracking network intrusions, and a fondness for kernel-based spyware and surveillance tools. An interesting character, Rogers' transfer into the discipline was a good move for him and the Service, unlike a number of his compatriots in the field who were there for the kiddy porn investigations.

"We already have. There's an aspect of this lead that needs a personal touch."

"I suppose Ed's waiting for us?" Ruben stood, closed the file, and dropped it in an open safe drawer. Pushing it home, he yanked the lever to set the locking bolts. As he spun the dial, he turned to Benson. "Let's go."

The NCIS Far East Field Office aboard Yokosuka Naval Station—also known as Fleet Activities—had twenty-five special agents working in the Service's primary core missions. They investigated felony crimes and fraud, conducted protective service and force protection, ran foreign counterintelligence, counter-terrorism and cyber operations, and managed an array of other mission support responsibilities. Just like the other field offices around the world they were under-staffed and under-budgeted. Somehow they got it done.

No secret, really. Ruben had served with a few whiners and malcontents, but the majority of pistol packin', badge totin' SAs were fully aware they had the coolest jobs on the planet. He was no exception. In his seventeen years with the organization he cross-trained in most of the core disciplines, and had working knowledge of the rest.

He took a right out his door and followed the hallway around to the left. Instead of going directly to the office of the Assistant Special Agent in Charge of Counterintelligence, he took a detour to the coffee mess. Benson didn't bother to follow—he made his own coffee and Carver understood his distaste for forced civility. Alone for a few minutes, he could mull over what he remembered about Chinese hacking and information piracy in general.

Ruben reflected on his first Japan tour beginning in 1991, at Misawa airbase in the Shimokita peninsula. He remembered those days as his quiet period. Stuck in country at the end of the cold war, it was a three-year counterintelligence assignment, that turned into five. A two-man office, he and his partner were busy with sexual assault allegations, theft cases, and dead bodies. He calculated they processed fourteen death scenes in the years he was stationed there. Four or five that were truly gruesome.

The information collection program was fairly aggressive, with frequent visits to the police departments in Japan's seven northern prefectures, along with some door knocking at the Public Security Intelligence Agency and the Maritime Self-Defense Force. Carver had a few bullshit counterintelligence operations targeting the Chinese and Russian Consulates in Sapporo, but the shitstorm he started with the CIA, and the catalyst for his understanding of Chinese tech transfer gambits, was his intelligence collection operation against Russian merchant seamen.

Soviet merchant ships frequented the port in Hachinoe, seventeen kilometers south of the base, bringing in cornmeal and timber. Before the wall fell, all the ships had political officers aboard to keep the crew in line. Contact was spotty and difficult, but Carver raked in some good information. Most of it intel on domestic port conditions, commercial shipping, and foreign trading activity in Chinese and North Korean ports. Areas that were closed to the West.

After the fall, the political officers disappeared and the void was quickly filled by members of Russian organized crime. Mercenary, to say the least, Ruben could get those Ruskies chatty for chump change. The reporting improved almost overnight, with additional intel on Russian criminal activity in Japan. Drugs, guns, and blonde prostitutes, all at very reasonable rates. Everything was hunky-dory until the CIA started asking questions about where he was getting the information.

In those days, NCIS received nearly all funding for its CI and collection operations from the CIA. Langley, always suspicious of its junior partner's conscientious spending, periodically conducted audits to make sure they were getting their money's worth. When they found out what Carver was doing, notwithstanding the solid reporting, they got a major case of the ass.

The Agency prohibited NCIS from using foreign assets in its operations without strict CIA oversight. The Assistant Special Agent in Charge of counterintelligence at the time needed a backhoe to dig him out of the mountain of shit deposited in his lap, and Ruben found himself sitting on his hands.

After several weeks, he finally got the go-ahead to continue domestic collection operations and had to decide where to refocus his attention. With a little help from his buddy on the other side of the base, a special agent with the Air Force Office of Special Investigations—or OSI—he was introduced to a new, but quickly growing threat: Chinese academics in Japan.

The OSI agent, Bob Logan, a fifty-year-old Air Force retiree with a long history in the land of the rising sun, was a prolific collector. The Air Force had a sizable cache of goodies and source funds to spread around, which helped. Until years later, in light of a number of bribery scandals, it was common practice—and expected—to ply their sources, referred to as customers, with a twice yearly round of gifts. It reminded Ruben of tithing. While NCIS could only afford booze and logoed trinkets, OSI was handing out sets of golf clubs and sportswear, and picking up the tab at expensive restaurants and hostess clubs. With Bob's fluent Japanese and deep pockets, he was the life of the party.

Ruben, always willing to accept a helping hand, allowed Bob to mentor him in the fine art of tapping the inscrutable Nipponese for information. After the merchant-shipping debacle, Bob threw Carver a bone. He'd developed some intel on the activity of thousands of Chinese grad students and research scientists in country on grants and fellowships. The Japanese government opened the doors to these scholars at the end of the eighties as a form of exchange with China because of the increased business and trade between the two states.

The Japanese saw a utilitarian benefit in the arrangement. After opening factories in a number of China's provinces, production was hampered because of significant barriers in language and culture. They believed once these students and researchers completed their studies, they'd go back to China, language trained and indoctrinated in the island country's business model, and bring order out of chaos at the factory level. It certainly seemed like a good idea.

The Chinese didn't argue. They recognized a nice set up. The cooperation did, in fact, extend to better economic Japan-Sino relations, but Ruben mused that just like any miracle drug promising a harder dick or better bowel movement, the side affects made it difficult to enjoy. *The Chinese weren't called the yellow peril for nothin'.*

The intel Ruben and his buddy Bob received—and what they reported in tandem in a series of Intelligence Information Reports—concluded the Chinese had the proverbial keys to the store and were robbing the Japanese blind.

By the mid-eighties, Japan's Ministry of Education had established a computer network called the National Center for Scientific Information System or NACSIS. It connected all the universities and several of the large corporate donors' research facilities, where they shared data and mainframe time. A pure research tool for university faculty, and the erudite pursuits of corporate R&D.

Another system, created later in the decade, was the Widely Integrated Distributed Environment, also know as WIDE. More of a grass roots network, unaffiliated with NACSIS, it connected a smaller number of academic institutions, but included a larger corporate membership. The creators envisioned a commercial application to networking and reached out, cross border, using Internet protocol to communicate with organizations such as the U.S. National Science Foundation.

The Chinese students and researchers, while in Japan, had full access to both systems. Since the Chinese loitered far behind the other industrialized countries in science and technology, and didn't have the economic strength or wherewithal for development on their own, they felt justified in stealing whatever they could.

According to two or three sources within the Public Security Intelligence Agency, they were indiscriminate.

They copied everything they accessed to floppy disks and walked them into the Chinese Embassy in Tokyo, on what became regularly scheduled visits. The embassy staff would then bundle the disks with hard copy notes to explain disk content, place them in diplomatic pouches, and send them to Beijing on a weekly basis.

The reason the PSIA felt compelled to reveal this activity was because much of the information these particular foreign academics were helping themselves to happened to be licensed U.S. Technologies. The military critical, and dual use variety. Apparently, no one cared until they realized the volume of data being sent to the middle kingdom. It wasn't a single burlap bag with "D Pouch" stenciled on the side. Surveillance detected material stacked on covered pallets going out by the truckload.

A half-quart-sized coffee cup in hand, Ruben headed for Ed Johnson's office, still thinking about the Chinese move into the cybersphere. The global history of computer hacking, going back thirty years, was replete with the likes of post-pubescent pranksters, disgruntled employees, and cross border activists causing trouble. They defaced websites, crashed servers, stole or changed data, and in some cases went as far as robbing banks and threatening national security. Americans, Russians, Romanians, Croatians, Brits, Filipinos...the list went on and on, but no one outside the military talked about the Chinese. Before 1996, they weren't much of a threat.

After the advent of the World Wide Web in '96, however, the Chinese hacking attempts grew so pervasive, that, by 2005, some folks believed they owned the NIPRNet—the DoD Nonsecure Internet Protocol Router Network. More amazing is they did it through run-of-the-mill social engineering and phishing. After years of security briefings that included computer and email security awareness, people continued to open attachments containing rootkits, worms, or bagels that, within a few hours, infected entire networks.

As Carver walked through the door, Frank Rogers and Ray Benson were standing at Ed's desk. He couldn't help wonder what a semi-literate computer user could do about a problem that had the best experts in the field on the ropes.

"Morning, Ed. You wanted to see me?" Carver always walked with care around Ed Johnson. Although not afraid of the man, he simply didn't like the hassle of dealing with his short fuse and bellicose temper tantrums.

They came into NCIS the same year. Ruben in Long Beach, California and Ed, farther north in Port Hueneme. A smart and aggressive investigator, Ed made a name for himself early, in General Crimes. He developed the lasting relationships he needed for promotion, though, in foreign counterintelligence, tying himself to the coattails of the rising stars during his tour in the Philippines.

Along with a gruff personality, he had the political acuity, outside NCIS, of a bull goring a cape. He made the mistake, on at least two occasions, of going toe-to-toe with the CIA Station Chief on a matter of "principle". The loss of those duels nearly cost him his career. They also put an immeasurable strain on the integrity of the NCIS CI brand in the Far East, and his relationships with his sugar daddies in DC.

His management style didn't garner much popularity, either. Discussions turned to brow beating quickly if he didn't like what he heard. Ruben figured Benson's bridle towards him had something to do with the daily assaults he suffered in meetings with Johnson. The kind of badgering Ed was capable of would wreck anyone's confidence over time, but for some reason, he left Carver alone. A fact that irritated Benson.

"Yeah, Ruben, come in and close the door." Leaning back in his ergonomic chair, he rested his hands on his chest, fingers interlaced. "I don't know how much Ray has filled you in, but we received a lead from headquarters this morning I'm assigning to you."

Ruben noticed Ray's reaction, subtle but telling. As the Supervisory Special Agent, the responsibility of delegating work, load-balancing cases, and reviewing operational planning and execution belonged to Benson. The fact the assignment was coming directly from Johnson meant Benson took it in the ass yet again.

"Okay, what is it?" Ruben made eye contact with his boss in spite of the reflection off of Ed's thin, round tortoise shell glasses.

"According to our cyber squad at the DC Field Office, a Chinese hacker has successfully acquired the technical data and schematics for a new drone program."

Carver felt like yawning. "Drone technology? Chinese hacking? We're talkin' issues so common they're almost passe." Ruben, rarely negative about anything that would get him out of the office, couldn't mask the incredulity.

Always ready to take his shot and impress the boss, Benson piped in, "This is a matter of national security, asshole." Benson preened and Carver became even more skeptical.

"Look, Ray, you may think something like this is extraordinary," Ruben said, being purposely patronizing, "but the number of savvy hackers sitting behind the bamboo curtain eyeballing the U.S. can't be counted. Not only do they have their own version of the NSA, apparently located in Shanghai, but they've also got private, semi-private, and government controlled individuals and groups scattered all over the country. What do you think I'm going to be able to do?" He could tell the only person listening was Frank, the computer geek. "At the end of the day, all of it is state sponsored. It's still a communist country."

Johnson, surprisingly calm in a conversation that was getting testy, replied, "We're aware of all that. Frank here keeps us up to speed on China's capabilities. The drone technology was classified secret, but the problem goes beyond that. The hacker knew exactly who to target at the government research facility, as well as at the contractors'. On top of that, he found an exploit in the SIPRNet protocol that got him into several classified databases." Ed paused, peering at Carver. "You're going to Shanghai to find this guy. We want to know who he works for and where the data was sent. The folks back in DC don't believe he's Chinese."

"Why's that?" Ruben's curiosity grew.

"Because he whaled them through a series of highly technical, and highly literate, emails to accounts that are LIMDIS. Someone with access had to give them to him." Johnson referred to email addresses with limited distribution.

"Okay, I got it. You realize I can't just buy a ticket and go to Shanghai. The PLA know who I am. We've had our differences in the past. I'll have to go through the standard visa protocols with a letter of invitation, and declaration of intent for the purpose of the visit. That has to be managed through our embassy in Beijing. What's the cover story?"

"Advance for the visit of the Commander, Seventh Fleet next month." His reply was uttered with a straight face.

"Okay, but there's got to be something else. I just got

back from admin leave after a nasty 2B. I'm on the Director's shit list. Why me?"

"Three weeks ago, the Army sent in one of their best CI guys. He was trained at the Farm. His mission was the same as yours. They found his body floating in the Huangpu river last week."

Fuck me...here we go again.

CHAPTER THREE

The Dragon Lady

His hand shook as he tried to swipe his access card. Anxiety-driven perspiration dripping down his back, he gripped the small, flat piece of plastic with both hands to guide it into the slot. As the door opened he glanced at the nameplate set at eye level—Randall I. Hodges, Regional Manager - Power Elite Computing—and once again questioned the direction of his life.

His mind dipped into its memory reserve as he fumbled the card on the floor.

They said I was safe.

He arrived in Shanghai as Ryan Henderson, on an airline named after the city. Not a great traveler by air at the best of times, it was a two and a half hour white-knuckle experience from Guangzhou. On edge at arrival, he forgot about the new moniker and spent another hour in the Hongqiao airport waiting for his ride. A driver with his name on a placard finally approached him, and life as Randall Ian Hodges began.

When he left Zhanjiang—certain at the time NCIS would somehow ferret him out—he was thankful The Board found him new digs, a new identity, and a suitable occupation. He accepted the instructions for his escape and assignment with reluctant relief. A simple gig, with an opulent lifestyle compared to the half-year he lived aboard the Blue Ridge, he trusted the outcome would finally give him both physical and financial independence. He still didn't understand, however, why he couldn't do their bidding in the good ol' U.S. of A.

It took over an hour of city driving to get to his drop off in Pudong. The driver didn't leave the wheel, just handed Randy the card key for the elevator and his door, and drove away. His only luggage was a backpack, nearly empty, save for a copy of Eric Steven Raymond's manifesto, *How To Become a Hacker*. A magnum opus to legitimize a questionable activity and hackneyed expression. Randy thought it pretentious and self-aggrandizing, but, in some way, it helped him keep his head in the game. *I'm a hacker, not a cracker...*

He also had Simon Singh's, *The Cracking Code Book*, a nice history of cryptography and cryptanalysis. A toothbrush, a pair of dirty gym socks, and an iPod rounded out the inventory.

He rode the elevator to the twenty-fourth floor, and on exit, found only two doors; one on either end of the hallway, both unmarked. He tried the door to his right but the light on the card swipe blinked red. Using binary logic, he went down the hall and tried the other one. A green light, the last color he'd see after gaining entry. To describe the interior in a word: white. Not ivory, cream, or Navajo. Stark, almost blinding white. Every room, every piece of furniture, fixtures, and drapes. Even the floor was quarter-sawn oak, bleached colorless and lacquered.

The single feature of the space that didn't make him feel like he was standing in a light bulb was a floor-to-ceiling, wall-to-wall picture window. A panoramic view of a forest of high-rise apartment buildings stretched out before him. From his vantage, the city to the north was partially visible, with a sliver of green, between the concrete, he would soon learn was Century Park. He noticed one other thing as he peered through the glass. Like a grainy photograph lacking the customary hue, a brown-gray haze lay draped over the sprawl.

I'm in hell.

With his head edging toward despondence, he dropped the backpack in the middle of the floor and went looking for the bathroom. Never a favorite with the ladies, he spent the last several years trying to strip himself of a dweeb persona. Lasik surgery, classes on men's fashion, a lean, cut physique…he was getting there. Even in the Pen, running from the hirsute love-starved, he obsessed on image reconstruction. Convinced Goldstein and Maslow had missed the boat on self-actualization, he embraced the notion to reach one's full potential, particularly with regard to sex, you had break the code on cool. Pretty simple. It turned out to be a painful and expensive road to pave.

Now this. As he squatted on the porcelain, forearms on knees, he wondered, *How you s'post to pull serious trim when you live in a cancer ward?*

The next forty-five minutes heartened him somewhat. In the bedroom closet hung a dozen suits, three sports coats, slacks, and starched shirts on the left side. On the right, an assortment of in-style casual wear. *How'd they know my size?*

There was also a tie rack with a dozen Jerry Garcias, along with the standard spot, paisley, and striped. A two-tiered stand was filled with various dress and casual shoes, and trays of folded sportswear. The dresser drawers contained underwear, socks, and accessories from belts to cuff links and collar pins.

The refrigerator, freezer, and pantry were also well

stocked and the kitchen accoutered with enough professional quality pots, pans, and cutlery for him to think about learning how to cook. Perusing again the arctic tundra-colored apartment, he figured it wouldn't be a bad idea to take a few lessons since he'd probably be eating alone a lot.

As he stood leaning against the counter by the kitchen sink, he realized he'd reached the end of the line. The instructions didn't take him any further, and once again he was stuck waiting. He noticed something else about his sterile environment: no telephone, television, radio, or clock. The only feature in the place that gave him a sense of time and space was the picture window.

Dude...Rod Serling didn't die...he moved to Shanghai.

Not hungry, he found the liquor cabinet while rooting around, and after pouring three fingers of Jameson over ice, he headed back down the hall. Time for a bath and then sleep. A good plan interrupted by a knock on the door.

Before he could respond it opened and in stepped another surprise. Taller than Randy by at least two inches, even without the six-inch stiletto heels, she wore a full-length black sleeveless dress with mandarin collar, and a slit up the right leg to the thigh. Her black hair was thick, straight and glossy, and parted slightly off-center, falling down her back, waist-deep.

Slim but curvaceous, Randy was on his way to horn dog heaven until she turned and faced him. Not ugly. On the contrary—a stunner, but scary. Han Chinese with the classic heart-shaped face. A chin that could put out an eye and cheekbones sharp enough to shave with. Her eyes, with epicanthic monolids, were hooded slits, slanted at thirty degrees; her heavy, drawn-on eyebrows shaped at the same angle. A bijou mouth, with full lips like ornaments painted bloodred, sat pouting under tiny oval holes. The nostrils were elfin folds of flesh.

She said nothing as she slowly pushed the door closed.

What does the nice dragon lady want?

"Hi, Randy Hodges. May I help you?" He patted his chest with the palm of his right hand during the self-intro.

Without uttering a word she sized him up head to toe. Then, spinning left on the soles of the nude pumps, moved into the living room as if gliding on ice.

A year ago, Randy would have stormed after her demanding an explanation. Now, tired and in a funk, he shrugged it off. "Make yourself at home! There's beer in the icebox!"

And for the next thirty minutes he soaked in a hot tub with his cold whiskey.

Skin soft from the bath, he performed a full body shave, then went to the bedroom and picked out a few duds with relaxing in mind. A white linen, short sleeve Cubavera with a blue L-shape engineered stripe; cornstalk linen drawstring pants; and a pair of blue Tommy Bahama beach dweller slip-ons. He didn't bother with underwear. *Gee, I hope I'm not showin'.*

Still wanting a nap, he made his appearance. Dragon Lady was sitting on the sofa, legs crossed, staring out the window. Hodges poured himself another three fingers, this time neat, and settled in the armchair to the woman's right.

He detected a subtle mix of vanilla, musk, and something else. Nose slightly tilted, he thought, *What is that...ginger?*

He said nothing, focusing instead on a point in the achromatic wall. Hodges discovered during the desperate years of his geekhood that conversations with the opposing gender required the ability to listen or at least give the impression of listening. He learned three very useful expressions handy in all occasions: "Really?", "Is that right?", and "No kidding?". If a guy wanted to be daring he could also throw in "No way!" but usage could be a little tricky.

"Mr. Hodges, why have you kept me waiting?" British English, husky voice. No inflection to signal her mood.

"I'm sorry, was I expecting you?" Randy was perturbed yet attracted. She had to be fifteen or twenty years older than him, but he couldn't help wondering what she looked like naked.

"I am Control."

"No way!" He threw it out there too soon.

"Excuse me...what did you say?" Flashing coal shards flickered behind narrowed slits.

Uh-oh. "Sorry, no offense intended," he said, trying to regroup. "Control's always been a disembodied voice and never a woman."

She simmered. A constant and natural state, he would soon learn. "The Board felt it necessary for you to have a physical presence."

"Logically, it seems a good idea. I don't speak Chinese. I have no idea where I'm at, except it's somewhere in Shanghai, and no clue why I'm here. I'm assuming it's got something to do with computing, maybe networks, more than likely hacking. Am I close?" Hodge's natural state was wise-ass—a factor of his nerdified DNA and one of the major obstacles in attaining cool actualization.

"You will find your instructions waiting for you in your office," she said, staring through him as opposed to at him. "From now on I am your connection to The Board and you will follow my instructions when they are not available in writing. Is that understood?"

Hodges drained his glass and, with a palm on his chin, twisted his head until his neck cracked. As he stood, his reply was more of a declaration. "I'm hungry. Let's see what's in the fridge."

A try at granny's knickers no longer held any interest for him, but as he started for the kitchen she cut him off. The diminutive mouth with the full round lips now stretched into a grimace across clean, even teeth. The blow on the side of his head was hard enough to knock him down. Dazed, he realized as he gazed up at her that she'd hit him with her fist.

"Did I make myself clear, Mr. Hodges?"

"Lady, you can beat on me all you want but I don't respond to that kind of foreplay."

The next strike was a kick to his abdomen, sending him sliding to the back of the sofa.

"You're not hearin' me, Madame Butterfly. Homeboy ain't playin' your game." He was ready for the next assault. Control had removed her shoes, rolled her dress to her hips, and moved in for a heel strike. Hodges caught her foot with both hands and spun on the lacquered floor, sweeping her planted leg at the ankle with his left foot. She slammed flat on her back and Randy heard the air rush from her lungs.

Up on one knee, he rubbed the side of his head above his left ear, and stared at the woman as she performed a straight-legged kip to a standing position.

What is her problem?

As she came at him again he held up his hand, palm out. "Stop! What's the matter with you?"

"Do you understand me?" Her voice came out breathy.

"Listen, I don't want to get into who can kick whose ass the hardest. I understand you. Now you understand me...I don't work for you. You're just another one of The Board's hired guns. You're here to watch my back and make sure I get to work on time. I will not take orders from you." Now on his feet, he took a boxer's stance with hands up. "Seriously, do you really want to do this?"

He could see she pondered the question, cocking her head to the side, reassessing the young man in front of her. She dropped her hands and uttered, "Fine."

Grabbing her shoes, she didn't bother unrolling her dress as she went to the front door. "I'll be back in two hours to take you to the office."

"Great! I'll have a list prepared of the things I want, starting with a color palette."

"What's that?" Eyes pierced through him once again.

"I want the apartment painted. I can live with the furniture but this whole THX 1138 thing has to go."

"I don't know what you are talking about."

"Look around, lady. Do you live like this?"

"You will address me as Control."

To Randy she sounded like one of the nuns at his parochial grade school. "Oh, for cryin' out loud, Control is a voice on the phone. Give me a name."

"You may call me Miss Qu."

Suzy fucking Qu. "Okay, Miss Qu. I'll see you in a couple hours... Oh, and I want a clock, a TV, and DVD player..."

The door slammed.

Flicking the light switch, Randy was back in the present. Two florescent tubes fluttered then popped to life, illuminating the four-meter cube he'd occupied for three months. Centered in the gray, softly lit cell was a Formica table with a single drawer. On top, a quad array of seventeen inch Dell flat panel monitors, an adjustable-angle split keyboard, wireless mouse, and speaker phone. Under the table was a computer tower he pieced together with parts he found locally. With dual AMD 4GHz processors, two ATI video cards, sixteen gigabytes of random access memory, and five terabyte hard drives in a Linux MD RAID 5 array with a hot spare, it got the job done.

As he flopped into the black high-back, it rolled away from the work station. The thermostat was set at twenty degrees Celsius, but even with the dry, cold air blowing on him the sweat continued. Somehow, he'd been tagged.

His operation ran through dozens of proxies scattered through five countries. The sniffer he loaded on target systems was a variant of snort and dsniff, buried in a rootkit that was designed to detect and defeat anti-malware applications by spoofing a legitimate root directory executable file. He grabbed data at the source, before the packets were encrypted, and flagged the information he wanted with a subroutine that attached a separate IP header and packet to a legitimate email. It went out like a blind copy, avoiding detection by a packet logger. It was a beautiful thing.

Even if the intrusion was somehow discovered and cyber sleuths tracked the packet through the myriad proxies, the proverbial buck stopped at China's door. The core of this onion he created was in a server at the PLA's own Unit 61398, China's cracker central for all things network nefarious.

With the help of Miss Qu, Randy learned the Chinese used the Linux distributed Community Enterprise Operating System, better known as the CentOS, on all their boxes. Turning the tables on the zipper-heads, he had Qu craft a sweet spear-phishing message to one of the operators in the unit with admin rights. The guy thought he was running a valid update from a CentOS repository. It looked and responded just like the Yellow Dog updater, the default package manager.

What he actually installed was a custom kernel with a

modified network module. At that point Hodges owned the kernel, and controlled the file system. All of his hacking and cracking was managed through the PLA system. He even used their hard drive storage for his big jobs. It couldn't have been a better set-up. Yet, he'd been found out. By the U.S. Army, no less.

Over the speakerphone came a smoky timbre. "Mr. Hodges, you'll find your new target in the drawer."

"I'm not doin' it today." A quivering intonation exposed his frustration and fear.

"We have already been through this. Your security is assured."

"Yeah? I've heard that before. You ever hear the expression 'waking the sleeping giant'?"

"The American agent had gotten too close. The Board sanctioned the solution."

"Don't you get it? To keep our operation on a roll, I have to know how the guy found out about me. If, in fact, he did. I need to know what kind of footprint I'm leaving...how they ran a trace. If the U.S. Army can do it, so can the Chinese."

"I will make a few inquiries with our sources inside the PLA. Perhaps they can shed some light."

"PLA? You can't go the PLA with this. I operate off one of their servers."

"They are aware of your presence. The Board and a number of Chinese Communist Party members have a...cooperative in place. We exist at their largess."

Oh, shit! "Listen up, Mizz Qu, Americans don't like losing their people. They will send more, and next time it won't be to just shut us down. They're gonna be pissed off and lookin' for some payback."

"In that you are correct. I have anticipated the response and will continue to clear the field. You will now read your instructions and get to work."

Fucking bitch! I can't deal with this.

CHAPTER FOUR
Hassles

Four o'clock in the afternoon and the gym was packed. Carver hoped, as he walked in the locker room, he'd be able to get a solid hour on the weights. Not a chance. With the bodies on the machines and benches, even a simple back and biceps workout would take a couple of hours. Too long. Too many things to do. After his meeting with Johnson and Benson that morning, he spent six hours trying to get the wheels in motion for the trip. Two of those hours he spent with Frank Rodgers, trying to get his head around a few things Frank had uncovered.

The intrusions the Army had under investigation did indeed involve the compromise of drone technology, but not from military research facilities. The targets for the data uploads were two of the Army's primary contractors, Raytheon and Northrop Grumman. A system administrator in one of the civilian sites picked up two anomalies on IP headers while testing a packet logger the company considered using. When the news filtered to the Army's program manager at the Pentagon in Arlington, Virginia, the order went to all the contractors to check for the same type of incongruity. Several were identified, but the data regarding the classified tech rang the bell. Nobody, until then, had successfully breached the classified databases.

Ruben didn't understand the particulars of the tracking technique, but apparently the brainiacs at NSA pinned the IP header destinations to China. That bit of deduction didn't surprise or confuse anyone. The location and purpose of the building in Pudong, where the data wound up, was well known in military cyber circles. It was home to hundreds of PLA computer specialists and hackers. What Frank didn't understand, and what no one was fessing up to at the Army's 310th Military Intelligence Battalion, was the reason the Army agent was there in the first place. In Frank's droll opinion it was a waste of time, money, and the life of a good man.

As Carver strolled out of the MWR fitness center, he thought about Frank's rant: "The right way, the wrong way, and the Army way...". There was something else, though. Something he understood from the half-dozen years he labored at that same till. The Army sent the agent into China looking for something, or more specifically, some*one*, who couldn't be identified any other way. The same reason Ruben was now being sent in.

When NCIS cyber specialists discovered servers beaconing data at the Laboratory for Autonomous Systems Research, a department of the Naval Research Laboratory, all indications suggested they had been active for weeks. The bug the intruder used was identical to those found at Raytheon and Northrop Grumman. Johnson said the hacker who targeted the scientist at LASR had produced a whale so convincing, he thought nothing of opening the attachment. Even the documentation it contained was valid. Dated, but valid.

The offending email was discovered in the NRC server archives. Analysis of word usage and syntax garnered a consensus. Whoever duped the scientist was a Westerner, probably an American, and male. Even though the person responsible for the intrusion could be anywhere in the world, NSA expressed confidence he resided in Shanghai. Once the data reached Pudong, it didn't go anywhere else. Ruben didn't need the Army's confirmation the dead agent in Shanghai was there to bag the dude.

Something else about the scenario itched at him, but he couldn't quite claw it out.

June was the rainy season on the Kanto plain, and as Ruben headed back to the office on foot, a crack of thunder signaled a downpour. He jogged as far as the Chief Petty Officers' club before it fell in sheets.

The NCIS Far East Field Office was across the street, on the second deck above the Naval Security Group Activity and Afloat Training Group WestPac. Something about the sprint up the stairs to the door finally dislodged a cognitive connector. The dark spot he had floating above his brow all day fizzed bright, like a match being struck.

Before going back to his cubbyhole, he walked around the corner to the Sensitive Compartmented Information Facility, a fancy term for a large, windowless room used for all things top secret. They referred to it as the SCIF. Ruben figured he'd find Junior Prosser inside reading the TS message traffic. A habit of his this time every day.

Prosser received the Special Agent of the Year Award for the very same Southeast Asia operation Ruben just flashed on. Dropping his cell phone in the tray by the door, Ruben buzzed himself in. As expected, he found Prosser lounging in front of the Joint Worldwide Intelligence Communications System terminal, also known as the JWICS.

"Hey, Junior."

"S'up, Rube?" Junior looked a mess with bloodshot eyes, necktie askew and shirtsleeves jammed up his arms to the elbows.

"You have a rough night or what?" As Ruben got closer he could smell the broad Junior had been with from five feet away. "Whoa, boy, you look like shit and smell like bad fish. You need to go home and wash the stank off."

The two analysts housed in the facility snickered.

"Wha...?"

"You heard me. You're stinkin' up the place."

"I didn't...know..." Prosser stuck his nose in a pit.

"Well, never mind for now. I need you to do something for me." Ruben crossed his arms and waited for his words to register.

"Yeah, okay. What?" Extending his arms over his head, Junior pulled and stretched until his eyes focused.

An unresolved issue from the Southeast Asia caper five months prior, and this new assignment, now waved for Ruben like a lantern. "You remember the computer geek off the Blue Ridge who went missing in Zhanjiang a few months back?"

"Yeah, of course. The contractor everyone wanted to believe was the mole Smith was supposed to contact."

"That's the one. I need you to pull all the information you can on the guy. I want a background profile with pictures, work history, schools, any law enforcement run-ins, shit like that."

"That's a big job. When do you need it?"

"Yesterday." Carver stared at the floor, ruminating. "With his access the guy must have had a clearance. Most of what I'm asking for would be in his SF-86. Check with the DSS and see if a background investigation had been completed. The guy may have been operating with an interim clearance. It takes more than two years to fully adjudicate clearance applications these days."

Slack jawed, Prosser peered up at Carver. "You doing that cognition thing—pulling pieces of a puzzle out of thin air?"

"That's right, Junior, and what I want you to do is use that stellar counterintelligence acumen you've been officially recognized and rewarded for to get me some answers,pronto."

"Okay, okay...I'm on it."

Carver was an Okie in the truest sense of the word. Born the year Dwight Eisenhower was elected to his first term and Mr. Potato Head was introduced, Ruben was the oldest of four children, raised in a ramshackle three-bedroom in a wide spot in the road south of Seminole called Bowlegs.

His dad, a former Marine and combat vet, worked as a roustabout in an oil patch leased to Sinclair Corporation. In Ruben's mind there never lived a coarser, more uncouth individual than his old man. At the same time, however, he believed a more courageous and strong-willed son-of-a-bitch never walked the earth. Compared to his pop, as gross and disagreeable as he could be, Steinbeck could take Tom Joad and shove him up his ass.

When Ruben was four, his mother came down with rheumatic fever and suffered a stroke that stole her ability to use the right side of her body. During the years it took to relearn how to walk and talk, his father doted on her, but Ruben was sent to live with his grandmother.

A strict, bible thumpin' authoritarian, she took him under her wing and through her tutelage he developed a love for learning, and an appreciation for good table manners. She was a knuckle banger, though, and Ruben found himself in a situation where, if he didn't find a way to memorize scripture along with his times tables, his fingers would have been too bruised and crippled to write his name or throw a baseball.

Prosser used the expression "cognition". A term Ruben heard after he grew to adulthood to describe what he could do starting in grade school. He developed the ability to chunk information in such a way as to give him an enormous working memory.

Throughout his formative years he taught himself how to parse information into useful deductive strings almost instantaneously. Mathematical formulas, random number sequences, pages of a book, TV dialog...it didn't matter. He had a way of grouping information contextually that allowed him to remember everything he saw, heard, or read.

When he turned nine he went home to help his mother and watch over his little brother, Claude, a carefree and rambunctious five-year-old. The next eight years taught Ruben some hard-learned lessons in responsibility and accountability. That period of maturation and life experience added to the cognitive exchange going on between his ears, and became the catalyst for his knack of entering a state of intense clarity.

It was most effective under duress or in stressful situations. The answer to a vexing problem came to him so quickly the people around him often scoffed, declaring he'd crapped the conclusion. Even if he happened to be correct. He had school psychologists, and later, Army shrinks, try to define the phenomenon as pattern recognition, high level gestalt effect, even epiphanies. Ruben didn't care. He didn't suffer from any delusions about being a genius, in the classic sense of unprecedented insight or creativity. He just knew how to remember shit and apply it to his circumstance.

Back in his office Carver picked up the handset from his STU-III desk unit and punched in the number of the Defense Attaché's office in Beijing. He'd already dialed the digits earlier in the day and talked at length with the Naval Attaché, Captain Roy Williams. They needed to get the process underway to obtain a letter of invitation from China's Ministry of Foreign Affairs. Without it, there'd be no visa for entry.

Ruben waited as the phone rang a half-dozen times before it connected.

"Commander Williams speaking, this is an unsecured line."

"Hey, Roy, it's Ruben. Can you go secure?"

"Hi, Ruben...yeah, just a sec. I have to get the STU key out of my safe."

After about a minute, Carver heard the unmistakable sound of a safe drawer sliding open.

"Okay, I'm back. The key's in and ready to go."

"I'll push secure on this end." Carver watched the digital read-out, and within thirty seconds it read: line secure. "Can you hear me?"

"Yep, a stable connection."

"Have any good news for me about the letter of invitation?"

"We finally got the PLA to acknowledge the request. It may take forty-eight hours to get the letter signed and forwarded to the Chinese Embassy in Tokyo. I know from our conversation earlier you've got your boss up your ass to make it happen faster. Have you got your visa request prepared?"

"I'll fill one out as soon as the letter of invitation is ready and waiting for me. If my experience with the folks at the embassy holds true, they'll probably dick me around for a week before they're ready to issue the documentation."

"I hear ya. Is that it?"

"No, I've got another request. Can you get a list of registered expats living and working in Shanghai?"

"Sure, do you have a time frame?"

"Not really. While his actual entry would be sometime in February this year, I'm not sure that would be helpful."

"Why's that?"

"It's not likely he's traveling in true name, and if he's got back-stopping the entry dates would show him landing much earlier."

"That's going to be a long list."

"Yeah, more than likely." Realizing the size of the order, he shifted his approach. "Is the Army Attaché in?"

"Sure is. How do you think he can help?"

"The MI agent who was killed in Shanghai had to go through the same process I am. Ask your Army counterpart if he got a similar request from his guy about American expats."

"Sure."

"In particular, find out if the agent focused on anyone. It could even be the company he works for or his line of business."

"I'll see what I can do."

Ruben cogitated for a few seconds before continuing. "Do the expats register with photos?"

"Don't know. It can be done online so I don't believe it's necessary."

"Are the Chinese providing information on the progress of their death investigation?"

"Nope. We're like a patch of mushrooms to those assholes. They keep us in the dark and feed us shit. That case will never be solved."

38

"What about the Army or Air Force? Do they have more agents coming in?"

"Kinda tough right now. The Chinese are scrutinizing every visit request closely. Yours will probably be approved because of the Admiral's visit next month."

"Do what you can to expedite the process. It's a hassle but I appreciate it."

"Oh, almost forgot. You need to come to Beijing first. The Defense Attaché wants to meet you, as does the Legal Attaché and the Chief of Station. They received a briefing on your Singapore adventure and would like to lay out some rules of engagement."

Great. "I'll buy my tickets as soon as the visa's in my passport."

As he put the phone in the cradle the idea of his first stop being Beijing irritated him. On second thought he changed his mind. He figured the folks at the embassy had more to say about the dead agent than they were letting on. Asking the right questions would likely jar some recollection.

Ruben rolled his chair to the door, opened it, and yelled into Frank's office.

"Yo, Rodgers, you in there?"

"Whaddya want?"

"With the work you've done on the MI angle, where was the agent stationed?"

"Fort Meade, but I believe he got his marching orders from the Army Cyber Command at Fort Belvoir."

"If I located his command support, do you think someone there would talk to me?"

"Not a chance. They don't play well in the sandbox— you already know that. With those pricks, if you ain't CIA or NSA you ain't shit."

Yeah, the right way, the wrong way...yada yada. "Well, they may get more friendly if they find out I'm the only game in town."

"What does that mean?"

"Never mind." Ruben closed the door and rolled back to the desk. He opened his SIPRNet email box and typed a note to Jason Hartley, the GS-15 in charge of NCIS CI operations globally, referred to as Code 0022. Out of courtesy and good sense he cc'd Johnson and Benson.

CHAPTER FIVE

Fatal Attraction

She waited until the exact moment the conference call was to begin before she joined.

"Good morning, Qu." The words were spoken with halting modulation, a slight echo, and metallic tenor, a bad connection on the secure line.

"Good morning." The dragon lady, always reserved during the weekly report, gave the impression she had better things to do.

"We're pleased you continue to control Mr. Hodges' production. The results are within expected parameters." The remark, while benign, contained an unspoken "but".

Get to the point. "Maintaining focus is problematic, but I've found the more complex the target, the easier to manage his inherent fear. He tends to obsess until he finds a solution."

"Yes, you've shown a deft hand. However, there is another issue we need to discuss."

Spit it out. "Please be direct." The words judicious, but pressed. Patience was not an attribute she extended to mincing conversations.

"We have some concerns about the way you handled the sanction. It was to appear as an accident. Our friends have informed us the body shows signs of extreme interrogation. There is also the matter in which you deposited the remains."

"The instruction I received implied determining what the man may have discovered. He proved to be more resilient than your intelligence indicated. I applied techniques necessary to elicit believable responses. I suppose we could have handled the disposal in a more efficacious fashion."

"What did you find out?" The question exhibited a shared impatience.

"He was fishing. Analysis of the hack on the defense contractor in the U.S. suggested native American English incongruous with the beacon destination. Hodges was not identified."

No response, only a soft hiss. She wondered if the connection terminated. She opened her mouth, but before the words formed the voice spoke again.

"There is another problem."

Finally, the tail of the fox. "I'm listening."

"As expected, the response to the agent's demise was a number of entry requests by individuals from each of the U.S. Military establishments. The Air Force and Army visa applications have been denied." There was another "but" resting like an unwanted pregnancy.

"I'm still listening."

"The Navy has presented a compelling reason for its visa application. Approval, while pending, will be granted. The person coming is someone we've had the displeasure of encountering before. An irritatingly willful individual, he is a special agent with the Naval Criminal Investigative Service. While not necessarily the reason for the failed mission in Malaysia, he was certainly the destructive force behind the collapse of our operation there."

It was obvious the agent was a source of considerable annoyance, judging by the way the voice spewed the statement in a single breath.

Impressive. "What is his name, and what do you want me to do with him?"

"His name is Ruben Carver. He is traveling on official business, which means there will be surveillance not only by the PLA, but most likely the Ministry of State Security as well. From what we understand, the Chinese believe he has successfully run operations in country. They have not been forthcoming in regard to what those suspicions entail. We suspect Carver was running counterintelligence operations under the nose of the MSS." The speaker paused as if checking his notes.

He continued. "Yes, well, at any rate, they don't care for him any more than we do. However, he has not as yet been declared persona non grata. We suspect the Chinese wish to catch him *in flagrante delicto*. It is for this reason they've been adamant about you not killing him on their patch. They have, for all intents and purposes, staked a claim. If you elect to eliminate, it has to appear accidental—to everyone. Our friends will, of course, suspect you. Providing them with plausible deniability, or better yet, convincing evidence to the contrary, will help maintain our associations."

I like this Carver already. "I understand. Is he traveling from Washington DC?"

"No. He's stationed in Japan at the NCIS office on the Yokosuka Naval Base. One more thing, Madam Qu. If you miss, he'll come after you. Set your calendar for our regular briefing—same day and time next week. If the situation changes, and requires an earlier call, please follow the incident management guidelines provided for this project." No salutation—the call terminated with a dead line.

* * *

She remained seated, sipping tepid jasmine tea from a thin glass mug, reflecting on the discourse. Once again she'd been given the green light to approach this new threat at her discretion. Pleased they placed that much reliance on her ability to deliver, the issue of local stakeholders and their claim to this Ruben Carver was a conundrum.

Qu hadn't been completely forthcoming with Hodges. Contrary to what she advised the hacker, who had become her albatross, the PLA had no knowledge of his activities. For his—and her—health and welfare it needed to stay that way. There was no PLA contact with whom she would confer regarding the American Army agent. Just as her intimate encounter with the delicious Yank the week before could not be known to the communists, neither could her sudden growing interest in Carver. Her little white lie to Hodges was necessary to tighten her psychological grip on a surprisingly slippery psyche.

Tapping the armrest with the nail of her right index finger, she began the exercise. Firm but soft, with a high back and adjustable head and armrests, Qu designed her chair for relaxation and meditation. It gave her a sense of reclining in an upright position, her feet flat on the floor. It supported her weight with comforting assurance, yet was pliable and giving along her thighs, lower back, and the base of her neck. She sat without the distraction of feeling the chair.

The room was a fifteen-cubic-meter windowless shell. Sound-proofed but wired for sound with speakers and microphones embedded in the walls and ceiling. A pure, flat white, with her chair the only piece of furniture visible. She controlled panels in the walls from keypads located in compartments at the end of each armrest.

This was her living room, meditation center, gymnasium, dance studio, and office. Raised in a classic Chan Buddhist environment, fused with Maoist indoctrination, her meditation techniques were pragmatic, comfortable, and effective; never a spiritual étude, played for spurious enlightenment. For Qu, solving problems didn't rest solely with the intellect and subject matter knowledge. She relied with confidence on her *Qi*.

She didn't view it as the "life force" dictated by the monks she suffered under growing up—that came through external sources she discovered in puberty. Her meditative state unlocked that part of her brain where intuition resides. Physiologically, she understood what took place. Relaxation and controlled breathing released serotonin and melatonin, as well as neurotransmitters such as endorphins and gamma aminobutyric acid, or GABA. The hormones helped clear the mental clutter and provided the sensation the mystics referred to as a flow of energy. A pleasant, but unnecessary, side effect.

What she was capable of went beyond what modern psychology called recognition primed decision making. The visceral, gut reaction to an analytical process. One hemisphere of her brain gave her the empirical, rational options to problem solving—linear, with multiple vectors. In her meditative state, using the other hemisphere, she could direct her *Qi* against the quandary like a scalpel, dissecting the divergent parts of the plight with precision.

Her *Qi* immediately added perspective and volume. Qu saw it as the difference between studying a map of a city and being in the city walking the streets. When she came out of a meditative exercise, as she did now, the solution invariably presented itself.

Slipping from her seat, she touched a button on the

outside of the left armrest. A faint change in air pressure occurred as a large wall panel opened and the chair rolled into the vacant space. As the door slid closed she assumed the mountain pose, *Tadasana*. For the next twenty minutes she performed a yoga routine, beginning with the forward bend, her face between her straight legs, *Uttanasana*, and then the three warrior poses, *Virabhadrasana*.

Now finished, she didn't bother with further relaxation. Rather, she stepped out of the office into the apartment that shared the floor where Hodges lived. Visually spartan, the only furniture in the rest of the place was in the bedroom—a wood frame with a futon mattress, and a thin Sferra Savoy queen-size cashmere blanket. With a secular mindset, she in no way attributed her lack of interest in accumulating things with spirituality. She realized, however, the asceticism in her youth may have planted the seed that would one day grow into personal choice. In her mind, it was easy to keep clean.

She also preferred to go without clothes, and lived naked in her space, dressing only for conference calls with video feeds. The only aspect of her life she couldn't will into submission was her sexual appetite. Through her fifty-two years, she researched, explored, and experimented to find the partner or activity that would sate the *eros*. Ultimately, like everything else in her life, she discovered a simple truth: she liked to get laid and found it more convenient and compatible with her lifestyle to just pay for it. In her experience, working with a professional always proved satisfying.

After her shower, she donned a saffron blouse and drawstring pants, and went back into her office. A remote control hung on the wall next to the entry. She thumbed in a code and the section of wall hiding her throne opened. Within a minute she was mounted, and looking at a sixty-inch flat-panel screen.

"Wèi." A long angular face, high cheekbones, and hooded eyes came into focus. A baldpate, with a number one cut on the sides and back, his skin was the color of tarnished bronze.

In Mandarin she said, "Hello, Feng. It looks like Tokyo agrees with you."

"Qiu Hu, I hope this is a wonderful surprise." Feng didn't bother to mask a circumspect attitude.

"Relax, baby brother. This is a simple request." *I could always make him cry.*

"You shouldn't call me here. There might be people around." His mewling tone came from a down turned mouth.

Always with the whining. "You wouldn't have picked up if there were. Now listen, this is important. An American by the name of...do you have a pen ready?"

"Yes."

"...by the name of Ruben Carver, will be submitting his visa application within the next few days. You may have already received his letter of invitation. I need you to send me a color scan of his application and passport as soon as it is submitted."

"Is that all?"

"You need to call Mom. She complained the last time I talked to her that you're not staying in touch."

"I've been very busy."

"Feng, be the good boy and call your mother. If you don't I'll come for a visit and dial the number for you."

"That won't be necessary. I have to go. Do you need anything else?"

"How's that wife of yours? I haven't noticed her snooping around lately."

She could sense him bristling, heard it in his voice.

"You leave her alone. Mother wouldn't like it if any harm came to her."

"Listen to your big sister and get me the information." She touched a button on the armrest console and the screensaver appeared.

After the lengthy email to Hartley, Ruben threw in the towel and went home. He wanted to spend the evening at his club in Tokyo. He and a retired Air Force OSI agent pooled their money to invest in a live blues club just after Ruben's return from an Iraq deployment. With a former Tokyo police officer as co-signer, they opened on a back street in Nishi-Azabu.

It was supposed to be a swanky part of town, but to anyone who'd spent time in Tokyo—or any town in Japan, for that matter—it all looked pretty much the same. While sections of the city did attract the crowds, such as Shibuya, Shinzuku, and Roppongi, exclusivity was determined by who lived, or hung out, there. This part of the metropolis was the haunt of politicians, sports personalities, celebrities, and the generally famous or wealthy who didn't want to be bothered by the mobs in Roppongi or Shibuya.

For Carver, it was a matter of convenience. The club was a five-minute walk from a small U.S. Army-run compound known as the Hardy Barracks, the only place in central Tokyo were the American military could land choppers. It also housed the OSI and Army MI detachments, a two-man office of NCIS, the *Stars & Stripes* newspaper production site, and the Japan base of operations for the Naval Research Laboratory.

The barracks facility it was known for ran like a hostel for military personnel who came into the city to party down. Carver parked there for free and often crashed on the sofa in the NCIS office when he'd drunk too much to drive.

He planned on taking the stage with his band that night, for three thirty-minute sets. Unfortunately, he couldn't afford that kind of "me" time and had to cancel.

After throwing a TV dinner in the microwave, he took a shower and started organizing the crap he would take to China. In bed by ten, he was up at the butt-crack of dawn and in the office by seven.

A knock at the door. Ruben turned to see Junior leaning against the frame, three or four pieces of paper in hand.

"Whaddya got, champ?"

"I found some information on the contractor who went missing off the Blue Ridge."

"Great, let's hear it." Carver spun his chair to face Prosser directly.

Junior wheeled his in and sat down. "Okay..." Prosser stared at the top sheet for a few seconds. "The dude's name is Ryan Henderson. Here's a photo." He handed a scanned black and white image to Carver. "He went aboard about five months before the start of the southern swing. September ninth, 2004, to be exact. You were right about the interim clearance. The cursory they did for his hire didn't pick-up any criminal record. No wants or warrants." Junior scanned the sheet and continued. "PhD in Computer Science from MIT..."

"Who'd he work for?"

"Uh, he worked for a small subcontractor called Power Elite Computing. The home office address is listed in Boston." His eyebrows arched and his speech became slightly halting.

"What else?" Ruben didn't need a crystal ball to tell him Junior discovered a missing piece. Prosser liked things in order, in a columns-and-rows-fill-every-box sort of way. Ruben could tell he'd stubbed his toe on something.

"Just a couple things...like the company. It has a website, corporate registration, all the normal stuff. Taxes are paid on reported earnings of five or six million every year..."

"So what's bugging you?"

"The only contract I could confirm this company has, or had, both government and private, was the Blue Ridge. Henderson's SF-86 shows him employed by Power Elite since 1996." Another pause.

"Why are you pingin' on that?"

"Because he worked nine years for a firm on contracts that didn't actually exist, or at least can't be confirmed. The listed corporate officers are either dead or residing out of the U.S., and Ryan Henderson appears to have been the only employee."

"Good, we're on to something. The company was a shell, but for who?"

"Don't know. So, what are we on to?" Yawning and rubbing an eye with the knuckle of an index finger, Prosser leaned back in his chair.

"Let's assume Henderson was the plant. He was working for someone who wanted him to install some pretty nasty malware on the systems aboard the Blue Ridge. He was supposed to receive the virus, or whatever it was, from David Smith, the Cultural Affairs Officer stationed at the embassy in Kuala Lumpur. When Mr. Smith fails to deliver, Henderson sees the writing on the wall. Afraid he's going to be found out, he jumps ship at the next port-o-call, Zhanjiang. So, what does he do?" Ruben peered at Prosser over tented fingers.

"Hey, man, this is your story. What does he do?"

"He leaves Zhanjiang, probably with a new identity in place, and makes his way to Shanghai. The same folks who hired him for the Blue Ridge gig have set him up in the big city to start a hacking campaign. See where I'm going with this?"

"Yeah, pretty thin. You've got nothing to support it."

"We got the right time frame, a guy with the skill sets, an organization with resources to finance it..."

"What organization?" Rubbing his nose and shaking his head, Prosser wasn't buying it.

"Yeah, well, you said the guy was a PhD candidate at MIT, right?"

"Uh-huh."

"Send a lead to Boston to have an agent contact his thesis advisor. We're assuming he was going by the name Ryan Henderson at that time. A fair assumption since his resume and SF-86 would list something easy to confirm. His college transcripts might even have the name of his advisor."

"Then what?"

"Come on, Junior, did you leave your brains on the pillow last night? Get a copy of his project proposal or his dissertation. Give it to the same analysts who determined the hacker was an American male, and find out if they believe it's the same guy. We also want to get his advisor to provide us with a bio on him. Determine his habits, likes, dislikes, family, girlfriends or boyfriends, and find out where they're located. We'll send leads to have 'em interviewed."

"Okay." Prosser squirmed in his seat.

"As part of the lead to Boston, have an agent go by the address listed for Power Elite Computing and see if they're still in business. If so, have an interview sheet prepped with questions to ask."

"Ya know, I can't send a lead without an OPEN." Junior referred to the NCIS documentation necessary to initiate a case.

"Grab a new case control number and put Henderson in the Subject block. Reference the 'ONLY' Singapore put out about his disappearance, and in the 'Purpose' paragraph outline our theory."

"Hey, man, it's your theory."

"What? Junior, this your chance at another plaque on the wall. I need you on this, pal."

"Bullshit. You just want me to manage the paper—again." Prosser's head drooped with his chin resting on his esophagus. With his arms crossed over his chest, he extended his legs one ankle on top of the other.

"Look, I have to prep the advance on the Admiral's visit to maintain my cover. I'm still working on the Army angle and I've got to get my visa application in and approved. I need you to run some of these other issues to ground so I have somethin' to work with when I get in country. It's some critical shit, bud."

"I'm on it, but you owe me—again."

CHAPTER SIX

June 2, 2005

By 09:00, Carver received a heads-up from CDR Williams the Chinese issued the letter of invitation. It was waiting for him at their Tokyo Embassy. Due to the frequent trips into China since 2000, Ruben kept a small stack of visa request forms already filled out in the bottom drawer of his desk, each one stapled with a Xerox copy of his official passport photo page. With one of those, and two passport-sized photographs he snipped from a strip he kept in the top drawer, he was good to go.

He hadn't heard from Hartley yet about a contact at Army MI, and Junior was plowing ahead on the Henderson angle. The Consular Section of the embassy stopped accepting visa applications at noon, so he had to hustle to make it. The sooner he attempted submission of his package the quicker the visa cha-cha started. The Consular Section always refused acceptance on the first try, the excuse usually being failure of the U.S. Embassy to provide written verification of official business. Then there was always the matter of a typo either in that document or the letter of invitation, if it could be found. The process invariably took four days. No more, no less.

As he headed for the door, Benson cut him off. With jutted jaw and furrowed brow, his skin was tight across his forehead.

What did I do now?

"What's the idea of enlisting Prosser to help you out on your China mission?" Benson spat the words.

Carver spoke in a measured tone, with a steady, careful response. "There's lots to do and very little time to get it done. I need Junior to do some research and send some leads."

"He wrote an 'OPEN' for an inquiry on Ryan Henderson. How is that related to your case?"

"Ryan Henderson is the guy we're lookin' for." *Make it simple for the myopic.*

"What? How did you make that jump?" A small vein on Ray's forehead pulsed.

"Did you read the 'OPEN'?"

"Yes, I read the paper and I don't agree with the assumptions. I'm not gonna approve sending it."

As they locked eyes Carver had to restrain his reaction. Arguing with this asshole would get him nowhere. He had to be on the road now if he wanted to submit the visa application before the window closed for the day. He spun, and walked away with crisp, long strides.

"Hey, don't turn your back on me. I'm not finished."

We'll see. Carver came to a halt in front of Johnson's door. Ed looked up from his monitor. At first it was only Ruben. Seconds later, Ray, in an obvious snit, was at his shoulder.

"Rube, have you upset the Supervisory Special Agent for Counterintelligence?"

"Yeah, same ol' shit different day. I have to get to the Chinese Embassy before it closes. I got no time for a question and answer session with my main man here." He threw a thumb in Benson's direction.

"Wait a minute!" Benson elbowed his way into

Johnson's office.

"Hang on, Ray. What's the beef, Rube?"

"I need your official approval to use Prosser for support on this China gig. I need him doin' leg work for me here, while I'm in Shanghai."

"Fine, he's yours." A definitive response.

Benson lost it. "Ed, he's got Prosser on a fool's errand."

"What about that, Rube?" With pursed lips, and eyebrows ascending over the tortoise shell frames, he leaned back in his chair.

"When was the last time I blew an op or failed to close a case?" *I got no time for this.*

"Singapore was a close call." Johnson's rib was more like a poke in the eye.

Poised to take a step into a mound of shit, Carver focused on Johnson while pointing a finger at Benson. "When was the last time the SSA did anything other than play devil's advocate or naysay initiative? You give me the reigns and I'll trot your pony back to the barn."

"What is this bullshit?" Benson flopped in a chair in front of Johnson's desk.

The ASAC looked at Carver and then dropped his gaze to Benson. "Sign off on anything he wants," he said, pointing at Ruben. "Anything except C&CI funds or other expenditure requests over a hundred bucks. Those come to me. Now get outta here."

In the hallway, Benson groused, "You stepped over the line this time, Carver. I won't forget it."

"That's what you said the last time I went over your sloping forehead, asshole." Ruben kept walking.

He drove off the base through the main gate, making a right on Route 16. It was a couple kilometers to the tollbooth for the Yokohama Yokosuka expressway. From there, the drive would take about an hour and twenty minutes to get to the Hardy Barracks. Once he parked, it was another twenty-minute walk to the embassy.

The old adage, "all roads lead to Edo", for the most part, held true in modern times. He had any number of routes he could take, but he preferred going up the YokoYoko to the Daini-Keihin into the city. He could pick his way through traffic on surface streets easier than sitting on the parking lot called the C-1, a beltway circling central Tokyo. By 10:20 he was on the Gaien-Nishi Dori, a broad avenue with smooth traffic flow. At 10:40 he stepped out of his government vehicle, pulling his boxers from the crack of his ass. He made good time, without smashing too many motor vehicle laws in the process.

The Chinese Embassy was located in Motoazabu with the Consular Section entrance on a narrow road not far from the Roppongi Hills complex. A large, gray, windowless structure with the visa application counter was on the third floor. A favorite sento of Ruben's happened to be directly across the street. Located walking distance from his nightclub, he found the clientele colorful—literally. The place was a hangout for local Yakuza members, many with irezumi sleeves from mid-thigh to collar bones.

Out on the street those bōryokudan wouldn't give him the time of day, but soaking in a hot tub they got gabby. Often, the best intel Ruben collected on the activity of Chinese Embassy personnel outside the compound came from that bathhouse.

Carver stood at the back of the line with fifty minutes to spare, but the queue had stalled. A woman at the counter, waving her hands, gave the clerk grief about denied entry for her Nigerian boyfriend. While doing his best to ignore that tiff, he wasn't altogether oblivious to his surroundings. He noticed three security cameras with red blinking lights had turned in his direction as he waited. After five minutes, a tall, bald Chinese gentlemen in a navy pinstripe suit approached him. He spoke passable English, but was more comfortable with Japanese. Ruben decided it best not to speak Mandarin.

"Are you here for a visa?" The man used sonkeigo, a polite dialect with a smattering of bikago thrown in to really flower up his language.

Carver followed suit using the humble kenjougo. "Yes, can you help me?"

"May I see your application?" He reached for the paperwork before Ruben's reply. "Mr....Carver?"

"That's right."

"I believe we can expedite this for you." He extended his arm in the direction of an open counter with a smiling Chinese woman waiting for him.

"You are most gracious, thank you." *They've been waiting for me.*

Within ten minutes the application process was finished. The woman behind the Plexiglas instructed him to go to window number six on the ground floor at 3:00pm. The application fee had been waived and his visa would be ready to pick up.

What's wrong with this picture?

Shanghai was a prison. In what felt like solitary confinement, Hodges' days and nights revolved around "the office" and his apartment. Nightlife in his current state meant no life. He could wander the city during those few days each week when a target scenario was pending, but his movement was monitored. In fact, he was convinced everything he did was being recorded for posterity. *I can't take a crap or jack-off out without Suzy Qu knowin' about it.*

Money wasn't an issue. He had boatloads of cash. No

bank account, but he received an envelope every week stuffed with bills. The dragon lady didn't seem to have a problem with him going out, but he quickly learned to expect an interrogation the following day. She'd bring photographs and voice recordings of the people he talked to. Background checks were done on hookers he had sex with more than once, and several pubs he enjoyed banned him because of the intimidation imposed by the bitch on the owners, bartenders, and staff.

The spyware Qu installed on his system prevented any online socializing. She captured all activity. She even showed up with an avatar in the multi-player game he downloaded. Randy was in a fix and going nuts living his life in a fish bowl. Then he found Mingwang Internet cafe on Fuzhou Road. Not hidden by any means, it was close to a pizzeria he went to on his days off, and he found after his first try, his prescriptive patron said nothing about the visit.

Now predictable in his off hours, the babysitters left him alone when he stayed on his regular routine. The occasional quick detour was either ignored or not spotted. In most cases, Internet cafes in Shanghai didn't shine to foreigners. The requirement to present a second generation ID card, swiped through a reader to verify identification, was difficult to get around. Mingwang let him in with a visual check of his passport. A relatively painless process, the second time he entered as Ryan Henderson.

Aware of the time he could spend, he reserved those precious minutes for drafting coded emails to the only person he believed he could trust: a doctoral advisor with whom he'd established not only a close working relationship, but a physical one as well. The only woman who'd ever shared his ardor, and tolerated his lapses of weird social insecurities. She cut him off when he got busted. Apparently, her acceptance of his power-to-the-geeks antics had its limits.

Using the proxies he set up at the office, he spoofed email headers with names associated with events or people in which they shared an interest and discussed ad nauseam. The subject lines were unmistakable with regard to authorship. He hoped time healed the wound he inflicted with his arrest and she would answer him. He needed his advisor once again.

After sending the first email he didn't think it wise to go back to the cafe too soon to check for a response. He followed his routine. If he learned anything from his time in the joint, it was life got easier by keeping his mouth shut and following the rules. He went once a week, skipping a week if the two guys who followed him had been replaced. The new team had to be broken in. It didn't take long before the boredom had them slacking off.

Randy got a gas out of running them around town until they were tired and hungry. He then went to the same pizzeria and ordered a medium pepperoni, extra cheese, and a Coke. The new guys always came in at first, but it didn't take long for them find a better place to have lunch. It gave Randy a chance to skip out with the pizza to go and spend a half hour checking his email.

He had no idea if the surveillance ever came by when he wasn't in the restaurant chowing on a tomato pie. If they did, they never said anything to the succubus. *Man, if I were one of 'em I wouldn't, either. She'd bake their cojones for hors d'oeuvres.* Ryan had no idea how close he was in making that quippy assessment.

When he finally received a reply he wasn't sure how to take it. A rambling missive about life choices, morality, ethical conduct, betrayal of trust...on and on. After some analysis, he figured there were two positive aspects of the feminine philippic. She took the time to write the didactic drivel, and she didn't end it with eat shit and die. She was ready for him to ask her for help.

"Hello, little brother. Do you have the information?" She spoke with a crisp monotone, all business.

"Yes, but I can't risk sending an email or fax. They're monitored." Feng gunned the words in rapid fire. "I put the documents in a drop box we use for processing applications. You'll have access for the next thirty minutes. I'm sending you an SMS now with instructions on how to open the file. Do not download the information and do not attempt to open any other file you see listed. If you want a copy, take a screen shot."

Qu understood the security issues. She didn't want to burn Feng, but more importantly, she didn't want the exposure. Operating in a totalitarian system, notwithstanding the many concessions made to capitalism, required stealthy finesse. "Thank you, Feng. A deposit into your offshore account will go out tonight."

She touched the disconnect.

The instructions were simple, and within fifteen minutes she stared at the face of the new nemesis, Ruben Carver. The home address went out in an encrypted text message to a contractor she recently acquired. His reputation preceded him, and he did, in fact, exhibit a deft hand in managing troublesome busybodies.

The man rarely accepted jobs with a tight deadline, preferring detailed planning that left little room for error. The actual operation, invariably executed by a subcontractor, never left enough evidence at the scene to cast any suspicion on him or his clients. Qu hoped he would make an exception to the rule, considering the hit was offshore, involving a single, unprotected individual.

She was about to sign off, expecting a response in two or three hours, when the reply came. He accepted the contract, but advised the price would be three times the normal scheduled rate. While money rarely became an issue, Qu was sensitive to price points for service. Any change to an expected fee signaled concern regarding the cost of completion. She then remembered the expression used for Carver as a "destructive force", and pounded her keyboard.

Seconds after she hit send, a reply came: "I know the mark. You would be wise not to place this contract. If you choose to go forward, the price stands."

Qu split the screen, opened a web page for a bank in Abu Dhabi, and proceeded to transfer half the monies requested. Confirmation of funds receipt was immediate.

As she sat pondering this interesting turn of events, she began the exercise. Touching her *Qi* with this new revelation, and the act she set in motion, she explored the possible outcomes. Through all the permutations and combinations, the final and most obvious result was an image that ripped her from her treasured state. While uncommonly troubled by what she sensed, she also became aware of something else: the dampness between her legs. She was dripping. *Ruben Carver...*

CHAPTER SEVEN
More Questions

Out of the embassy by noon, Ruben considered grabbing a cab for a short ride to the New Sanno Hotel on Takeshita Dori in Minami-Azabu. An all-ranks hotel, run by the U.S. Navy, it was a nice place to lodge for military and DoD personnel either transiting through, or vacationing in Tokyo. The rooms reminded him of a Ramada Inn, but it had a decent bar and could plate an outstanding cheeseburger, with grilled onions, and avocado slices.

It made his mouth water thinking about it, but settled on washoku at a little three-stool joint near the Hardy Barracks. A ninety-five pound sexagenarian with a dishrag twisted and tied across his brow like a headband, ran the place for the last forty years. He wiped his hands on a grease-stained bib apron as Ruben ordered the shiosaba teishoku—grilled mackerel accompanied by miso soup, pickles, a bowl of rice with fermented soybeans called nattō, and a raw egg. Ruben took his time, but was still finished in fifteen minutes.

He had a couple of hours before the visa would be ready, and wandered over to the two-man NCIS office. It was on the third deck of the building housing the *Stars &*
Stripes newspaper production site, and Naval Research

Laboratory. The guys that sat there weren't special agents, rather Intelligence Operations Specialists responsible for maintaining liaison with the various Japanese agencies. They had window sources with the Tokyo Metropolitan Police, Customs, Immigration, the Maritime Self Defense Force, and Coastguard, as well as number of other intelligence organizations such as the Public Security Intelligence Agency and Cabinet Intelligence and Research Office.

After 9/11, Ruben had worked closely with these two fellas, collecting information from the Japanese on possible terrorist activity in northern Asia, and running a few limited-scope operations. He had his own desk in the space and liked the quiet environment. Benson wasn't around to bang on his door.

When Ruben walked in, he found one of the IOSs crashed on the worn brown Naugahyde sofa. He had the look of an all-night pub crawl. One foot parked on the armrest, the other flat on the floor to keep the room from spinning, he'd passed out. The guy hadn't even bothered to loosen his tie or take his suit jacket off. The racket from his snoring was interrupted intermittently by apnea, but he could still be heard in the hall.

Ruben tapped the man's heel with the tip of his shoe. "Hey, Larry...wake up." One more time, a little harder. "Hey, man, time to get up and go home."

"Huh...wha..." Larry's eyes opened, out of focus. "Dude, lea' me 'lone."

"Hey, buddy, you need to get up. It's one in the afternoon. I need to make some calls and your disturbin' the peace."

Larry moved into a sitting position, scrubbing his face with his palms. "Fuck...I didn't get in until five this morning. OSI had a sobetsukai for a transferring agent. It got pretty ugly."

Ruben turned his back on the sodden wreck and went to his desk, grabbing the phone.

"Prosser."

"Hey, Junior, have you heard anything?"

"I got an acknowledgment from the NCIS rep in Boston. She's busy, but will run out to MIT in the next day or two to try to find Henderson's advisor in the graduate program. She's also gonna visit a couple Boston PD contacts—see if our boy Ryan was ever arrested."

Ruben scratched his head. "I thought you said his record was clean."

"Yeah, his SF-86 shows no criminal history, but that doesn't mean he's never been arrested or convicted of a crime. Even if it's been sealed or expunged, there should still be some record of the incident, either at the police department or the court house."

"What about the MI agent?"

Prosser's sigh of frustration punctuated his response. "You know what it's like dealin' with the Army—they're not great at sharin' information."

"Yeah, I know. I got an earful from Frank Rogers yesterday about the same deal."

"Well, it's true. Anyway, the guy's MI unit in Virginia has definitely slammed the door on this thing. We're not gettin' any sympathy from the Pentagon, either." Prosser took a breath and continued. "Some good news, though. Hartley cc'd me on an email he sent to you, and apparently, while the big green machine has battened down the hatches, the Army Attaché is willing to brief you when you get to Beijing. You should get some answers."

Ruben looked at his watch and decided to head out. "Okay, no surprises. Stay on top of the lead to Boston. I'm going back to the Chinese Embassy now. Maybe they'll have my visa ready. I'll work on my travel arrangements tomorrow. I still need to set up meetings to prep for the Admiral's visit next month. I'll see you tomorrow."

"All right, later."

It was apparent Junior had settled into the task. He was pushing everything along as best he could. The answers would eventually come, but if Ruben wanted to really move the needle and pull the case together, he had to be in China. He rolled away from the desk and stood, looking at Larry. He'd fallen asleep again, in a sitting position, drooling on his tie.

Who says this job ain't glamorous?

When Randy finished his email to his old advisor, Helen Parsons, he believed with certainty it was akin to a suicide note. He also realized it wasn't only his life he was jeopardizing. He was placing her at great risk as well. What made him click the send button, after several minutes of hesitation, had to do with the bigger picture. He may not have been the end recipient of the data he pirated, nevertheless, he was fully cognizant of what he was collecting, and what it was doing to his future.

In many ways, his role in China forced Randy to come to grips with the consequences of his misspent youth. Unlike the year-and-a-half blown in residence at the Allenwood Federal Correctional Institute—which only convinced him to be more careful—he'd finally started the process of self-evaluation, pondering his life choices. He never got into progressive idealism—the Utopian view of supervised entitlement. He didn't agree with the notion of a free ride in exchange for freedom of choice. He also never understood, however, until recently, what it meant to take responsibility for one's actions.

In the beginning, his naïve rationalizations led him to the conclusion that as long as no one got hurt, and he didn't get caught...why not? In his mind, he definitely believed that if you could, you should, and had constructed a flexible morality around his conduct. He could exercise his naughty side—let the dog out—without completely trashing his conscience.

Randy never counted himself as one of the criminals he was incarcerated with. The idea of stealing from people never registered with him, and killing folks was strictly anathema. He had ethics when it came to shit like that. He didn't even learn how to fight until the joint, and then it was a matter of self-preservation. When the Army spook was wasted by Miss Qu, the stark reality of his situation was in his face. The quintessential wake-up call.

Randy remembered the cat. A regular guy he ran into two or three times at a drinking establishment he was now no longer welcome in. A place where a ton of American and British expats hung out. The conversations were, in Randy's mind, innocuous. As he thought about them later, the questions the man had about Randy's work and the circumstances around what brought him to Shanghai were probing, but nothing that made him feel uneasy or suspicious.

The man singled Randy out because he was an American—a homeboy. The unfortunate joe, however, popped up on the bitch's radar and the video recordings and subsequent surveillance of the guy convinced her he was a threat. Now he was dead, and it was Randy's fault—sort of. For sure, if what Suzy Qu had intimated was true. Randy captured data that made him a threat to his country's national security; he'd be considered a traitor and subject to the death penalty if apprehended.

I'm not safe...I'm fucked.

He wanted out, and while he didn't know how Helen could help, she was the only person he trusted. She was also the smartest person he knew, and if she was willing, she' find a way.

At Roppongi Dori, Carver turned left and walked up the hill. To reach the Chinese Embassy he had to cross the busy boulevard, and it was a hundred and fifty meters to a traffic light with a crosswalk. A drizzly rain had begun to fall, but Carver barely noticed as he mulled over aspects of the China scenario that continued to bug him. Johnson said the MI agent arrived in Shanghai three weeks ago. If that was true, did he enter on official business carrying a brown passport, or did he enter on a tourist visa with his blue passport?

Traveling to China on official business required more than a plausible cover story, and it would, in fact, have to be bona fide. He'd have to be there doing something other than looking for a hacker. That might explain how they identified him so quickly. Ruben wondered if a missing persons report had been filed, and if the cops were on the lookout. And another thing, if he was official, what about the constant moving surveillance? In Ruben's experience, they weren't subtle. They got so tight sometimes when he was out roaming a city, he thought he'd shit a couple of them before bed.

If he was unofficial, traveling as a tourist, it was unlikely he carried a U.S. Army ID card. Fingerprints or DNA would have taken days or weeks to get results, and if the Chinese didn't have the guy in their system it would take even longer. The Army certainly wouldn't have informed the Chinese authorities they had a man missing. Not under those circumstances.

He lands in China three weeks ago, and two weeks later, he's a flesh cork bobbing in a shipping lane. *I don't think so. That chump wasn't a newbie. Somebody in Shanghai knew exactly who he was...and that somebody was either PLA or police.*

After Ruben crossed Roppongi Dori, he took a detour to Roppongi Hills, a large, integrated urban center, with offices, apartments, restaurants, shopping—the works. The centerpiece of the development was the fifty-four-story Mori Building. A landmark in that part of the city. Carver wanted a coffee for-the-road and bought a tall House Blend at Starbucks on the lobby level of the skyscraper.

Twenty minutes later he collected his rather fat official passport, with a fresh visa pasted inside; and thirty minutes after that, he'd tucked himself behind the wheel of his g-car, ready to go back to the naval base. Ruben thought about sticking around to chat up his bartender at the club regarding the band playing that night, but risked running into his partner, Barry. The place opened for happy hour at six, and if Barry were there Ruben could see himself hanging around until one or two in the morning. *Gotta show some discipline...*

He left the city the way he came in, taking the Yokohama Yokosuka expressway straight south. He didn't expect the results of the leads in Boston to come in for at least four or five days, and that would be a quick turnaround. He could forget about the Army until he landed in Beijing. Any further fussing with questions he had no answers for was a waste of time, and Ruben was getting hungry again. He decided not to go back to the office.

He lived in a two-story house in a quiet bedroom community in southern Yokohama called Tomioka-nishi. An old firetrap, it had worn-out carpets, clogged plumbing, and exposed wiring in some rooms. The place was also too big for one person—hell, it was too big for two people—with five bedrooms, a den, living room, formal dining room, kitchen, Japanese style bath, and a tatami room in the far back of the house. It even had two toilets. A great place to entertain if he was so inclined—and if the domicile wasn't such a dump—but he liked it. He got up every morning to a spectacular view of southern Tokyo bay on one side, and Mt. Fuji on the other.

He jockeyed his wheels into the concrete carport in front of the house, and punching the locks, shuffled up the ten steps to his front door. Before he went in he pulled a lighter-sized remote control from his trouser pocket to deactivate the alarm system he installed when he first moved in. Basic magnetic contact sensors were on all the windows and entry points.

He then checked the small piece of Scotch tape he'd applied to the bottom of the door and frame. A habit he began years before in Los Angeles and continued everywhere he'd lived. Ruben didn't think of himself as obsessive or compulsive, let alone both, no matter what the psych evals indicated. In his mind, good habits shouldn't be discarded, no matter how benign the environment.

The shoes came off in the genkan, a small recessed patch of floor after the threshold. Stepping up onto the hardwood in his stocking feet, he headed down the hall to the kitchen, briefly looking in and sniffing each room on the ground floor. In the kitchen, he opened the refrigerator and pulled out his sixteen-inch, telescoping ASP baton and shoved it in his hip pocket. He had tools of the trade stashed in various cubbyholes throughout his humble abode. One never knew when a rat might crawl through an opening.

He spotted the couple in a Mazda 6 sport wagon when he started parking. The station wagon was staged in the only spot on the street where a surveillance team would have a good view of the front of the house. The neighbors rarely parked on the street and he knew what they drove. Delivery vans and the vehicles repairmen used had profiles he recognized. This was different. The Mazda had Osaka plates, and the two inside hunkered down slightly when he peered at them from the steps.

Going into the living room, he checked the back. The hill he lived on was terraced, and below him, adjacent to his wrought iron fence, was a public access path. Beyond that was a small playground where stay-at-home moms would take their toddlers in the afternoon. He saw nothing suspicious. The second floor was also clear. From an upstairs window that looked out on the street, he could see the car had moved.

He didn't mind making mistakes when it came to situations like this. It was always better to exercise care, and he never rationalized away uneasy feelings. He was still hungry, though, and the only things in the refrigerator besides the ASP were a six-pack of beer and some moldy cheese. He held onto the baton as he went back out the front door, this time to walk down to his favorite ramen shop across the street from the Tomioka-nishi train station. A bowl of ramen noodles in a tonkotsu broth, with garlic chips and pork slices, would definitely hit the spot.

They were waiting for him when he got home.

CHAPTER EIGHT
Sending a Message

Another habit Ruben had gotten into over the years was establishing multiple avenues of ingress and egress, wherever he was at. It didn't matter if he was going to and from work, taking a walk in a park, going on a date, or in this case, walking down to the train station to get dinner. On foot, he had three options exiting the house. Within fifty meters he had a half-dozen more avenues to choose. While living in Japan he'd gotten lazy, falling into patterned routines. He rarely varied his routes, taking the fastest or most direct path to a destination; but after spotting what he perceived as possible surveillance, decided to take the long way home.

Tomioka was a residential area and he didn't have the benefit of large picture windows or store fronts to detect anyone, either behind him or moving parallel. He had to listen, use the terrain, and the intertwining streets to allow brief 360 degree scans that wouldn't look odd to someone following him.

The two people he'd spotted at the house didn't appear in, or around, the ramen shop and he didn't pick up a tail leaving. He began to believe what he thought was an observation point was just a young couple parked for a chat, suddenly intimidated by the big white man staring at them. About a hundred meters from home, however, he saw the Mazda 6 again. Reflexively, he ducked right under a large cherry tree that blocked the light from the street lamp.

He couldn't see much from that position, but was fairly certain the vehicle was empty. *Just 'cause your paranoid...* An old, pithy adage he continued to live by. The car was across the street, but far enough away from the house that he could leave the shadows and approach it without being seen. Certain now there was no one behind him, he moved in a half-crouch to the back of the vehicle. The streetlight illuminated part of the interior and he figured he could hazard a peek through the rear window. It wasn't the rolled plastic sheeting that got his attention so much as the two large butcher knives and a hacksaw.

Now convinced his initial assessment was dead on, he wondered if the two he burned earlier were the only pair he'd have to deal with, or if they'd brought friends. He also had to find them first, and take them out without bothering the neighbors. If they'd gone inside, they would have had to breach the alarm system, and if they did that, he knew he was dealing with talented desperadoes. It wouldn't be an easy take down.

He had his cell phone and could call the cops, but preferred to be in a situation where he could ask some questions or collect intel afterward. NCIS backup was clearly an option. Ruben knew a number of young agents who had no problem bangin' heads, but he didn't like putting his teammates in harm's way. Besides, the folks who came calling had conveniently brought the means of their disposal. A call to Johnson after he was finished would be enough.

What to do? Carver thought a frontal attack would be a bold move, but again, he had to consider the neighbors.

Instead, he backtracked, electing to advance from the rear on the public access path. The advantage came from concealment. The walkway was dimly lit and he could stay almost invisible using the shadow from the retaining wall to his left.

Apparently, that's exactly what one of his attackers was thinking. Carver didn't see the guy until he was almost on top of him. Surprise causes people to do some weird shit, but for sure, even with the best trained, reaction is binary: action or inaction. There's an immediate response to either freeze, with a kind of momentary paralysis, or go offensive with defensive muscle memory. That generally meant swinging wildly or yanking the trigger convulsively in the general direction of the assault.

This dipshit was the former. He stood for an instant, motionless, confused by what he was seeing. Carver had already deployed the ASP, the matte black steel rod fully extended; and as the baffled one tried to bring his pistol into play, Carver trapped the gun hand at the wrist with his left hand, and struck the man in the mouth with the baton. Tooth shards flew down his throat as the top and bottom incisors shattered. He gasped for air, and Carver struck him again at the bridge of his nose. As he dropped, Carver used his tool like a dagger, ramming it twice into the solar plexus, and finished him with a blow to his larynx.

He had to move with haste. While not exactly a fracas, the encounter wasn't without some noise. This nimrod's compadres probably heard something—so where were they, he wondered. As he knelt next to the body, Ruben felt around for the pistol, finding it next to the man's right thigh. A QSZ-92. Even in the low light he recognized the standard issue weapon of the PLA. This one was modified to fit a noise suppressor. He dropped its magazine into his hand and checked the rounds. It was chambered for 9mm. 9X19 parabellum, he reckoned.

Re-seating the magazine, he pulled the slide back a fraction and saw a round chambered. He was a little puzzled until he looked at the decock lever. The punk had the safety on. That's why it didn't fire when their brief interlude began.

I wonder if his friends are any better?

He couldn't leave the body out on the path. There was a good chance someone would come by, even at ten o'clock at night. He had to pick it up and carry it into his backyard. No other choice. The prick wasn't heavy, but still, dead weight. Carver grabbed an arm and pulled him over his left shoulder. Once he got his feet under him, he straightened his back and pushed with his legs. He had the body in a fireman's carry, the ASP in his left hand, left arm draped around the shitheel's left leg. The pistol was in his right hand, safety off, and in a ready position.

He used the suppressor to unlatch the gate, and slowly pried it open. The hinges squealed a bit, but he managed to get it wide enough to take the four steps up to his yard without hooking the body on the wrought iron. He stifled the urge to drop the burden, and squatting, rolled the body to the ground.

They must know I'm here...

That's when he noticed the curtains had been drawn.

They're in the house. One of these fuckers does have some talent.

Chewing over his next move, he figured if they posted a guy in the back, maybe there was someone in the front as well. There was only one place he could stay out of sight, and Ruben retreated to the path. Once out of what he considered earshot, he jogged to the street, turned right at the corner, and stopped.

He wanted a free hand, and kneeling on one knee, smacked the business end of the ASP against the pavement. The shafts released into the handle and he slipped it into his hip pocket. Up and moving again, he went to the next corner where he made another right. At that point he was more concerned about the neighbors and someone out for a late night stroll.

As he walked past the Mazda he looked again, more closely, at the interior—very clean. Then he saw the sticker on the windshield. A rental. He tried to keep the weapon out of sight, but as he moved to the concrete wall of his carport, he had the pistol up in a two-hand grip.

Okay, smart guy, what now?

He cogitated for a second, making assumptions about this crew based on the pistol he had in his hand and the way the dimwit was dressed. An idea emerged he thought was worth a try. In Mandarin he whispered, "Hey, I got him. He's in the back."

Like magic, a muffled, disembodied voice came from behind the g-car. "What? Where are you?"

"Here." Ruben's Mandarin was near native but he still had an accent. He didn't want to say too much. Luckily, he didn't have to. He could hear the guy scraping past the fender. He was coming out. Ruben counted to three, bobbed left just enough to acquire the target and double tapped. It took less than a second. The first-round pop was a little louder than he hoped, but both rounds hit the jizzpack in the ten ring.

Yeah...give the man a cigar.

Moving quickly, he went to the fallen Chinaman and looked him over. Still breathing, but bleeding out.

Oh, man, this is no good.

Ruben took three steps back, put a bullet in the oriental brow, and returning to the body, tried to avoid the puddle that formed. The guy was wearing a spiffy knock-off Adidas warm up suit—black with white stripes—along with matching black Adidas trainers. Next to him lay a firearm with suppressor, the same model as the one in Ruben's hand.

Buy one, get one free...

He had a clean-shaven head, a gold ear stud, and a black spider web tattoo visible on his neck below the left ear. When Carver searched the remains, he found a car key, but nothing else—not even spare change. A sudden memory alert had him pinging on events of the not-so-distant past. He grabbed the guy's right arm and shoved the sleeve up to the elbow.

No, fuckin' way...

If the cutlery in the car was an indicator, it was kitted for three. He'd taken care of two, leaving an intruder in the house. One of the occupants of the Mazda he spotted earlier in the evening he thought was a woman. Male, female, it didn't matter. Clearing a house—especially a big, dark house—was his least favorite thing to do. He couldn't sit there all night, though, and as he tried to wrap his head around the current quandary, he focused on the car key he'd been juggling in his left hand.

So far, the nitwit ninjas had been falling for some basic ploys. He calculated one more for the hat trick, but he had to hurry. The suppressor worked well, but shooting in the carport amplified the sound, and he worried about the folks across the street looking out their windows. No longer able to avoid the blood, he pulled the stiff over his shoulder in the same fireman's carry. If the person in his digs wasn't looking out the kitchen window, he could leave the carport unseen. He took the chance.

In less than three minutes he had the body laying in the cargo bay of the station wagon. A couple of minutes after that, it was covered in blue plastic sheeting. Before getting behind the wheel, he stretched the Adidas warm-up jacket over his frame and did a magazine exchange with the one from the dead man's gun. The engine cranked with a quick twist of the key, and after a three-point turn, he slid the gear lever into reverse and backed the wagon up the road until it was at the curb in front of his crib.

Two short blasts from the car horn. He waited...forever.

Come on, sweetheart, your ride is here.

He kept the engine running but put the car in park. The front door wasn't visible from his position and he had to depend on his rearview mirrors to spot the mark. Ruben didn't see the figure until he was at the left rear quarter-panel. Definitely a man, with hair to his shoulders. He'd stopped to glance at the lump in the cargo space. As he continued to the passenger-side door, there was something too familiar about his gait. He confirmed Ruben's suspicion when he opened the door and plopped himself in the seat.

The man's expression was utterly smug, until he turned his head to face the driver. "*Arre?*"

Nihonjin.

"Don't move!" Ruben, speaking in Japanese, trained his pistol on the man. As he watched surprise turn to anger, he got the impression having a chinwag with this numskull was out of the question. The bullet shattered the passenger-side window as it exited his cranium.

Ruben checked his watch and calculated the whole process took less than fifteen minutes. Still too long. As far as he could tell, he hadn't disturbed the neighbors, but the fact no one came out to complain didn't mean anything. The Japanese had a habit of leaving notes on doors to avoid face-to-face confrontation. The police box, called a Koban, was only five-minutes away by car and he wasn't hearing any sirens. A good indicator he may have gotten away with the mayhem.

The dead guy in the backyard turned into a real hassle. Carver drove the car down the hill and around the corner, stopping at the start of the path. He didn't want to run to the spot, fearing the sound of footfalls echoing along the hillside, but he couldn't mosey, either. In the end it didn't matter. He still had to carry the load, and when he finally tossed the carcass on top of his soon-to-be-stiffening comrade, Ruben had broken into a full sweat.

As he put the car in drive and headed east down the hill, he arched his ass off the seat to pull his Blackberry from his right front pants pocket. He toed the break to provide the brief pause necessary to thumb in the pass-code, and then continued after hitting Prosser's number he had on speed dial. He'd need a ride home in about an hour.

Junior's voice came on. "What happened?"

Taken aback, Ruben's response was stilted. "Whaddya mean, what happened?" He felt like he got caught with his fingers in the cookie jar.

"You never call me this late unless you've got a problem."

Is that true? "That's not true. Well, in this case it is true, but it's not always true." *I'm babbling.*

"What happened?" Prosser was just busting his balls, but now realized Carver had, in fact, jammed himself up—again.

"Never mind that now. I need you to meet me at Umikaze Park." Ruben started wiping a plan out of his ass.

"Umika...what?" Not a clue.

"You remember the place where the joggers found

that dead marine last year?"

"You mean the skateboard park, with the basketball courts? Down by the water?"

"That's right. It has a waterfront walkway. Anyway, meet me in the parking lot, and bring clean dish rags and bleach."

"Oh, man..."

Prosser was waiting for him when he got there. Ruben slowly drove the parking area before pulling into a slot next to Junior's car. A few other vehicles sat empty in the lot, and Ruben guessed they belonged to folks doing some late-night fishing. He picked the place because he remembered it being poorly lit and had no CCTV.

When Prosser saw what was inside the Mazda, he freaked. "No way...uh-uh. Are you crazy?"

In a voice that suggested just another day at the office, Ruben replied, "Get a grip, Junior. We have work to do."

"No, man! What's goin' on?"

Ruben wanted to wait to explain, but realized his young protégé was losing it. "You remember Sonny Xú?"

CHAPTER NINE
Complications

When Ruben came in the office the next morning, Prosser was waiting for him. "Are you going to tell the boss what happened?"

"No, and neither are you. We just leave it for the coppers to scratch their heads over."

"What if we missed something? They're gonna come knockin' on our door." Prosser was stressed to a near frenzy.

"Close the door," Ruben said in voice that jarred Prosser into compliance. "Now, listen,we've got a mission to complete. Do you understand?"

Prosser folded his arms and rocked on his heels, but nodded in the affirmative.

"Those three so-called hit men were sent my way because of the mission."

Ruben was speaking with authority but Prosser, shaking his head, wasn't allowing the words to penetrate. "You don't know that. Sonny Xú would definitely have a bone to pick with you over what went down in Singapore. The timing is, more than likely, pure coincidence."

"No such thing. We know Sonny had a lively enterprise in murder-for-hire. What's the main principle for a professional in any field? We've talked about this before." Ruben stood with his eyes fixed on the younger man.

"A professional doesn't do anything for free," Prosser parroted as he stared back.

"That's right. With Sonny it's all business, and he's not gonna risk his business for a little payback. That wouldn't be his style." Ruben looked down and pulled his chair from under the desk. As he sat down he said, "He got my address from someplace, and it's not like it's listed in the White Pages. The last place I provided my personal information was the Chinese Embassy. If Sonny got it that fast—fast enough to put those three zhlobs onto me —then whoever hired him for the hit either works at the embassy or has a close connection with someone there."

Prosser had begun to breathe. "You think the hit was state sponsored?"

"I don't know. Two of the guys had Chinese firearms, but exports of those are pretty common these days. One guy was Japanese, but he wasn't sportin' the gang tat. I don't want to get my head wrapped around it too hard. Pay attention to the news, maybe the cops provided some information on identities.

"Anyway, you need to cool your jets. Those characters wanted to spread my body parts around the Kanto plain. We did them the favor of a nice Shinto funeral. Now go to work and get me some information on Ryan Henderson. I have to buy my tickets and make some hotel reservations."

"What's in the bag?" Prosser pointed at a thick plastic fifty-gallon trash bag Carver had walked in with.

"It's their clothes. I'll throw this in the dumpster down by the crew barge after lunch."

As Prosser, shaking his head, opened the door and disappeared down the hallway, Carver stretched his legs and twisted his head until his neck cracked. He only had a few hours of sleep. After getting home he cleaned up the carport with a bucket of water and bleach, then had a few odds and ends to deal with in the house. The naughty nip had wandered around with his shoes on, helped himself to a few souvenirs, drank two out of the six-pack, and took a dump in his kitchen sink.

What a rude motherfucker...

Ruben rarely had moments of self-doubt, but while the attempted hit was a bold move, it was something he should have been better prepared for. He prevailed, but was lucky on two counts: the three stooges Sonny sicced on him had a lousy game plan and he forgot to set his alarm system as he went out the door for dinner—something that never happened.

Fuck. I got to keep my head in the game. I'm not eligible for a full retirement, yet.

If the alarm was set, it would have either scared them off or all three would have tried to take him outside. Bad odds for Ruben and the neighbors, since the stooges wouldn't be keen on witnesses.

Logging into the system to order his tickets, Ruben cogitated a bit about Sonny. He wondered if he was the man responsible for offing the Army agent. That thought fractured in a direction even more troublesome: who hired him?

"I expect the balance on the contract to be paid." A simple, clipped statement came from Xú Bao-Zhi, known to most as Sonny Xú. He hated using the phone. In fact, after his less-than-auspicious exit from Singapore, he developed an aversion to any form of personal contact with a client beyond encrypted email, but Qu insisted.

"Your team failed to fulfill the conditions of our

agreement."

Sonny was aware Qu was seething, but had kept the discussion strictly on business terms. Nevertheless, she seemed disinclined to let Xú Bao-Zhi off the hook.

"There was, I believe, an implied caveat when I accepted this job." Sonny disliked excuses even more than phone calls. They were anathema. He didn't want to hear them, and didn't want to use them, but he'd warned the bitch about Carver.

Weeks of surveillance and planning may not have been warranted for a simple hit, but if his experience in Singapore taught him anything, Ruben Carver didn't fall in the "simple" category. The man was a wrecking ball.

The two subs he had in Tokyo he'd placed there a few months prior, to open an office and establish his brand. Neither one was ever going to win an award for scholastic excellence, but they did have the ability to follow instructions, and had a proven track record in executing planned assignments.

They'd even shown some initiative in recruiting a new member, a Japanese thug on the outs with a crime family in Osaka—not a first choice of Sonny's, but a start. The youngster had exhibited a certain psychological bent for the work. He liked killing people, and was trainable. Sonny had him running errands, to confirm his reliability, before Carver put an end to his career plans.

Within the niche Sonny Xú was competing, strict quality control and customer satisfaction were critical elements for longevity. And not just for the business. Too many missed assignments and he'd be carved up like sushi.

Along those same lines was another principle he also relied on: never buck the odds. Sometimes, no amount of money was worth the gamble. He wished, now, he followed his experienced based instinct, and refused the woman. Carver had once again jacked up his operations and set him back several months in gaining a foothold in Japan. A market Sonny believed had great high-yield low-risk potential.

Qu interrupted his cogitation. "I'm aware there was a certain concern regarding this target. The price you requested was accepted with that understanding." She pressed on with, "You haven't provided, as yet, a reason for your failure. Is there an explanation?"

Qu wasn't the first hardboiled ball-buster Sonny had the displeasure of dealing with, but she was now pushing his buttons. At one time, he excelled at putting a bitch like this one in her place, but decided not to rise to the bait.

He responded, "From the information I've been able to glean, he killed them with their own weapons. More than that, neither you nor I really need to know. He is, as I warned you when you let the contract, someone better left alone."

Qu took a few seconds to digest what was said. "The wicket stands. Do you want to continue bowling?"

It was now Sonny's turn to deliberate. "You pay me what you owe, plus ten percent for replacement costs, and I want twice the last contract price on this new one."

"I'll agree as long as you give me a guarantee of delivery against a penalty for a second miss."

"What kind of penalty?"

"Please, Xú Bao-Zhi, do you really have to ask?"

"Defense Attaché's office. This is a non-secure line, may help you?" A staccato monotone came from a female voice.

"Captain Williams, please."

"Who's calling?" No perfunctory "may I tell him" or "please".

"Ruben Carver," he said, in his most mellifluous intonation. *The woman needs a hug...or somethin'. Maybe I should bring Junior with me and turn his newfound mojo loose on her.*

For all intents and purposes, Ruben was ready to go wheels up. He just needed confirmation from Roy Williams he had the logistics set for his arrival. He wanted to spend as little time as possible in Beijing, and hoped a single afternoon would be enough to satisfy the country team about his mission parameters.

"Captain Williams."

"Hey, Roy, it's Ruben."

"Didn't we just talk?" Cordial but clipped, Williams was already trying to get off the phone.

"Catch you at bad time?"

"Yeah, well...kinda, but it's good you called. I've had the Army and Air Attachés in a couple times today trying to wrangle an angle to get the approval for an OSI and MI agent in country."

"The PLA bein' hard-nosed?"

"You have no idea. Anyway, intractable would be the best way to describe it. The PLA knows why they want to come, and they aren't buyin' the song and dance we're tryin' to shovel past 'em. At one point, the Army even pressed NCIS to provide credentials so their man could travel on your invitation."

"Yeah, I bet that went over well." The irony of this cooperation thing with the Army was that they definitely got a serious case of the red ass when they didn't get their way. In Ruben's mind, though, MI had a serious gripe—it was their man who went down.

"I'm not gonna bore you with the details, but the Chinese are getting tired of us asking. If we're not careful, we'll wind up queerin' your approval. So, whaddya need?"

Captain Williams lit the fuse on the conversation, giving Ruben the feeling he had about three minutes to make his point. "I need to see the Intelligence Information Reports the MI agent put out. I'm assuming, as a case officer, the guy had some kind of reporting requirement. You might as well tell the Army Attaché I ain't believin' for a minute the guy had only been in China for a week before he got burned.

"Also, I'm gonna need a car and driver in Shanghai. Can you impress on the person who works for you at the consulate there, to provide someone who's been trained in defensive driving? I don't need a good English speaker, I need a good driver."

"Okay, I'll see what I can do. By the way, the Naval Attaché at the consulate in Shanghai is Captain Doug Fairbanks. A former aviator. His call sign is Zorro."

"Yeah, all right, cute. I'll just call him Captain. So, anyway, has my PLA liaison been identified? My so-called cover is Seventh Fleet's visit next month, and I've still got an advance to conduct."

"That would be Major Zhao Bao-Yu. You'll meet in Shanghai at a police station on Datong Road."

"Zhao Bao-Yu? A woman?" Ruben liked women—he was crazy about 'em—he just didn't like working with them. The X in his heterogametic chromosome combo was definitely lowercase when it came to his cuddle quotient. The other side of that coin was, women had little time for Ruben in the workspace—he was apparently considered insensitive. He gave up trying to figure that one out.

Roy picked up the vibe. "You gonna have a problem with that?"

"Ah, no...not really, uh-uh...nope..." *Maybe Junior would be a better fit...*

"Listen, I gotta go, Ruben. Is there anything else?"

"I'll be there tomorrow night. I fly out of Narita at 15:15, on China Air, flight 926. I'll arrive around 18:00. I know it's a pain in the ass, but is there any way I can get a pick up?"

"Sure, I think I can arrange something. Is that terminal two?

"Yeah."

"Okay, see you tomorrow."

"Oh, hey, wait. There is something else, and you need to keep this to yourself until we sit down with the country team. Whoever did the Army agent knows about me already. I had a couple visitors come by my home last night. I haven't said anything to my management about the encounter yet, but let's just say, whoever hired them are now short a few headcount."

"Ruben, you're not sayin' anything to brighten my day. Do you have any idea who was behind it?"

"See what your intel analysts can find out about a former Singapore crime boss named Sonny Xú. I don't know his Chinese name, but I have a hunch he relocated to Mainland China sometime this year. I'm pretty sure he arranged the hit, but whoever used him for the contract is connected at some level with the China Foreign Ministry and the PLA, maybe even higher."

"You're talkin' state sponsorship, Ruben. Our government won't listen to that kinda talk."

"Well, let's just entertain the notion of state condoned, then."

Ruben cradled the phone, and as he stood to stretch, Junior was at his door, a piece of paper in hand. His expression suggested he'd gotten over his jitters, and Ruben waited for him to drop whatever bomb he had clutched in his tight little fist.

"Oh, man, you are gonna love this!" Junior was now

waving the single piece of paper.

"Well, are you gonna tell me or tease me? You better not fuckin' ask me to guess."

"The NCIS agent in Boston called me. She located Henderson's graduate advisor...a Professor Helen Parsons, at MIT. Apparently, our boy was a budding star for a while. He was working on coding algorithms that had the potential of revolutionizing the way computer scientists viewed feasible AI...artificial intelligence."

"Yeah, I know what AI is. Is that it?"

"No, that's not it. Prof Helen and Ryan were close, on and off the court, if you know what I mean, but the prodigy had some ethical issues Helen couldn't feature. Anyway, Ryan got busted for some major league hacking and was sentenced to five years at Allenwood medium security. The Professor told our Very Special Agent that she cut Ryan off—wouldn't have anything to do with him after he was sentenced. Sounds kinda bitchy to me but..."

"But, do we have a point to all this?"

"*Yes!* Let me finish. He only served eighteen months. I haven't confirmed it yet, but apparently some mysterious international philanthropic organization arranged for his release. Had his record expunged—if you can believe that—and set him up in the computer software business we already know about. Now, here comes the good part. Ryan is in Shanghai, going by the name of Randy Hodges—I don't know what the deal is with the whole RH thing—but he's been in touch with Professor Parsons.

"You ready for the punchline?"

"Uh-huh."

"He's been 'forced'—that's Parsons' term—to hack for an organization with ties to the PRC. Some bad things are—or have—happened, I'm not sure which, and he's tired, scared, and wants the Prof to help him find a way out."

Ruben said nothing for several seconds. His brain was grinding through the possibilities this new information provided. As he settled on a couple scenarios, he glanced at Junior's bobbing face, with its wide eyes, raised eyebrows, open-mouth toothy grin and said, "Okay, let's go talk to the boss. It looks like we're on a rescue mission."

CHAPTER TEN

Transition

After laying down a basic game plan with Ed Johnson to put the grabs on Ryan Henderson, aka Randy Hodges, Ruben went home to pack. He decided not to crash at the house that night, but rather, got his buddy Barry to do a little string-pulling, with the security manager at the New Sanno Hotel, for a room.

Carver figured he wouldn't be shooting in and out of China this trip and packed for a two-week stay. Unlike his last outing in Singapore, the uniform of the day for the next fortnight would be suit and tie. Never one to throw caution to the wind, however, he did pack a few items that went with him nearly everywhere: a photographer's vest with Kevlar patches for ballistic protection, a pair of khaki Blackhawk tactical pants, his Timberlands with speed laces—his lucky boots—and a navy blue Vertex Coldblack polo. He had the vest repaired during a shopping trip to Hong Kong in May. A few patches were damaged by some rounds he took during the last operation and needed to be replaced.

Shanghai in June would be warm and moist. Not unbearably hot, with a mean temperature of twenty-four degrees Celsius, but it was the rainy season and he could expect heavy precipitation at least three times a week, and high humidity the rest. With that in mind, he folded four custom lightweight cotton-linen suits into the case. Even when they got wet, they still kept their shape.

He had most of his dress clothes made by a tailor at the Arcade on Fenwick Pier in Hong Kong. The place was officially known as Fu Shing and Sons, but everybody called the owner Fat Tony. During fittings, Ruben had Tony make a few minor alterations, with reinforced belt loops for pistol carry on the hip, and extra room under the armpits for easier concealment with a shoulder holster. He also had Tony sew in denim-like fabric inside the jackets under the armpits and on the side-seams. It cut down on wear and tear. The rubber sleeve on the grip of his Sig Sauer P226 would rub a hole in the standard lining of a brand new jacket in a week.

Along with the regular assorted accessories and toiletries, he tucked in an extra pair of Geox Dublin Brogues—lightweight with rubber soles, they were waterproof and easy to run in. When he was finished, the suitcase was heavier than he preferred but he still made sure he had his ASP telescoping baton and his Recon 1 tactical folding knife fastened to the case's metal frame. It generally got through x-ray scans without question.

Packed and ready to go by 16:00, he threw his bag in the trunk of his '99 Toyota Corona and headed north toward Tokyo. Traffic had picked up, and he was an hour and forty minutes getting to Hardy Barracks. He'd made arrangements to allow him to use its lot for long-term parking.

From there, it was a five-minute taxi ride to the New Sanno. Barry was waiting for him in the bar. Instead of going out to eat, Ruben and his business partner sidled into a couple of easy rollers at a table in the bar's lounge area, and ordered martinis and cheeseburgers. When they'd finished the last fry, they dropped a couple twenties on the table and went to their club. Ruben was the last man out, after putting a major dent in a new bottle of Tanqueray. He was feelin' A-OK. That would start changing in about forty-eight hours.

Over the last week, Randy's laundry list of tech data, and the likely targets where it could be acquired, had grown to five pages, single spaced. It was no big deal, really. His strategy, from the beginning, was to infect selected networks with multiple kernels, each with a separate function. Only one kernel at a time beaconed information. The others were used in a random cycle, with search algorithms he developed, to hunt for the data The Board wanted.

More than a hundred government contractors and research facilities involved with projects The Board was interested in, were knocked-up with his little babies. He had the ability to tag data files, email archives, chat logs, address registers, and other detailed information on research conducted, and papers submitted. He had gotten to the point where workarounds for acquiring information from the toughest sites had been established.

As an example, if The Board wanted information on the current status of DARPA's efforts in creating stealth clothing, Randy didn't bother trying to crack a DARPA server. He searched the records across his mal-net to find individuals involved in corollary studies that referenced DARPA findings or breakthroughs. He'd then craft an email, spoofing the researcher's name and address, or use his own nom de guerre, depending on the target, and reach out to DARPA in a text format.

In Randy's experience, what a scientist wouldn't discuss outside the office or lab, he was often too willing to discuss with someone he perceived as a fellow sojourner in the same arcane pursuit. This was especially true if he'd talked to, or had correspondence with, the guy before. It became virtual pillow talk. He felt like lighting a cigarette afterward.

The sudden jump in activity, and Qu's daily demand for updates had nothing to do, though, with the success of his endeavors. On the contrary, the bitch cracking the whip on production could only mean one thing: she was getting prepared to tear the office down. Since she hadn't been particularly loquacious of late, he figured his services to The Board were likely in question as well.

Yet, with all his concern about the future of the gig, he could have probably gutted it out if Qu's grip on his after-hours activity hadn't also increased. She'd already put a major bend in his hose when it came to his limited sex life, but now, she began to dictate which part of the city he was allowed to spend his time in.

Places where he could kick back and find respite in conversation with other foreigners were off-limits. The escort that used to give him space, now stayed with him. He found the pizzeria was still a safe haven, but for only short periods—no more than fifteen or twenty minutes. He wasn't sure how much longer he'd be able to use the Internet cafe before that important outlet would be trashed.

As he sat staring at the monitors, the contemplation over Helen's last email returned. She wrote about the visit from the NCIS agent and her decision to reveal his location. Randy had never really struggled with mixed feelings about anything—he either liked something or didn't. In his current state, however, he discovered the true meaning of ambivalence. His old paramour and confidant had agreed to help, but the help she decided to provide probably meant he'd have to go back to jail—a prospect he wasn't ready to entertain.

For sure, he didn't want to wind up like the G.I. Joe—a bloated floater in the Yangzte—but his options were very few. Now, effectively shackled to the dragon lady, his only out appeared lodged squarely up Uncle Sam's ass.

Fuckin' NCIS. Not those guys again...

As if on cue, the door opened, and in glided the bane of his existence.

"Good evening, Mr. Hodges." Her eyes at half mast, were piercing and derisive. "Do you have an update for me on the new assignments?"

"Hey, lady...update this." Hodges yanked at his crotch.

"Mr. Hodges, your childish charm was appreciated in Boston, I'm sure, but this expression is lost on me—an update, if you please." Qu's weight was on her right foot, her left hand propped on her hip.

"Update? What update? When I get the data, you get the data. There's no mystery here. So before your go and get physical—and I wish you'd try it again...really I would—what is it you really want?"

"What do you mean?" Her weight now balanced on feet shoulder-width apart, arms akimbo.

"What I mean is, you don't come in here unless you want me to do something besides my job. So, what is it?"

As if evaluating the veracity of the remark, Qu was silent for a few seconds, then responded, "Your assessment, in this case, is correct. There is something I need you to do. I want you to search the hotel registries in Beijing for a man by the name of Ruben Carver. He'll be traveling from Tokyo, today, or tomorrow. Once you've located the reservation, I want you to upgrade his room assignment to either business or luxury, but make sure the room has active surveillance capability. I want access to those feeds, both audio and visual, and if needs be, the ability to turn it off. Do you understand?"

"You're speakin' English. Yeah, I understand. Is that it?"

"Once you've located the hotel and made the adjustment to his lodging, I want you to assign me the room next his. I'll give the you the name I'll be traveling under in an encrypted email."

Hodges recognized Carver's name, but played dumb. "What's your interest in this guy?"

"Let's just say Mr. Carver and I need to get acquainted, and leave it at that."

Hodges' fingers started on the keyboard, and he mumbled, "How many days?"

"I beg your pardon?"

"How many days...how many days do you want the reservation for? I'm *workin'* here."

Qu's hand came forward as if to cuff Hodges in the mouth, but restrained herself. "Time my stay with Carver's. While I'm gone, make sure your mobile phone is charged and on you, or near you, at all times. If he makes it to Shanghai, I may require your further assistance—I'll let you know. In the meantime, your assignments have been laid out."

Qu then spun, and slithered out the way she came in. That instant—those three or four seconds—as he watched her ass move under the fabric of the dress, was the only time Hodges didn't mind seeing the cooz.

Qu had no more interest in spending time with Randy Hodges than he did with her. She sensed a strength and intelligence buried in the man, that, if harnessed, could be formidable. The problem of reaching it had to do with the thick coating of adolescent obstinacy. The man was a construct built around misguided notions of chic sophistication. The video and audio coverage of Hodges forays into the Shanghai nightlife convinced her that the man-child lacked any natural social adroitness.

With an unrestrained libido, he used his constantly erect penis like a divining rod, following its lead without discretion. In conversations with both men and women, he invariably used the same single-syllable word to describe something he liked, he thought was attractive, or for which he exhibited a covetous desire. It was always "cool". Qu had purposely restrained Hodges' activities with the specific intent of breaking down this spurious shell he wrapped himself in, to more effectively gain access to the man's true talent.

She had allowed him one outlet: contact with the woman Helen Parsons. Qu knew of Hodges' outreach from the very first email, but let it slide. Every caged beast needed a treat from time to time. A certain amount of controlled freedom fed a sense of hope, which in turn fueled mental acuity. The background on Parsons suggested she'd be the perfect emotional release for the man-child. Fifteen years his senior, she not only got him to focus for extended periods, she rewarded him with an introduction into carnal gratification he'd never imagined.

Like most good academic progressives, she understood great sex and how to get off. Qu also recognized, in that same vein, the woman had very little interest in real world scenarios, denying the empirical, and embracing the Utopian. Until the last email, Hodges' Oedipal pen pal was a harmless tool. She'd have to be dealt with.

As her apartment door slid closed behind her, she removed her shoes by hand and placed them in a tall cupboard by the entry. The teak parquet flooring under her bare feet gave the only texture in the vacant space as she padded to her sanctuary. The chair slid from its walled compartment, and after taking her repose, the comm systems came alive.

She sent Hodges the information necessary for her hotel reservation, and then dialed a number on the secure channel. It activated with several long beeps in a perfect B-flat.

The metallic voice, with a slight chambered echo, clicked on. "It's early, Qu. Is there a problem?"

"The termination of Carver in Tokyo did not transpire." Qu was careful not to reveal her excitement. She'd been pondering the unexpected physical response from her *Qi* exercise after the contract was initially let. The anticipation of meeting this apparent force of nature had her feeling something she thought was dead for the last forty years. She had a crush. She also accepted and anticipated the outcome. It would end deliciously, in the same way as her first infatuation—with a razor edge against pliant flesh.

"Yes, we are aware. The actual police reports of the condition of the bodies when found, suggest a certain striking sociopathy."

Once again, Qu ignored The Board's evaluation as biased. "While I would like to believe there is a chance at recruitment—he'd be a excellent asset—the truth, I feel, was simply one of expedience rather than psychological preference. He found a location he could dump the bodies in a fashion that would not turn local law enforcement his direction. The man may be nefarious with regard to our interests, but he isn't stupid."

"Once again, we stress caution and avoidance. Our operation can be well-placed in another location, and encourage you to consider relocation sooner, rather than later. Our cost-to-benefit analysis indicates using Mr. Hodges in his current role connotes at least twelve more months of positive jaws. Please keep that in mind before taking a course that would not only risk our exposure, but have pernicious impact on our relationship with the administration."

Quit with the whining!

"What's your next move?"

"I've learned Carver has a stopover in Beijing. I've decided it's time to get acquainted. I know him only by reputation and your idolized image of him as Perses, the god of destruction. I need to get a feel for the man."

Except for the slight hum on the line, it was quiet—no response. They'd switched off the mic to deliberate—a sign of some objection. The wait lasted almost two minutes.

"Madame Qu, do not light a match you can not blow out."

Where did that come from...a San Francisco fortune cookie? Cao-ni-ma! "Yes, gentlemen. A very wise sentiment, to be sure."

They've made me wealthy. That's all that matters.

As she clicked off, a soft tone from the wall speakers signaled receipt of an email. Her hotel reservation had been made. After alerting her flight crew to prep the plane, she had time for a workout, twenty minutes of meditation, and a shower. Her bag was already packed.

Before she left the apartment, she let Sonny know where she'd be. She didn't want him interfering with her playtime. His crack at Carver would have to be in Shanghai. Qu left this bit of news out of her discussion with The Board. Their reaction would likely be churlish, and she wasn't in the mood for anymore chop-suey bon mot.

CHAPTER ELEVEN
Beijing

Beijing, a bleak, achromatic morass of choking smog, gridlock, and construction cranes. Ruben hated coming here. As he exited the airplane, he could feel the air—like acid prickling his skin. From a sky window, he could see renovation on the airport's Terminal One had finally finished, only to be replaced with groundbreaking and foundation work for the new Terminal Three construction. With the advent of the 2008 Olympics pointing at the city like the barrel of an AK-47, the People's Republic of China was on a massive clean and sweep.

After Mao, the Chairman, finally kicked the bucket, the Communist Party broke the faith. It willingly accepted the realty that redistribution of wealth, state ownership of industry, and forced submission of the populous to enslavement under incompetent rule was great for the revolution, but lousy for business. By the turn of the millennium, it also recognized modernization with worthless currency was impossible and threw open its doors to world investment with a single-minded intent to rake in foreign legal tender.

Leave it to the Chinese to establish one of the greatest shell games of all time. The establishment of a market system, trading floors, property ownership, banking, and financial trusts were like peanut butter to rats. Every major and not-so-major corporation on the planet fell prey to the Siren's song: one billion people just waiting for foreign goods and services. A con game of historic proportions, and while companies came in with expectations of profits beyond their wildest dreams of avarice, they found themselves fleeced from regulatory payoffs, skyrocketing property prices, discriminatory business practices, fraud, and government corruption.

Some stuck it out and opened factories, only to have their products counterfeited, technology pirated, or business models copied and then used against them with domestic companies formed to compete. The industries' stories of corporate muggings at the hands of the Chinese were replete in boardrooms, stockholders' meetings, media outlets, and the Internet. And yet, while armed with the full understanding of who they were dealing with, the alluring lilt of Persephone's lovers continued to shipwreck corporations against a rocky China shore.

The truth was, Carver gave a shit less about foreign business interests. *If you want to stump break a dragon, expect to get burned.* He had his own issues with the Oriental horde. For him, it was the irony of counterintelligence. He protected his country's secrets by stealing others'—in this case China's. The fact he was sporting a bayonet scar and a bum knee that ached in cold weather, was all on him. They were just trying to keep him out of the meat locker.

Once he cleared Immigration and paddled through the sea of unmetered taxi drivers, he saw a placard with his name on it. Ruben checked the man's ID and followed him out.

Hallelujah. Williams came through.

The car was parked at the curb thirty feet out of the exit, with another guy waiting at the wheel. The young man with the poster board sign grabbed Ruben's suitcase and tossed it in the trunk. As Ruben climbed into the backseat he noticed something else that struck a chord: a single individual standing on the curb, with a banner. He was either protesting or commemorating, Carver couldn't tell which, the anniversary of the 1989 Tienanmen Square demonstrations. *I forgot what day it is...this poor dumb bastard hasn't, though...gutsy.* Ruben couldn't help tipping an imaginary hat.

The hotel was about twenty kilometers away, near city center. His watch read 19:45, and considering the traffic he saw as they came out of the airport, calculated at least an hour and a half ride.

Aside from the involuntary hackin' and wheezin' brought on by the air quality, or lack there of, he was once again impressed by the building going on along the expressway. It reminded him of Hollywood backlots with the elaborate facades—all image no substance. A mishmash of high-rise set designs built for the international stage, which would never see a tenant.

What did the man say? Perception is reality...

The guy next to the driver, a young Marine by the look of him, handed Ruben an envelope from Capt. Williams. It had his itinerary for the meetings at the embassy, starting at 08:00. When they pulled into the driveway of the Beijing Marriott Northeast, its twenty-eight story glass spires reflected blue against the night sky. It was just after nine. The driver made good time.

The lobby had golden marble floors and walls, with chairs, sofas, and wall coverings in red and yellow. Its most striking feature was an arched, and back-lit, aqua-colored glass ceiling that looked to be at least a hundred feet in diameter. Ruben's reaction to the visual stimulus was markedly blasé.

Where's the bar?

When he stood at the front desk, a cute little twenty-something with a Bai Ling pageboy took his passport and, checking her monitor, spoke without looking up. "Mr. Carver, you've been ungraded."

"That's nice, but I don't really need an upgrade. I'm only staying one night." Ruben didn't like surprises. He looked around the lobby again, and didn't see any activity to suggest the hotel to be so full as to offer an upgrade.

"Yes, sir, but it's the room we have assigned to you. The embassy rate we're charging you is the same price as the deluxe room." She had Lim on her name badge, and she spoke with a heavy estuary accent—east London or maybe Essex, Ruben surmised.

"Yeah, okay...do I check in here?"

"No, sir, please follow this lady." She waved at someone to her right with the flat of her hand. "She'll take you to the executive lounge on the twenty-fifth floor."

Never one to argue with a freebie—too much—he followed the young woman as directed. Ruben had picked this hotel because the Marriott, aside from the bombing in Jakarta two years before, had some of the best security in the Far East, was walking distance to his morning meetings, and he satisfied the bean-counters at the office by getting an embassy rate for the stay.

As he slipped the card key into the scanner assembly on his door, he suddenly felt a change in the air around him and saw movement in his peripheral vision. Thinking it was the persistent bellhop from the executive lounge check-in desk, he didn't bother a glance—until he heard her voice.

"Hello..." The husky greeting brought Ruben to a full stop.

First rotating his head to get eyes on her, the rest of his body quickly followed suit. Maybe an inch shorter than him, she wore a red, sleeveless lace overlay cheongsam with a gold and silver fire pattern. It hugged her body like it had been painted on. This was not a young woman, but a knockout just the same. She had curves that made him downshift his roving eye, but when he saw her face he couldn't stop staring—even with the visual feast she carried below her chin.

It was the irises on those shuttered orbs. The coal black seemed to etiolate the longer he peered at them. He also realized she wasn't really looking at him—it was more like she was looking in him.

This broad may be smokin' hot, but she's kinda creepin' me out.

"Uh...hi." His palms started to sweat. This jingyàn shèng nu had tractor beam allure and there wasn't another thing he wanted more than to hear the next words coming through those crimson lips.

She's doin' this on purpose. She knows who I am.

"Are you coming or going?" Her mouth curved up on the ends and those teeth...the perfect Colgate smile.

"Uh, yeah. I'm uh, just getting in. How about you?" *This is what you think it is, not what you hope it is.*

"Me too, a few minutes ago." She stood leaning against the door, her right hand on the nob, left pulling a few strands of hair. With her weight on her right foot, she toed the carpet with her left.

Ah, fuck it. He took a step toward her, right hand extended. "I'm Ruben Carver, what's your name?"

Accepting the offered hand, she cooed, "I'm Lisa Chin."

"Well, Lisa, I'm gonna force myself to go in my room now, but in about fifteen minutes I'll be in the lobby bar, if you'd like to get acquainted."

There was a slight rise in an eyebrow, as she sucked in her cheeks and pursed her lips. "Hmmm, maybe."

Then her door opened and she disappeared.

Suitcase on the bed, Ruben pulled out the suit, shirt, tie, and shoes he'd wear in the morning. The shave kit went in the bathroom, and one final grab, the tactical knife, he put in his pocket. He thought about calling Junior and Ed Johnson, but changed his mind. He didn't like to think his cynicism was the dominant characteristic of his personality, but along with his tendency toward careful deliberation—also referred to as paranoia by most—meeting the hammer next door didn't forecast a fortuitous event. The woman definitely had "trouble" stenciled on her T-back.

Just because his little head screamed "go for it" didn't mean he shouldn't at least find out what she was up to. With the card key in his shirt pocket, he yanked the door open, applied the tape to the top of the door and frame, and headed for the elevators.

Who knows? Maybe I am irresistible.

Two minutes after she entered the room she was naked. She had to clear her mind and strip away the unexpected physical response to her first encounter with the man. She'd pushed her *Qi* to attract him and it backfired. It had never happened before, but, then again, her method of seduction was almost always against those with a predisposition to the licentious. She should have anticipated at least a marginally different reaction with this westerner.

Then again, he wasn't what she expected: older, bigger, and with the unmistakable odor of...sex. This Carver was swimming in pheromones and it bothered her she couldn't control her physiology. Her breasts were sensitive, their nipples hard, and she could feel the swelling and moisture between her legs.

Before meditation she spent ten minutes performing a Tai-Chi routine to cool down. The concentration helped break the spell. Without her chair, she positioned herself on the bed in a lotus form, and it took longer than usual to go deep. He would wait. The expression on his face told her that much, but other than that, a blank. She couldn't get past the smell.

They said he was dangerous, but they have no idea.

Tripping in the metaphysical cosmos, she once again examined her options but perceived only chaos. As she pulled herself from the less-than-satisfying state, she sussed the only path: for her survival she had to devour this gwailoh. There was also something else that lingered. Something analogous to exposure. She now assumed Carver was on to her and wondered if coming to Beijing to meet the man was such a good idea after all.

The lobby bar had open seating with overstuffed chairs and sofas in olive and brown fabric, along with nine or ten tall wood-back chairs in front of a curved counter. It was well stocked, with bottles stacked on illuminated blue glass shelving. The uniformed bartenders, in white shirts, black vests, and black bow ties, were wiping glasses and pushing crap around on the counter top when he dropped onto a stool. So far, he was the only customer.

As Ruben bellied up, he ordered a Tanqueray martini, extra dry, with three olives—he didn't like drinking on an empty stomach. He had it shaken for the extra chill, tiny chips of ice and foggy appearance. Forty-five minutes later, a jazz sax was on the sound system and his third drink, delivered with precision, sat on a coaster in front of him. He was thinking about ordering grilled chicken wings and a plate of niuroubing, a pastry with spiced beef in the center, when she finally walked in.

Ruben stood at her approach and pulled out the chair next to his. She had a long, smooth stride that made him think of a shuffle beat, and her waist-deep black hair, now in a ponytail, swayed like a metronome. He could sense, however, a distinct shift in the woman's mood. Her allure was still there, but not as piercing. The difference between a cathouse musk and Sunday-go-to-meetin' floral. She even toned down her clothes, wearing a dark gray pinstripe pantsuit, with a two-button blazer, and a black silk blouse with a modest neckline. The string of pearls gave her age away.

Gee, I hope it's not somethin' I said.

The throaty timbre remained. "Mr....Carver?"

Ruben smiled and nodded. "That's right, and you're Miss or Mrs. Chin?"

She swiveled slightly right, her head bent to the left as they made eye contact. "Please, call me Lisa."

Ruben wasn't intimidated by beautiful women, but small talk wasn't a talent he'd bothered to develop. It was a wonder he ever got laid. "Well, Lisa, can I buy you a drink?"

She pointed at his and said, "If that's a martini, I'll have the same."

Carver signaled the bartender for one more. He had only one question for the woman, but held his tongue. He wanted to get at least one drink in her before he spoiled the tone. His instincts kept him alive, but that didn't mean he didn't commit a faux pas now and again—especially when it came to the opposite sex.

"So, Lisa, what brings you to Beijing?" A soft start.

"I'm doing research on a problem my organization is currently facing. It's more of an obstacle than a problem, really, and I've been assigned to do some troubleshooting."

Her drink arrived, and after the customary clinking of glasses and perfunctory "cheers", Ruben responded with, "That's interesting. I've had assignments like that. They can get a little dicey at times."

"Yes, as a matter of fact, I believe the issue I'm dealing with will be...dicey."

"Really? By the way, and I hope you don't mind me askin', but, where 'bouts in China are you from?" Ruben couldn't place the underlying accent.

"I grew up in the interior. My primary years were under the tutelage of Chan Buddhists. Very archaic. I believe the modern term in the west would be Zen Buddhism. However, like so many things that evolve over the centuries, what's practiced today is only a dim reflection of what it once was—what was imparted in me."

"Interesting, but you couldn't have spent your entire formative years there. Your English is excellent, maybe central London posh?"

"Very good. You have an excellent ear. Yes, I've had opportunities to travel. I studied abroad—London—as a teenager."

He watched her take the final sip from the long-stemmed conical glass, the olive going untouched. The gin had brought a hint of a blush to her sharp features and once again the attraction to this femme d'âge mûr had him feeling...erect. Coital interest aside, he was conscious of the fact she hadn't bothered to poke around his edges. The cognition: *She already knows who I am.*

"So tell me, Lisa, who do you work for?"

"I'm not at liberty to say, other than it's an international philanthropic conglomeration."

Carver slowly nodded. "Ya know, as much as I'd like to take you upstairs, strip you down and lick you 'til the cows come home, I got a feelin' we've started somethin' here that's gonna play out in whole different way."

"Excuse me?" The sultry she-devil's guard came up, and the coal shards behind the epicanthic folds pierced him with undiluted malevolence.

Oh, yeah...there you are.

"When you get back to Shanghai, tell Ryan I'm comin' for him."

CHAPTER TWELVE

Unfullfilled Expectations

Ruben checked his watch. *Maybe I've got time to get a massage.*

Lisa Chin, if that was her name, made a chilly exit after Carver called her out. No threatening remarks, no long menacing glare, or even a nice-to-meetcha-thanks-for-the-drink. It was as if she switched off. Hookers and drug dealers often got that look. The vacancy behind the eyes after a completed transaction. In Vietnam they called it the thousand-yard stare.

The lonely walk down a deserted hallway. *So what if she was supposed to use and abuse me?* He really felt like he'd missed out on something. As he passed her door, he considered knocking, but thought better of it. She didn't seem the type to forgive and forget, and he certainly didn't want any black widow action.

The encounter firmed up a of couple things, though, which to that point, had only been conjecture: Ryan Henderson was indeed the hacker, and, whoever hired him, had Carver in their crosshairs. The woman in the red dress was an aggressive move and he placed her in his brain's grab bag of shit to check on. He reckoned the next time they met wouldn't be over an adult beverage.

* * *

Indentured servitude required as much willingness on the part of the person chained to the oar as the belief of control by the coxswain beating the drum. For months, Randy Hodges, now once again Ryan Henderson, accepted the contrivance he was trapped in a situation in which there was no escape—bound to a postulate: the only safe place lay in the warm embrace of the The Board.

He couldn't deny, for the most part he was comfortable, but a Bubble Boy existence wasn't what he'd signed on for. The sense also continued to grow that this ride would end sooner than later, and he would invariably end with it. When Helen Parsons dimed him to NCIS, he initially pictured himself doing a swan dive from the frying pan into the fire, but when he saw the live surveillance feeds from the Marriott in Beijing, enticing possibilities started to effervesce.

After the hacking he'd been doing, a black bag job on the Marriott's systems was a walk in the park. He didn't limit himself to Carver's room, either; he had access to everything, and he was impressed. There was sight and sound almost everywhere in the hotel. *Ya gotta love a totalitarian state.*

Getting a look at Carver did two things for Ryan: he could pick him out of a crowd if he had to, and he was convinced Carver had the keys to Ryan's cuffs. It wasn't the way Carver acted or moved, so much as the way Qu responded to him. The naked Tai Chi thing, he had to admit, was a total turn-on, but watching Carver fry her in the bar really had him going. The capper was the tantrum she threw when she got back to her room.

Fucking priceless.

Qu would know he'd been watching and listening, and the grief he'd have to endure when she got back to Shanghai was enough for him to get a move on. He didn't want to be anywhere near her when she stormed through the door. The cloak and dagger he applied online would have to be transferred to the streets, and after his long walks on his days off, he had a few ideas about how to disappear. The first order of business would be to shake his shadows, and he had a plan already devised.

If he wanted to stay off The Board's radar, and out of the woman's reach, at least until the Feds brought him in, he'd have to construct a new persona. He had a dresser drawer full of money that would help catalyze the change, but it wouldn't last forever. He hoped Carver wasn't just blowin' smoke up Qu's world-class ass. He only trusted one person, and even she pushed the limit, but he was committed now. Before yanking the hard drives and throwing them in a shopping bag, he copied and encrypted several files onto a four gigabyte USB flash drive and coded a message to Helen, sending it to a drop box she had access to.

The email had only two words: Get Out.

When he got back to his apartment, he took a shower, knocked back three fingers of Midleton Very Rare, turned down the bed, and then turned out the lights. After making what he considered enough of a bedtime show, he tiptoed to the closet and got dressed in the dark. With passports in a pocket, cash and hard drives in a pillowcase, he descended to the avenue fronting his mammoth cocoon and hailed a cab.

When Qu departed the Marriott, her driver was waiting. She'd allowed herself a moment of self-indulgent fury over her brief, but enlightening encounter with Carver before she calmed herself. She perceived no value in remaining in the hotel, and had the chauffeur take her to the house she maintained in the Capital.

She had no doubt Hodges witnessed everything. That was the point of having him tap the hotel's security systems. It was to be an object lesson for the man; however, she'd been the one taken to school. Out of balance in mind and body, her *Qi* seemed blocked. She needed to regain her power. In a voice quiet, but commanding, she instructed the man behind the wheel to go to Sanlitun. He'd been in her employ for the better part of his adult life and understood what this deviation meant. She needed to feed the demon.

Considered a part of the diplomatic district, Sanlitun Road, a bar, and restaurant haven in Chaoyang, was close to the center of Beijing, and ran between Dongzhimen Road and Workers' Stadium North Road. Its bars and club scene were popular with Chinese and foreigners alike, and on weekends the open-air grills covered by orange tarps were packed. The smell of chicken on skewers sizzling on hot plates, mixed with stale beer, body odor, and trash littered thick along the street, assaulted her olfactory sense as she began the hunt.

Often, along with the party animals, were creatures of a different sort. Groups of four and five young Chinese toughs looking for trouble. If they couldn't find an excuse to jump a reveler, they'd make one up. If it was getting late, they didn't bother having a reason. They'd pick a target, generally a lone individual, or a guy with pretty girl friend, and jump in.

Street fights were never elegant or disciplined. Lots of pushing and shoving, errant kicks and punches, along with gang-ups and pile-ons that would generally send one or two people to the hospital. A set-to almost always involved idiot onlookers who recorded it on cell phones, with some chickenshit commentary, or made the sometimes-fatal mistake of getting in the middle of the brawl to try to break it up. Fights like these in Sanlitun were so common, the resident shop owners and food vendors paid little attention unless it affected them directly.

For Qu there was another benefit for her perambulation in this neighborhood: no police interest.

She had her kit in the car, and as they drove south on the side street of East Third Ring Road, she peeled off the jacket, pants, and blouse. She then slipped into a black leather jumpsuit and a pair of black socks, followed by black Reebok eight-inch tactical boots. The final piece of equipment was a one-and-a-half-inch wide, black snakeskin belt with a thick, flat black buckle she had custom made by a company in California. A cute little fashion accessory every girl on the go shouldn't be without.

When they arrived at the intersection of Dongzhimen and Sanlitun, Qu stepped out and headed south. The driver would meet her on Workers' Stadium North after she finished her workout. At the next corner, she turned right, and then left again, until she found what she was looking for. A group of rowdies, maybe five or six, standing outside a bar staring at passersby. They were on the prowl and she pointed her boots in their direction.

The heavy foot traffic on the sidewalk took a wide berth around the thugs and, as she approached, she calculated she had enough space to move. What she didn't want, was to find herself in a position where they could take her to the ground. At seven meters she began pushing her *Qi*, and like an omnidirectional antenna, her vibe was hitting everyone around her.

She had the gang's full attention at three meters, and as she closed, her appraisal of their numbers, how she would string them in a line, and who would go first, blossomed spontaneously. They had swaggered into the middle of the sidewalk to cut off her advance, spooning her with their versions of romantic epithets. As the tallest soon-to-be-dead—at about 180 centimeters—grabbed at her right shoulder, she spun right in an unaggressive pirouette, gripped the man's wrist with her left hand, and smiling, she took four sliding steps backward, pulling him along.

The others, seeing this as a positive sign, shambled in behind. As she watched them line up, she did a shuffle-step toward her new boyfriend, and with a single smooth action pulled the two-and-a-half-inch folding knife from its slot on her belt buckle, using the thumb stud to lock the blade forward. With knuckles down in a hammer grip, she buried the steel to the hilt. Her stab, twist, and rip started at his liver and finished five centimeters past his solar plexus, knuckles up.

She pushed him left and stepped into the next man, stabbing and ripping in exactly the same manner. Qu had two down in less than five seconds, but it was enough time to alert the others. Unfortunately, they weren't as game as she'd hoped, and she had to run a third one down. She didn't tackle him—she didn't want to scuff her leather. Rather, she did a running front kick to the back of his knee, and a palm strike between his shoulder blades and he went down hard on his face.

With a drop knee on his thoracic three and four, she pulled his head back, palm on forehead, and cut his throat. It was pandemonium in a twenty-meter radius, but Qu was less than elated. While the sport kill sated the rage and helped bring her back in balance, the source of her discontent remained. After wiping her blade on the dead man's T-shirt and re-seating it on the buckle, she stood, and strolled calmly to her waiting vehicle—Ruben Carver still on her mind.

As the driver merged onto East Third Ring North,

towards the S11, Qu reflected on her mistake in approaching Carver. The assumption she could manipulate the gwailoh like any other man, now placed her in a compromised position. The other American succumbed quickly. She'd placed herself in front of him in much the same way she did with Carver, but unlike Carver, he came to her with enthusiasm.

Her account to The Board regarding the necessity of aggressive interrogation was what she considered a tempered response. In truth, she had the information she needed before she started on the man. The activity afterward, was for her personal edification and nourishment. As she carefully carved away his strength, his screams had a lyrical effect she lazed in. She bathed in his life force as he slowly bled out, and, as she recalled the way his gonads smelled as they marinated in the ginger, garlic, star anise, and scallions, her mouth watered.

She then crossed her legs, musing about what she would do to Carver in their next tryst, and made a call to Shanghai. With no answer, she sent a text message in English: *He'll be in Shanghai in a few days. Are you ready?*

Within seconds her phone buzzed. In English she said, "That was quick."

"We saw you with him. You're making a big mistake fucking with this guy," came Sonny's curt rejoinder.

"That's no way to speak to a lady, Xú Bao-Zhi. Mind your manners. Now, are you ready?"

"We'll be ready," Sonny intoned.

"I don't want you to kill him. I would prefer you capture him instead."

Dead air for several seconds. "The contract was for termination."

"Please, you're being well compensated. Take him someplace of your choosing, away from the prying eyes of the PLA. I want to spend more time with him."

When the taxi dropped Ryan in front of the building housing the Mingwang Internet cafe, he had no idea how long he had before his handlers came looking for him. He'd known for several weeks, his companions were running in shifts. The guys following him in the afternoons were never the same guys who were with him at night. By varying his play times, he began to observe a pattern in the stints. One evening, when he decided to go out for a late toddy, he actually witnessed a turnover. 11:00pm on the dot.

He tested it four times and determined two things: it was unerring, and, for the few minutes it took place it was like he was invisible; they didn't notice him.

A month earlier he'd discovered the GPS trackers in the clothing. The Chinese may have had a knack for the devious but that didn't mean they were consistently good at it. What they gained through ingenuity, they lost in lousy quality control. A poorly repaired seam on a pair of trousers caught his eye. When he tugged on an errant thread, the diminutive device dropped on the floor. A random inspection of his pre-approved wardrobe found the same tiny tool, and he figured the rest of the rags had the same.

The clothes he wore to Shanghai were no help. Those went missing almost as soon as he was out of them. The previous week, he decided on the items he would take when it was time to split, and separated them from his daily wear. The trackers, from all the articles of clothing sat on the shelf above each. The shoes were old school, with the transmitter in a heel, but the way it was attached was novel. The heel didn't have tacks or dowels, it screwed on.

The cameras in his apartment were well placed, and

finding a blind spot where he could debug the attire was next to impossible, so he wore it to the office. The dragon lady was the only one who watched him there, and that was through the monitor, and his keyboard activity. Fortunately, all the trackers were installed in the clothing in exactly the same manner—inside inseams.

His first concern, when he walked out of his apartment was the light from the hallway. There were cameras there, as well as in the elevator and the lobby. When he got to the street without being challenged, he knew he had a chance. On top of that, the taxi passing by was a lucky break. It couldn't have been better timed. Thirty minutes later, he was sitting at a keyboard sending Helen a love note, with a coded message for Carver. Then he paid up and made his way to a gentleman's club in the Bund he'd heard about, with the intention of an extended stay.

CHAPTER THIRTEEN
June 5, 2005

Sleep came, but it was restless. The REM Zs played out like film noir. A mix of disjointed dreams orbiting the vision of a lady in a black cheongsam, with a long Fu Man Chu mustache swaying like a metronome. When the 06:30 wake-up call rang, he was already up, and out of the shower. The TV was on for the noise, and he could hear Wolf Blitzer using one of his better cause-for-concern voices reporting Marines crapping on the Quran in Guantanamo, or some such thing. Someone, apparently, needed to desecrate. *Well, I guess when you gotta go, you gotta go.*

Dressing for the embassy, he put on the beige suit with a powder blue, Egyptian cotton shirt, and a Rush Limbaugh tie in blue and gold. He'd brought a couple Jerry Garcias as well, and thought it more politically correct to knot one of those, but he was feeling particularly conservative that morning.

The knife went in his coat pocket, and the ASP in his thin, brown, Coach attaché. He never traveled to China with a laptop. The Chinese intelligence collectors were too inquisitive and not the least bit subtle. A few years back, one of his traveling partners made the mistake of leaving his in the room, and when he returned, found it in pieces on the bed. He figured the Chinese were disgruntled about the password protection and sent a message.

He didn't bother calling the office, deciding to wait until he got to the embassy. Checking his pockets for his wallet, money, passport, and badge, he picked up the card key. He didn't bother with the tape on his way out—housekeeping would be in later to straighten things up. The executive lounge had a small buffet set-up, and a guy in a white smock and tall chef's hat was standing at a portable stove making omelets. The breakfast area was about half-full with an even Euro-Asian mix. No casual attire. The sharks were shoaling early on a Sunday morning.

Before he sat down for his regular on-the-road fare of soft cheeses, sliced ham, hard-crusted rolls, and coffee, he stopped at the check-in desk to inquire about his neighbor.

"Good morning Mr. Carver."

"Good morning. Say, I uh...was supposed to meet someone for breakfast but she doesn't seem to be here yet."

"Is she a guest?"

"As a matter of fact she is. She's staying in the room next to mine."

"Oh, do you mean Miss Chin?"

"Yeah, that's right."

"I'm sorry, sir, but Miss Chin checked out last night."

"Do you know if she mentioned whether or not she was going back to Shanghai?"

The desk clerk smiled and said, "No, sir, I don't have any details." But, with a gossipy inflection, she whispered, "The person I took over for this morning did mention Miss Chin was very cold, and extremely rude."

"Well, I don't think it's anything to worry about. She

heard some bad news last night."

The U.S. Embassy was a fifteen-minute walk from the hotel. The smog was a constant, but that early in the morning the ozone level was down, and he could breathe without it stinging his throat. When he reached Tianze Road he hung a left. From there, the facilities housing the U.S. Diplomatic mission was a straight shot. The area was known as the Third Embassy District, and Embassies of France, India, Israel, Japan, and The Republic of Korea, to name a few, where housed along or no more than a stone's throw from the road he was walking on.

Since it was an early Sunday morning, there'd be few personnel on the grounds. Capt. Williams made a point of letting Ruben know in the itinerary the country team meeting would only last an hour. It was the day-o-rest, and with the exception of those on the duty roster, people wanted to go to church, spend time with their families, go shopping, do the laundry, watch sports on the AFRTS feeds; anything but get stuck at the embassy dealing with Carver.

He was cool with that, and appreciated the time they were giving him. Ruben wanted to be out of their hair as much they wanted him out of their hair. Beijing was a city he was always happy to leave. An environment, in his mind, if personified, would be described as someone in dire need of Prozac.

When he reached the gate, he presented his credentials and passport to the uniformed Chinese paramilitary policemen standing on the sidewalk next to the guard shack entrance. To save time he spoke to them in Mandarin, advising he had an appointment with Capt. Williams. It took more than a few seconds for it register he was speaking Chinese. Not that the accent was terrible, just the opposite. They had to get their heads around the idea the words were actually emanating from the gwailoh's face.

Within ten minutes, the young Marine who met Carver at the airport was signing him through. The knife and ASP were a concern, until he turned them over to the Marine. He was then handed a temporary badge with an alligator clip, that hung on his jacket lapel. The main building was about fifty yards behind the gate, and after climbing a dozen steps to the lobby, the Marine post where Ruben checked in was to the right. The sergeant behind the ballistic glass confirmed his authorized access and passed him another badge. Three minutes later he was walking down a hallway to the Defense Attaché's Office.

The DAO layout was typical. The Armed Services Attachés had small offices, big enough for a four-drawer standard issue desk, a bookcase, and two metal-framed arm chairs with padded seats and backrests. The admin personnel were all enlisted, and situated in the middle of the space, with a senior NCO as office manager—an E-7 or possibly an E-8. When Ruben walked in there were two or three people milling around, coffee cups in hand, and in civilian attire. With the exception of the Marine, he couldn't tell the service complement.

Ruben's escort pointed him toward Williams' cubbyhole, a middle office on the opposite side of the room. The Captain was clearly visible, but he acted like he hadn't seen Carver yet. Scanning the bullpen as he slalomed his way around a printer and two desks, he observed two other occupied offices: one with a guy pounding a keyboard; in the other, some dude tamping a stack of papers even.

Carver knocked on the doorframe, and as Capt. Williams looked up, he introduced himself. "I'm Ruben

Carver." Williams was posted to China when Ruben was in Iraq, and their only contact after his return had been by phone or email.

"Hello, Ruben." Williams extended his arm across the desk. "Come on in."

Ruben jostled around the chairs in front of Williams' desk and gripped his hand, followed by a single up and down.

"Do you want anything...cup of coffee, maybe?"

"What time does the country team meet?"

Williams looked at the clock on his desk. "We've got thirty minutes."

"A cuppa joe would be great." The coffee at the hotel was stale, and burnt, and he contemplated the possibility he'd get better here. The Navy floated on the stuff.

Roy Williams was taller than Ruben, maybe 6'4" or 6'5". He wore a pair of dark blue chinos and a dark blue, short-sleeved knit shirt with NAVY emblazoned on his left pec. Long legs and short frame, he was on the lean side, with narrow shoulders, but wide in the hips. Aside from his big hands and feet, he had a prominent proboscis in need of a trim job. The crew cut was fresh, and Ruben wondered why the barber hadn't taken the time to mow the nostrils.

He could sense Roy's beady, narrow-set eyes giving him a once over as they moved across the room to the coffee mess. In Ruben's experience, Attachés, at least in the Navy, were either incompetent fuckups or truly unlucky motherfuckers. In either case, they'd managed to piss someone off who had the juice to put a crimp in their careers. Ruben perceived early on never to ask an Attaché what made him decide to take that career path. Attaché and career were, on the whole, mutually exclusive terms.

Success in the Navy required being in the water, in the

air or in a supply and logistics assignment that kept fellow officers in the water or in the air. If a Captain in the U.S. Navy was assigned to a diplomatic post, it was likely he'd crashed too may aircraft, run a ship aground, or had done something else equally as deleterious in a critical mission setting. That, or he simply found it impossible to curry favor with the folks who controlled his advancement. At any rate, if an Attaché posting was in an officer's personnel jacket it was generally the last thing anyone would find recorded there.

Williams handed Carver a white ceramic mug, with a crossed-anchors emblem, from a dish drainer next to the sink. He poured the java from a fresh pot and pointed at a full-sized refrigerator. "Milk in the there if you need it."

After dumping two teaspoons of sugar in his cup, followed by the black stuff, Williams continued. "It's amazing how fast your entry approval came through. It may not be a record but nobody here has seen the Chinese cooperate quite like this. It's made us nervous."

"I can imagine." Ruben's mind was on the country team meeting.

From his experience, there was always a show of interagency cronyism for the benefit of the outsider sitting in. The jovial knuckle bumps or friendly chiding went on unabated until the Chair, the CIA's Chief of Station, cruised in. Unless otherwise delegated to a member who enjoyed being an asshole, the curmudgeon at the table was invariably the COS.

Once the meeting kicked off, the inveterate dick measuring contest, and political machinations began. Indigenous rivalries, common between the services, were invariably on display. They'd get around to a smattering of discussion about local events, or the latest issues revolving around something someone did to hurt

Chinese feelings. They would then deliberate about what the Chinese were doing to fuck with, and generally irritate, the Ambassador—an apparent favorite pastime of the pinko bastards.

As if reading his mind, the NA advised, "Ruben, you need to be ready to answer some hard questions coming from the Agency about your operation."

"Okay, that's to be expected. What's the gripe?"

"The COS is pissed. He's pissed with the Army for running an op under his nose without explicit Agency approval. He's pissed because they lost a man on his watch. He's pissed because even if we knew who killed him, and why, we probably can't do shit about it. But mostly, he's pissed and worried, because it signals an escalation in the way the Chinese respond to intelligence collection, and what it means to his NOC program." Williams was referring to CIA case officers with non-official cover. These were folks operating in China without diplomatic protection, and without any visible affiliation with the U.S. Government. They worked for Chinese organizations and multinationals in a purely covert capacity—otherwise known as spies.

"Fine. If I were him, I'd be going apeshit, too."

"Yeah, well...he doesn't see you as a solution to his, or the Army's, problem. Your reputation has preceded you. Your last two trips into Malaysia, and your tour in Iraq, as well as the unconfirmed body count in this country over the last five years, have him believing NCIS could have selected an agent less... controversial."

Williams watched Ruben's reaction closely, and continued. "Now, don't get me wrong. You've had your successes, and that's been acknowledged, but the COS has some rules of engagement he wants you to agree to." The implication in the statement being: if Ruben pushed back, he might as well not bother unpacking. The embassy would find him a ride to the airport.

Carver took a sip from the mug and licked a drop off the rim. Williams was spurring his horse down a well-traveled trail. He leaned against the counter, taking stock of Williams' words, and elected to reply, "Yeah, I understand. Whether or not I agree to his operational parameters, I'm still gonna go to Shanghai. I have to. The advance on the Admiral's visit has to be conducted, which is what you and I have to work on."

The country team in any locale could be very parochial about operations directed from offshore, and as much as he didn't like to admit it, Carver had a bad habit of peeing in other people's ponds. He knew Williams was counting on him to make a good impression with the country team HMFIC, and decided to play nice.

As he looked at the crease form between Williams' eyes, Ruben stated, "Relax, Captain. I didn't come here this morning, all dressed up, to be the party-pooper. Let's go hear what the nice man has to say and then get to work."

The meeting room was located in the Embassy SCIF. The entry procedures were standard fare getting through the outer door, but once inside, they were standing in a mantrap. The outer door had to close before the inner door into the SCIF would open. Captain Williams slid his coded ID card in the reader, punched in a sequence on another number pad, and then placed his thumb on a biometrics reader.

The entry yawned to a large space with a half dozen desks currently unoccupied. The computer monitors on each appeared to be JWICS connected but now displayed the approved embassy screensaver. The room also housed a twelve-foot by eight-foot by seven-foot soundproof box sitting on a steel scaffold. The U.S. Embassy had been under a 24-7 microwave barrage—care of the Ministry of State Security—for as long as anyone could remember. If embassy staff wanted to have a private conversation, the only place on the compound they could do that with certainty, was in the box in the SCIF.

The health hazards from exposure to the microwaves were never studied as far as Ruben knew, but it apparently never baked anybody's innards, and the youngsters were still getting it up. When they moved into the box, there were four people already seated: the Regional Security Officer, the Legal Attaché and the two guys Ruben saw in the Defense Attaché's Office earlier that morning; they were introduced as the Air Attaché and Army Attaché.

The hi-how-are-yas were quick, and then the regular gaffs about the NCIS TV show were bandied about. That ended as soon as the COS arrived. The guy had a reputation of being in a perpetual state of perturbed, and the expression on his face as he peered around the table suggested he was in his normal frame of mind.

As his eyes fell on Carver, he growled, "Is this the NCIS guy?"

There was something familiar about the way the COS moved, but it was the voice that rang the bell for Carver. Before Capt. Williams could say anything, Ruben intoned, "Lieutenant Sheppard?"

Sound inside the box was ordinarily flattened, but after Ruben opened his mouth, it went quiet as a tomb.

"My name is Art Sheppard." A snarky intonation. "Nobody's called me Lieutenant Sheppard in over thirty years. Do I know you?"

"Yeah, we met. On Thanksgiving day." Ruben squinted his eyes a fraction, trying to picture the prick younger. "Thirty-one years ago. I, and what was left of my squad, enjoyed the hospitality of you and your Marine platoon for a couple of days at a fire base, about five kilometers from the right side of the Laos border."

"Sergeant...Carver..." Recognition began to light behind his eyes. With both hands flat on the table he pushed himself up, and started moving around what had now become an obstacle. Ruben was also up and shuffling toward the COS. With right hands clasped they pounded each other on the back, laughing.

In almost a whisper, Sheppard said, "Shit, boy, I thought you were dead."

"So did I, until I realized the Army just transferred me to Germany. You did okay for yourself, though. But why the CIA? Seemed to me your future looked pretty bright with the Corps."

"That conversation is best had over a bottle of Scotch." He stopped, and gazed at the other, now dumbfounded, faces in the space and said, "If this is the man who's been brought in to unfuck your situation, then I'm satisfied."

CHAPTER FOURTEEN

China Doll

"Wèi."

"I have been trying to contact Hodges this morning, but he is not answering his telephone. Where is he?"

"He is still in bed."

Qu checked her watch: 10:40am. Hodges never slept this late on a Monday. *It's not like him to play...what do the Americans call it...hooky.* "Is he sick?"

"I don't know, he hasn't checked in." Hesitation. The chump hated this part—questions he couldn't answer.

"Have someone go to his apartment. I want him to call me." Qu had arrived home after midnight and, inasmuch as her phone had been silent, she assumed Hodges had been behaving. She maintained a pleasant demeanor, but she could feel her irritation growing, and cut the call without waiting for a response.

Her bungalow was in the Shunyi District, northeast of Beijing proper. It was a four-bedroom in a gated community called Yosemite; a neighborhood that favored monied foreign nationals. She didn't particularly care for the ostensible sophistication, but considering China's current attempt at gilding a dung heap, she understood the necessity to perpetuate the image. Besides, she could come and go in that environment without anyone taking notice.

Analogous to her apartment in Shanghai, her Beijing residence was equally sparse. Her meditation chamber was identical, and after peeling off her jumpsuit, she had no interest in going anywhere else in the house.

She didn't sleep, but stayed in a meditative state until the sun came up. Her intent was to, once again, explore her options regarding not only Carver, but her current association with The Board. The very real possibility of the operation's termination by an external force needed to be examined before it became inevitable. The more she pushed her *Qi*, however, the more she found herself undulating to her own leitmotif.

As Qu stood eating a breakfast of grilled salmon and congee with boiled potatoes, carrots, and onions, she reflected on her session from the night before. She rarely yielded to the past, but that's where she wound up, and she pondered its relevance to her present situation.

In 1952, the year of the water dragon, Qiu Hu was the firstborn to a young professor of economics at the School of Management, in the Harbin Institute of Technology. Considered an intellectual with a bright future serving the interests of the Communist Party, her father, and notably attractive mother, were allowed to sire a second child three years later. The all-important male progeny.

In the early fifties, the country wallowed in the throes of economic distress. It was also desperate to sustain the integrity of its borders from the then modern-day Golden Hordes: The Soviet Union and the United States. The path to relief that her father and a large number of his fellow academics quietly espoused, unfortunately, didn't sit well with the socio-political aims of the Chairman and most of the hardline party members. A lesson in the old adage that, just because the posited solution to a problem may be correct, does not mean it's acceptable.

In 1956, however, Mao started a campaign to encourage the intellectual elite to challenge the communist regime with opinions and recommendations. The concept being, through "constructive" criticism, new ideas would blossom into reforms that would enrich the ideals of the revolution. It became known as the 100 Flowers Campaign—from Mao's speech proclaiming: "Let a hundred flowers bloom; let a hundred schools of thought contend".

The initial response to this grand initiative was lackluster. No one wanted to pony up ideas critical to the party. They saw what happened to those who opposed the communists, when they took control of the country less than a decade before. Mao's patience, always on a short fuse, grew thin, and in the spring of 1957, he put the word out that compliance was mandatory. If he didn't get some criticism out of the country's brain trust, there would be hell to pay.

The motivation behind the program was never really certain; however, one thing was clear—to everyone—the Chairman may not have had a clue how to run a country, but he was a genius at running a revolution. A natural born campaigner, he believed by allowing this thoughtful contention, an overwhelming surge of support for socialism would pour in decrying China's roots in Taoism, Confucianism, and more importantly capitalism.

Boy, did he get it wrong. Within a month, the Premier's office was buried in an avalanche of letters, magazine articles, flyers for rallies, conferences, and symposiums.

The educated masses bitched about everything from communist cadre corruption to the lack of democratic governance. Some even called for the dismantling of the regime, demanding transitional governments with term limits. The young professor, in his zeal to impress and educate, wrote several long epistles addressed to the Man himself. He, like so many others, laid out in agonizing detail, economic programs involving private ownership of land, free trade zones, tax relief, and several other suggestions that would ultimately upset the commie applecart.

Mao wanted radical—he got radical—and it scared him. By the summer of 1957, the crackdown on counter-revolutionaries and right wing extremists began, and tens of thousands of intellectuals, students, artists, and activists who were coerced into sharing their opinions were rounded up for re-education, forced labor, and execution. The young professor was one of them.

Nearly destitute, his wife grabbed the kids and what she could carry on her back, and fled in disgrace to her family living in Jiujiang city—over two thousand kilometers south. The trip took more than a week, and after being raped, beaten, and subjected to daily humiliation and starvation, she reached the not-so-outstretched arms of her parents. They, themselves, had to endure re-education at the hands of the communists —as former landowners—and were labeled followers of Mao's hated rival, Chiang Kai-shek.

Assigned as an administrator of a farming cooperative, Qiu Hu's grandfather decided to take in her mother and son, but the extra mouth Qiu Hu represented was another matter. Arrangements were made, and she was dropped off at the door of Donglin, the local Chan Buddhist monastery, where she would travail under the tutelage of reformist monks for the next ten years.

Progressive Buddhism found a strange, and

compatible, bedfellow in Mao's China. It was seen as more of a science, than a religion, because it was based, they believed, on reason, not faith. The teaching of the eternal, unlimited, and absolute conception of the spiritual and material phenomena of the Universe that led to a final atheistic truth: there was no God.

Put to work immediately in the kitchen, Qiu Hu learned through frequent beatings and exhortations, to remain stoic. The tears dried up, as did the laughter and her childhood. Neither happy nor discontent, for the most part, she worked, studied, and meditated as directed, mastering the martial, as well as the spiritual.

Key to her remaining in the monastery past puberty, was a result of another of Mao's choice leadership decisions, which occurred between 1958 and 1961. It was called the Great Leap Forward, and the famine that accompanied the disaster claimed the lives, estimated by some historians at over forty million, of Mao's faithful constituents. Why this blip in history had her settled firmly in the lap of Buddha had to do with the irony of Buddhism in general. A belief system espousing love, peace, and understanding, the monks made their real coin from death and destruction.

Complaints of price gouging on Buddhist burial services may have ended under the regime, but the chaps in silk robes and shaved heads made up for the losses on sheer quantity. The Chan Buddhists, literally unable to keep up with the burial demands, had funerals on a production line. They made a killing, and Qiu Hu was able to furtively provide enough money and food to her mother and brother to sustain them. It came with the understanding that they were not to share with the grandparents. Fortunately, the two elders showed the good sense to die within the first year of the famine.

The years in training, along with the benefits of a

good diet and clean environment, allowed her to grow tall and strong. She had her father's physical stature and her mother's beauty, which may have been an asset in Hollywood, but at a Buddhist monastery, the abuse she was accustomed to changed.

The assaults from the younger monks were usually painful and frenetic. The older wise men preferred to take their time, a few with special perversions they enjoyed. Fighting only made the monks' nesting compulsions longer and more violent, and she began to accept them without complaint.

Her escape during these late night monastic love fests was her *Qi*, but in her anger and quiet despair, she penetrated something new and dark. Through strong, focused emotion, she discovered how to propel her *Qi* like a shield and sword, using it against her errant lovers. She sapped their strength physically and mentally, and while she drained them of spiritual energy, she burned with it.

About the time she began looking forward to the visits, they stopped. The bald cenobites, without accepting any responsibility, recognized the pernicious turn her spirit had taken, and aside from the continued training and education, she was left completely alone. It wasn't until 1967 that she found a purpose in the monastic instruction, aside from the constant, self-indulgent quest for mythical, universal enlightenment.

After the cessation of the Great Leap Forward, Mao was sidelined in favor of a new Chairman, Liu Shaoqi, and his political ally Deng Xiaoping. Two men who viewed political ideology as great food for thought, also recognized it didn't do much when it came to putting rice on the table. They brought the country back from the brink of complete collapse through the use of pragmatic planning, and a revision of priorities—agriculture, light industry, and heavy industry, in that order.

But, as everyone knows, you can't keep a good revolutionary down, and within four years, Mao had regrouped and regained favor with party hardliners and the military. There was no denying the man had a gift for power politics, and this time, through his new "continuous revolution" dogma, whipped the country's youngsters into a frenzy. He was back with a pure communism agenda referred to as the Cultural Revolution, and with it, the Red Guard.

There were millions of them, and they were tasked with rooting out old customs, old culture, old habits, and old ideas. It was chaos, as ideologically consumed youth destroyed libraries and museums, fired universities and schools, and defaced shrines and any buildings with historical relevance. They turned on their teachers and professors, who the Communist Party leadership considered anti-Mao—anyone, and everyone, viewed as lacking acceptance of pure communism. It was an entire generation lost in the destruction of the old, without any consideration for what would replace it. Mao's retort to those watching in shock and horror: *Hey, kids today...whaddya gonna do?*

Qiu Hu heard about what was going on from her twelve-year-old brother, wearing his green uniform, and spouting unintelligible Maoist slogans. Like any big sister, she thought he was nuts and ignored him. That came to an end when the Red Guard came knocking on the monastery door. She realized they weren't just about vandalism and violent diatribes, which was bad enough—these children were armed, and had arrest authority.

What she found appalling was not that they beat the monks senseless, or took hammers and gasoline to the cloisters. It was all the wasted energy spent in an exercise that resulted in nothing of value being produced. Nothing was gained. It was kids at play. They tried to destroy it for no other reason than it was there.

Her years at the monastery came to an end when a group of six to eight of the young revolutionaries found her in the kitchen. They had a head of steam up, and when they spotted her, it wasn't recruitment into the cause they had on their minds. After the years of abuse from randy monks tanked up on homebrew, this new threat was not met with fear or panic.

As Qiu Hu sprouted into womanhood, she'd learned to recognize the wanton gleam, but as they came at her, a thrilling sensation occurred, that radiated from her center. Not an adrenalin rush per se, although there was that. It was her *Qi*. As she hefted a pair of cleavers, she gleefully went to work.

The monks found her while doing a survey of structural damage to outlying buildings. Still in the kitchen, her arms were caked in blood to her biceps as she stood at the stove, stir-frying something in a wok. It smelled delicious. Then they spotted the bodies—what was left of them. Their blood-soaked uniforms lying in front of the wood-burning oven. The monks stood in awe as they peered into her face beaming with bliss. As she looked up, they saw her smile for the first time, and heard a question that sent chills through them: "Hungry?"

Dressed, and ready to meet her driver, the phone rang. She recognized the number, and without the usual greeting, began speaking. "Where is he?"

A three-second delay occurred before the response. "We don't know. He's gone. We checked the video recordings from this morning and last night, and saw him leave the building at eleven pm. "

"That's it? That's all you know?" Anger bubbled up.

"He got into a taxi, and that's all we know."

"How did that happen? Wasn't there a team outside?" She wanted to kill someone.

"We believe he slipped coverage during the shift change." A nervous quiver sounded in his voice.

Qu took a breath and centered herself. Screaming about incompetence, and demanding to know who was at fault wouldn't do anything but shut the idiot down. "Listen...he'll try to leave the city. Send people to the Heng Feng and Long Distance Bus Stations; try ticketing at the four train stations, as well as Hongqiao and Pudong airports. He doesn't have a drivers license, so check taxi and limousine services for a long-distance customer pickup.

"If you locate him, try and secure him but don't make a scene. Find out where he's going, and we'll intercept either along the way, or at his destination."

Qu paused to reflect on Hodges' personality, and his recent activity. She wanted to meditate, but needed to put her team on his trail before he put more distance between them. And then she remembered. "He won't leave Shanghai. He'll try and hide until he can make contact with an American coming from Beijing."

The man listening now sounded confused. "What do you want us to do?"

"Do everything I've told you, but don't spend more than enough time to confirm he hasn't tried to leave Shanghai. Post surveillance outside the U.S. Consulate and start thinking about places he could hide for three or four days." Qu again stopped talking—mentally surveying Hodges' possible options. "Tell the team watching the woman in Boston, to pick her up. Do not kill her yet, although some abuse would be prudent."

The emotional connection Hodges had to the Professor was easily discerned. If she were treated poorly, he'd want to protect and save her.

Qu finished with, "I'll be in Shanghai this afternoon. If you're able to reacquire, subdue but don't hurt him. That will be my pleasure."

As they terminated the call, Qu considered advising The Board, but decided against it. She was in no mood to listen to what would surely be trite admonishment. Rather, she grabbed her bag and went out the door.

CHAPTER FIFTEEN

The Briefing

Art Sheppard sat back down, and Ruben followed suit. The mood in the room, generally a composite of the Chief of Station's foul temperament and the other members' skittish solicitude, was heavy, but no longer oppressive.

Before he turned to Carver, he looked at the Army Attaché and asked, "Anything new today?"

The Attaché's name was Colonel Robert Brillson, a ring-knocker from West Point. Unlike most Naval Attachés, his career began in military intelligence, a successful grad of the CIA's Field Training Course in Virginia. He impressed some folks at the Defense Intelligence Agency after running a couple of noteworthy operations in the run up to the first gulf war, and they decided to redirect his career.

The DIA sent him to the Amy War College for two years to earn a master's degree in China area studies, and then dropped him in the Foreign Area Officers program, FAO for short. They packed him off to Monterey, California for eighteen months to learn Mandarin, and the Defense Language Institute had him speaking the lingo at a level 3/3 when he finished. He could eat with chopsticks and have a fairly fluent conversation about the weather. At least, that's how he thought about it, and exactly what the DIA wanted.

It was important for guys in that rarified field to be comfortable in their area of operation, understanding the political, cultural, sociological, economic, and geographic issues, without becoming too cozy in the environment. They had to remember who the foreigners really were—going native was frowned upon.

The guy was bright, and a standout in political-military planning, arms control, and clandestine operations. He'd had stints in the Defense Attaché's Office, both in Shanghai and Hong Kong, before this assignment, and was one of the COS's go-to guys in dealing with the PLA.

Brillson glanced at Carver and then Sheppard. Ruben could tell Brillson was wondering about what was obviously a St. Crispin's Day moment between the two.

I got some 'splainin' to do later.

Brillson began, "If you don't mind, Art, I'd like to use this time to bring Carver up to speed. He had several questions passed to me through Captain Williams."

"Yeah, go ahead. It'll help open the floor for discussion." Sheppard was no longer watching the clock.

"I won't get into the history of Chinese hacking, other than it continues to be a prevalent threat to national security. Up until a month ago, most of our efforts worldwide were primarily in prevention, with awareness programs, tight systems administration, and detection. After the Chinese, or what we knew to be China originated attacks, gained access to classified data—new drone tech, specifically—the Army decided to utilize an asset in country to attempt to identify and, if successful, neutralize the threat.

"From my last conversation with Captain Williams, I understand Special Agent Carver, here, correctly deduced the MI case officer—his name was Brody, by the way—had already been in country for a while before we put him on the scent."

Brillson paused for a few seconds, apparently distracted by Ruben shifting in his chair, then continued. "Our asset was an FAO who'd been in Shanghai completing a host nation approved sabbatical. He had less than a month left in that part of the program iteration, and the DIA approved his use."

With spittle flying, Sheppard interjected, "Oh, by the way, where is the DIA's representative?"

"The Defense Attaché is in DC this week," Brillson responded. "Apparently, he's trying to put the genie back in the bottle."

Carver thought this an interesting comment, making him wonder if Brillson's relationship with the DA was less than cordial. Since the Colonel hadn't continued the briefing, Ruben guessed they'd transitioned to discussion and asked, "With the fact that Brody went down, are you assuming he was successful with his first mission objective?"

"That is the assumption. Unfortunately, we didn't get anything more than a short list of possibles to go on, and some photos. The last name on the list was a Canadian computer tech, named Randy Hodges, who worked for a small subsidiary of an international..."

Carver finished his sentence. "...philanthropic conglomeration."

All eyes were now on Ruben.

Sheppard leaned back in his chair and in a low, but less-than-gruff voice, advised, "Special Agent Carver, it sounds like it's your turn to share."

"The gentleman's real name is Ryan Henderson, a former MIT grad student, ex-con, and an embedded civilian IT support contractor on the USS Blue Ridge.

He jumped ship and went missing during the Blue Ridge visit to Zhanjiang at the end of February. He's the hacker we're after."

The room was dead silent for five seconds, and then everyone started talking at once. The voice that cut through the cacophony was Sheppard's. "You want to tell us how you know this?"

Ruben spent the next ten minutes outlining the information Prosser obtained, the contact with Helen Parsons, the visit by Sonny Xú's men—avoiding the details that would confirm Sheppard's concerns about Ruben's reputation—and his encounter with Lisa Chin the night before.

Sheppard scratched his crown and countered, "Okay, so let's say everything you've told us is correct, and this knothead, what was his name...Henderson...wants to come in, say he's sorry, and get a start-over. Why didn't he just say 'fuck-all' and walk his computer-geek ass down to the U.S. Consulate in Shanghai and turn himself in?" Just because Sheppard and Carver shared a moment, didn't mean that thirty years of carefully crafted skepticism was goin' to the back of the bus.

"I can't tell ya. I haven't met the guy to ask him." Ruben hadn't had the pleasure of Art's company over the last several years to be intimidated by his management approach. The ol' questions-you-can't-answer ploy to keep the hired hands off balance didn't phase Ruben. He still remembered Art with a bullet hole in his ass, he had to tend to.

"But let's say he does wind up on your door step. After what he's been up to, he probably has a pretty good idea what to expect." Ruben centered his attention on the former Marine. "I know I would."

Sheppard didn't respond in words. He simply tapped the table top with the nail of his right index finger.

Ruben scanned around the box and continued. "Yeah, okay, look...we all know exactly what would happen. He'd be thrown in a locked room, interrogated for days, until you found a way to get him out of the country. You'd ignore his requests for a lawyer, laugh in his face about a deal, and threaten him with Guantanamo Bay, or some other equally undesirable holiday destination. That is, unless he unassed the goods—on everyone—and then he'd still go to jail, 'cause no one likes a traitor." Ruben now made eye contact with all his cellmates. "Is that about right?"

Captain Williams piped in, "The man can't go free, Ruben. He's a threat to national security." A comment that basically reinforced Carver's rant.

"Bullshit, Roy, we do it all the time. It's called the Witness Protection Program. The organization this idiot savant works for is worth knowin' about. If the operation on the Blue Ridge, and this set-up in Shanghai, is any indication what they're capable of financing, how long do you think Henderson would last in a lock-up?"

Sheppard held his hand up, claiming the floor. "Whatever this character's motivators are, we're all in agreement you need to go Shanghai, but there are some things you need to know first. In particular, a couple nuggets we put on close-hold about what happened to the Army agent. Bob, you want to do the honors?" Sheppard nodded at Brillson.

"Based on the information from the PLA major you're gonna meet in Shanghai, whoever put the grabs on Brody had him for a few days. He'd been tortured and mutilated. Somebody carved him up and kept a few pieces as souvenirs. He was missin' his family jewels, and apparently, it wasn't from fish nibblin' on him. In his last communication to me he was gonna meet with some Chinese cougar at the lounge bar in the Portman Ritz-

Carlton. That sound familiar?"

Ruben nodded and eyeballed the Regional Security Officer. "Do you have a contact at the Marriott Northeast who can get us a copy of the security camera recordings from last night? The feeds from the lobby bar, or the hallway on the twenty-fifth floor. We could run her picture through all the criminal databases and I'll show it to the major when I meet her tomorrow."

"I'll see what I can do."

Art Sheppard was looking at the wall clock again. "Well, gents, unless there's something else, I have to go." Sheppard glanced at Ruben and said, "Carver, do your best to find the guy, and please, whatever you do, don't get dead. Oh, one more thing, and this shouldn't be too hard for you from what I understand: if you have to waste someone, make sure you clean up after yourself. You don't have diplomatic status, and if you windup in jail, there's nothin' we can do for you."

That was the closest thing to a fond farewell he was going to get, and while the hacker was his mission priority, Carver had to keep up appearances. For the next three hours Ruben and Captain Williams discussed the Admiral's visit, which included his arrival time in a P-3 Orion, a four-engine turboprop ordinarily used for anti-submarine and maritime surveillance.

The Commander of the Seventh Fleet had a two-and-a-half day itinerary, sans the Blue Ridge, that started with the U.S. Ambassador at the consulate, a visit with the Naval Attaché, and then a country team meeting to discuss valid threats to U.S. interests by the Chinese.

Next were courtesy calls on the Commander of the East China Sea Fleet and the Mayor of the Shanghai Municipal People's Government, also known as the Mayor of Shanghai. While there were also a few dinners scheduled at locations run by the PLA, the three-star in charge of the most powerful naval presence in the Far East was more at risk getting caught with his pants at his ankles—the recipient of a slobbin' nobber from a working girl in the hotel bar—than any attempt on his life.

Carver would check the room assignments, the hotel layout, talk to the manager and his chief of security, run the routes for each of the meeting locations, as well as check the airport and hanger facilities. He had a PLA liaison—a woman—to get him into the meeting sites, and to coordinate local security support. The Naval Attaché had the names of the meeting participants he'd confirm with the PLA major. With a few other odds and ends to work out, the advance would take no more than three days.

After reviewing his plan, he remembered something the Army Attaché had said during his brief.

"Hey, Roy, what's up with this PLA liaison, Major Zhao Bao-Yu? Is she a registered source?"

"She has been officially assigned as our point of contact in Shanghai. She acts like all the other PLA stiffs we deal with most of the time, but once in while she can be candid. You mentioned you wanted to show her that woman's picture from last night. I'd be careful if I were you. She provided us a few details about Brody, that's true, but it was out of courtesy, and we're pretty sure it was state approved before she divulged it."

"That's even better." Ruben liked Roy, and was beginning to believe he was probably one of the unlucky Naval officers selected for this duty.

"How so?" Williams' wiry nostrils flared as he took a breath.

"If the major had been directed to provide information about a U.S. Army officer's torture and death on Chinese soil, then it's unlikely his demise was sanctioned by the state. You also gotta believe his activity during his sabbatical had been monitored, and if our commie counterparts thought he was committing espionage, he'd either be in jail or deported."

Williams nodded. "That's pretty much our read on it as well, but Sheppard saved a little space in the back of his mind, that the Chinese may have decided to make a example of Brody. He still worries about his NOCs."

"I know I can't trust Major Zhao with much information, but I need to have some idea how receptive she'd be in helping with our Ryan Henderson headache."

Not being contrary, Williams said, "I've met her a few times and just know she's typically officious, irritatingly bumptious, and arrogant beyond belief. Aside from that, I think she's kinda cute." One eyebrow went up, and with a half-smile, he shrugged his shoulders.

He then advised, "Oh, that reminds me, she's gonna meet you at your hotel, not the police station. I have her number here somewhere..." Williams pushed some papers around his desk until he came up with a small yellow slip he handed to Carver. "Give her a call when you get in. Her English is pretty good. Also, since she'll be hauling you around, Captain Fairbanks, the Naval Attaché in Shanghai wants to know if you still need a car and driver."

"Thanks. I'm not sure about the driver yet. I'll talk to Fairbanks about it when I get down there. I will need to have a chat with the driver who'll be schlepping the Admiral."

As Williams' head bobbed up and down, he stood, checking the top of his desk one more time. Glancing at Ruben, he announced, "Okay...so, if there isn't anything else to cover, I have to get goin'."

"Nah, I'm fine. Thanks for the support, but before you

go, is there a computer I can use to send an update to my office?"

Williams pointed at the young Marine who'd been Carver's escort. He was sitting with his feet propped up on a short filing cabinet, reading a dog-eared *People* magazine. "Talk to him. He's the duty NCO. He'll get you situated."

No rest for the frickin' wicked. A sleepless night. Henderson took a series of taxis from the Internet cafe to a "gentleman's" club on Luban Road, called the Jingyue Sauna. He'd never been there before but had a card with its address he'd picked up in a pub. He wasn't looking for action so much as a place he could lay low for several hours.

He went through the process of picking a girl for a nuru massage—a specialty of the house—twice. Afterward, he stretched out in a lounge chair in a bathrobe and slippers until a pretty young thing in a red business suit with earpiece and mic invited him to leave, advising, "This not hotel, mister."

It was nine in the morning when his feet hit the sidewalk. He may have hated the situation he was running from, but he already missed the comfort of the digs. After sucking down a bowl of noodles in a briny broth from a restaurant two doors down, he had to assay his next move.

The consulate was out of the question. It wouldn't be long before his nursemaids discovered him missing, and the first place they'd try to catch him would be there. Even if a cab dropped him at the gate, he'd be dead before he could show his passport. Then again, if he did succeed, he presumed it wouldn't be long before he wished he were dead.

English language in a taxi was hit or miss, but a cabby

generally understood a passenger wanting to go to a main shopping district. The taxi he attracted, he directed to West Nanjing Road, near Xijang Middle Road. It had a long pedestrian walk with a number of large malls. Most weren't open yet, and he decided to camp out at a Starbucks until the opportunity presented itself to begin his makeover. The first order of business, however, was to buy a prepaid cell phone—it was time to reach out.

CHAPTER SIXTEEN
Shanghai

For Carver, Shanghai was Beijing's obverse, the flip side of the coin. A banker once described it to Ruben as a sociological divide between politics and business. A person could say anything he wanted in Beijing, but in Shanghai, he could do anything he wanted.

Shanghai had always been known as the gateway into China. Since the first opium war in 1839, brought on by Queen Victoria's gunboat diplomacy, it became home to British, American, German, and French settlements described as concessions. They paved the roads, built a railway and other public transportation, established a telegraph system, water and power facilities, and generally relegated the indigenous population to domestic help.

Referred to as the Paris of the East, the New York of the West, it was neither. It was the product of Qing dynasty defeatism, and mechanized imperialism. While the Boxer rebellion had little or no affect on Shanghai, the issue led to the gang-bang of the Empress Dowager Cixi by the infamous Eight-Nation Alliance, which cemented a sense of foreign ownership of the metropolis.

At the turn of the 20th century, the Japanese moved in

with a military presence. After defeating the Chinese in the first Sino-Japanese war, they figured they'd earned a stake. The so-called White Russians flowed in after that, refugees from the revolution in 1917.

In Ruben's view, when discussing China's history and its place internationally in trade, commerce, progressive philosophies in religion and secularism, arts and sciences, as well as organized crime, political unrest and revolution, you were talking about Shanghai. It was the birthplace of the Chinese Republic under Sun Yat-sen, as well as the Communist Party under Mao, and the Nationalists with Chiang Kai-shek.

Up to 1949, it was China's economic center. After the communist take-over, the city went into decline—overtaxed and underfunded by the party hacks. Punished for its history of bourgeois capitalism and foreign influence, Shanghai spent the next forty years suffering a Communist Party shakedown.

It wasn't until 1989, when Jiang Zemin and the Shanghai clique grabbed power in the Central Committee, that things began to change. They cut the city's taxes and went on a rampage, encouraging both domestic and international investment. By 2005, Shanghai was challenging Hong Kong, once again, as the economic hub of China, and after growing to almost 2500 square miles in land area, it handled roughly a quarter of all trade passing through China's ports.

As much as he hated Beijing, Ruben tended to groove on the energy in Shanghai. The relatively new skyline along the riverside in Pudong gave the city a distinctive face, unmistakable from any angle. When the wheels touched down and he rolled his bag to the curb, he was looking forward to good dim sum and zongzi, a glutinous rice ball stuffed with spiced pork, and wrapped in a banana leaf. He had a reservation at the Portman Ritz-

Carlton, but decided it was time to eat. He took a cab, instead, to the Great World, an amusement arcade and entertainment complex that had been around for almost ninety years.

In the beginning it was run by a Chinese mob boss, Huang Jinrong. A multiplex, way ahead of its time, that featured six floors of jumbled restaurants, movie theaters, burlesque shows, and brothels. Since Huang also ran the police department, its gaming and drug dealing were protected. It sat at the corner of Yanan Lu and Xizang Lu, near the Bund, and had a yellow hexagon spire supported by twelve pillars as a landmark.

Now, it was a state approved tourist attraction, with the only thing remaining from the old days being the funhouse mirrors near the entrance. For Ruben, it had the best zongzi in town, and was also a great place to smoke out any surveillance.

With the exception of Lisa Chin at the Marriott in Beijing, he hadn't detected any trailers and was starting to feel neglected. Spotting a tail was a matter of seeing the same faces over time and distance—detection 101—and the way his brain worked, he remembered everything he saw or heard as long as he could put it in context. He looked for someone around him who stood out as a possible trigger to a moving surveillance, and then checked for vehicles that pulled into traffic after the taxi.

At one point, he had the driver pull over and stop in front of large department store. He handed him some bills with the instruction to meet him at the entrance on the other end of the complex. He took his time—he didn't want to lose those having trouble unfastening their seat belts.

Inside, it was a maze of hallways lined with small shops. Each was packed with boxes stacked floor to ceiling, glass showcases, and posters of products taped on walls, the shop owners might actually carry. It was eight pm on a Sunday night, and while there was a steady stream of customers, it wasn't crowded. For counter-surveillance the place was ideal. Plenty of corners to turn, and reasons to stop, look, and backtrack.

The Ministry of State Security, and the PLA may have developed some sophistication in electronic spyware, but when it came to boots on the ground, they often exhibited an astonishing lack of finesse. At first Ruben thought it was purposeful—they wanted him to know they were there. While that may have played into it, he also came to realize—and even empathized with—the underlying factor his nemetic counterparts faced: they didn't have the budget for training or additional personnel. Even the pinkos had to pay to play.

He made the guy in the third store he wandered into. Innocuous and non-threatening, dressed to blend, Ruben would have ignored the droopy shouldered bastard if he hadn't caught him peeking one too many times. He was alone, which meant the rest of the team had either moved into neighboring shops, or were covering the exits. Since they watched him get into the taxi, they saw his suitcase go in the trunk. If this were a team effort, then at least one vehicle would have stayed with the cab.

Time to go.

He'd confirmed the coverage, and he was hungry. His ride was waiting for him, and as he jumped in the back and gave the driver the destination, he watched the tail run to a waiting Volkswagen Polo. A nondescript guy in an equally nondescript car.

No wonder I didn't catch the movement at the airport.

When he reached the Great World, he gave the driver a healthy tip after he pulled his bag from the trunk. The guy was gracious enough to stick around at the department store and he hauled Ruben to journey's end in one piece. As far as Ruben was concerned, the expression "crazier than a Shanghai taxi driver" was more than a pithy quip. In his mind, they gave a whole new meaning to the term *vehicular manslaughter*. Hence, the double down on the gratuity. Yanking his bag behind him, he'd already witnessed the drop-off. His shadow's partner stayed with the car. There wasn't anyone else.

While the city was in a constant state of transformation, the one place that was always there for him was the zongzi stand at the entrance to the arcade. One of the banana leaf covered delights was a meal in itself, and he'd been looking forward to it. He hadn't forgotten about the company, but in the years he'd spent roaming the streets of this ancient burg, he'd never had anyone come at him in a public space. He did want to find out who his companion worked for, but the suitcase was an encumbrance. He couldn't leave it sit out in the open while he introduced himself.

What to do?

"Special Agent Carver." Not a question, more like a declaration.

As Ruben twisted in the direction of the statement, he found himself peering down at a youngish female, maybe mid-thirties, with a thick, pageboy haircut. She had large almond-shaped eyes; black, with heavy epicanthic folds. Her small, flat nose rested between round cherubic cheeks, and her mouth was heart-shaped, with full lips. She was wearing no makeup that Ruben could see, but her skin had a natural luster that didn't require any.

Maybe five feet tall, she had a gymnast's body concealed in a tailored, dark gray Mao jacket and pants, and her shoes looked like Doc Martens Shoreditch boots.

"Don't tell me...you must be Major Zhao, and I take it

that gentleman over there must be one of yours." Ruben pointed at the man who'd been following him from the airport.

"Yes, very astute."

Astute my ass...

Carver felt like he'd been burned. The little guy he'd spotted was a decoy. Someone he was supposed to be aware of while the real team lay invisible, covering him like a blanket. Scanning the room, there was no one he recognized, but the Major wouldn't have come alone.

She's rubbing my nose in it. Bitch!

Speaking now in Mandarin, Carver carped, "I thought we were meeting in the morning. What's with the cloak and dagger?"

Choosing not to answer directly, she chirped, "I was surprised you would come here from the airport, instead of your hotel. I would agree with you these zongzi are the best in the city, but why?"

"I was hungry." He paused, assessing the little China doll standing in front of him. "Since you've been on me, did you detect any other interested parties?" Taking a bag with two fist-sized zongzi, he handed the lady at the counter ten yuan and got back some change. Glancing again at Zhao, he tilted his head toward two unoccupied chairs at a beat-up card table, and moved in its direction.

Apparently more comfortable discussing this in English, she stated, "I'm not sure. We received intelligence that there were at least two people who showed some interest. We don't know as of yet who they are, but our sources are considered reliable."

She's not sure, yeah, right. "Did you get any pictures?"

"What do you mean?"

"Did you get any pictures of the people you weren't sure about?" Ruben unwrapped the banana leaf, and with wooden chopsticks, removed from a white paper wrapper, started to eat.

"Yes." It was a definitive, single-syllable response.

"You gonna show me?"

"Not at this time, no."

"Ya know...you might as well be forthcoming, 'cause the folks you're referrin' to are gonna come after me sooner than later. If you're around when that happens, some of the shit is definitely gonna get stuck to you. Now I have a photo I want to show to you, but before I do I want to see some ID."

"I don't believe that is necessary."

"Lady, I don't know you. I've never seen a picture of Major Zhao Bao-Yu, and if you are indeed her, I'd like to see some proof."

The Major tugged a small, folded wallet from a front pants pocket, and after opening it, flashed a photo ID in Carver's face. She held it up long enough for him to see her picture and the Chinese characters for the People's Liberation Army.

At that Carver wrestled a slightly crumpled piece of paper from the inside pocket of his suit jacket, and after smoothing the page open, showed a grainy photo of Lisa Chin.

There was recognition on Zhao's face. "How do you know this woman?" The tone was a stark contrast to her undeviating dispassionate mien.

"To tell you the truth, I don't know her." Carver wasn't hedging. All he had was an impression—a bad one—but an impression, nonetheless. "She approached me last night and we had a drink together. I will tell you this: she's somehow tied in with an American hacker, here in Shanghai, who's been especially naughty. He's someone I would very much like to have a sit-down with. This lady," Ruben tapped the picture with an index finger, "is, I believe, connected to the recent death of a

U.S. Army officer on sabbatical in your fair city."

Zhao's back stiffened, but she maintained eye contact. "You are out of your depth. You are talking about a police matter, and this is none of your affair. You're here to check security for your Admiral's visit, and will do so with my assistance."

"Please, let's not bullshit each other, shall we? You know exactly why I'm here, otherwise you wouldn't have bothered to showboat tonight. I need your help, and in doing so, you get to corral this broad." He tapped the picture again. "And shut down an operation embarrassing to the PLA. At the same time you can show the world a magnanimous China in the protection of property rights and poke the U.S. in the eye for all those unfair accusations about information piracy and illegal network intrusions. Whaddya say?"

"What do I *say*?" Pure aggravation sounded in each syllable. "You Americans, in your arrogance as the strongest nation in the world, think you can come here and tell us what to do. Make demands, and expect us to heel. You always assume 'right' is on your side."

She's been waiting to say that since she drew the short straw on this gig. "Yeah, so? America is the strongest nation on the planet and we didn't get there by being wrong. Think about it. Anyway, now that we've cleared the air, are you going to help me or not?"

Ruben could sense a shift in demeanor. A faint movement around her lips and the little muscles around her eyes, the frontalis, procerus, and orbicularis oculi relaxed perceptively. *Williams did say she was cute...*

"If we do this, it will be me allowing you to assist. Our file on you is substantial. To say to the least, it can't be read in one sitting, and while there are hints of effectiveness, we view you as an undisciplined rogue, with little regard for procedure or due process. You have also committed espionage in China, and we would very much like to put you on trial for crimes against the state, followed by a public execution.

"At this point, I'll have to talk to my superior and obtain his approval for any activity outside the scheduled visits and site evaluations. You have meetings at your consulate in the morning. I'll meet you in the afternoon with an answer to your request."

Great—she's hooked. I may be on her shit list, but she's definitely hatin' that other broad. "All right, I'm glad we have an understanding. Now that we're gonna be workin' together, can you tell me her real name?"

"Qiu Hu...my sister-in-law."

CHAPTER SEVENTEEN
Ryan's Run - Qu's Quary

Ryan found the Starbucks he was looking for, and, with coffee in hand, he only had to wait thirty minutes before the large department stores and malls opened. His first stop was the Westgate Mall. A shop on the second floor sold prepaid 3G SIM cards, and units to put them in.

He bought a monthly plan, and for 300 yuan he had nearly a thousand minutes of airtime. His next terminus was the hair salon on the fifth floor—a cut and dye job with a spray-on tan, and a charge on the phone. The sports center on the same floor had him in a warm-up suit and trainers, along with a gym bag for his cash, passports, and the hard drives. The last item on the checklist was a pair of fashion frames and sunglasses from Maochang Optical just down the street.

By two pm he was bop-stridin' toward East Nanjing Road, making a call to Helen. It was three am, on Monday, in Boston. She answered on the second ring and went hysterical when she heard his voice. Ryan remembered her throwing a similar fit when he was busted. In this state, there was no talking to the woman, but he had to force her to listen—to get a grip.

"Helen...*Helen...listen to me!*" He could hear a break in the sobbing as she sucked air. "Are you okay? What happened?"

"I read your last email and came to the office. I got a call from a neighbor a few hours ago. She said several men broke into my house. *They broke into my house, Ryan!*" Once again with the sobbing.

"Helen, where are you now?"

"I'm still at my office on campus. I've called the police. Ryan, what's going on?"

"I can't explain now, but if the police are coming, stay where you're at. I'm going to give you a phone number, and I want you to pass it on to the NCIS agent who came to visit you. Tell him..."

"It's a her."

"Okay, tell her to give it to Ruben Carver. You got that? Ruben Carver."

"Is that with a...su...su...'C'?"

"Huh? Yeah, yeah, with a 'C'." *What the fuck?* "Can you do that?"

"I think so."

"Do it, Helen. You'll be saving my life. I love you. I gotta go." He punched off, and thought about powering the phone down, but decided he couldn't risk a chance of missing a call.

A hotel room was out of the question. He'd have to provide a passport to check-in, even in a fleabag that would take cash. There were plenty of department stores, malls, restaurants, coffee shops, movie theaters, and massage parlors, but they'd be looking for him in places like that. He had to keep moving.

A city of twenty million, with a sprawl the size of New Jersey, and every second he was expecting one of Qu's bozos to come around a corner. His concern was certainly justified, but not because of chance. Had he settled into a place where he could sit quietly for hours—like an Internet cafe—odds-on he would have gone undetected. He'd made enough of a change in appearance to be passed over in a cursory check, but Internet cafes would be the first obvious choice of locations to look for someone like Ryan.

By five pm, he was on the pedestrian walk in East Nanjing Road, a wide avenue of constant foot traffic, laced with foreign shoppers. Focused on what was in front of him, he didn't notice the two men zeroing in from behind until they grabbed his arms at the wrists and biceps and pulled him to a stop. Startled at first, he instantly recognized the two troops and reflexively smiled with a nod.

They responded by stepping forward, pulling him along. What happened next surprised him as much as it did the two gong fei. He instinctively planted the balls of his feet, dropped to a squat, glutes touching calves and, as if bouncing, he performed a clean and jerk motion. He thrust straight up, smashing his elbows under their chins. Both bamboo goons had their mouths open, and the action, adrenaline enhanced, shattered the teeth of the man to his right, while the man to his left bit the tip of his tongue off. When they went down, Ryan added a bit of insult to injury by stomping on their heads until they lay motionless.

The mob, witnessing Ryan's gusto in his defense of self, neither repelled, nor chastised. After a brief, shocked silence, a few began to clap, and within seconds the gathering, which probably totaled two or three hundred, cheered. Ryan didn't want to hang around to admire his handiwork, but he was never one to let adoration go to waste. He waved, bowed, and exited stage right—chin up.

What he now realized, when it came to his babysitters, is that they didn't rely on what he looked like to keep him on a leash. Neither did they need electronics. His profile, his silhouette, the way he walked, were as unique as a fingerprint. They were also aware of the other areas in Shanghai he felt comfortable. He may have walked his handlers for miles around the municipality, but he had a pattern he fell into that he apparently hadn't recognized. They did.

As he thought about it an instant longer, he figured they probably started their search by teams, driving or walking in designated sectors, spiraling outside in. He also suspected a call was made to Qu before the two approached him, and leaving the area became an imperative. He ran to the end of the pedestrian walk, and after waving down a taxi, he ordered the driver to take him to Pudong. Assessing on the fly, he assumed the bitch's hired help would converge on the East Nanjing shopping district, and he elected to go to the one area he believed they'd look last—in the pub around the corner from his apartment.

Qu was in crisis management mode. The woman, Helen Parsons, evaded the men who were supposed to be watching her. It didn't require any further information to infer Hodges had been in contact with the woman, and she found a place to hide or barricade herself. In addition, Hodges had been spotted on East Nanjing Road but the two men who reported in had somehow been dispatched. She'd sent three teams to the area after the call, only to find two men dead and the police on their way.

Aside from the Hodges hindrance, Carver had arrived, and Qu had two men waiting for him at the Hongqiao Airport. The news he was being followed by the PLA was expected, but when they told her Carver was meeting with Feng's wife at the Great World, her rage boiled over, and with claws bared, she shrieked at the ceiling.

Under the circumstances, delaying further contact with The Board was ill-advised. She placed the call for a forum, and waited. Within twenty minutes the call began.

"We're on, and the line is secure."

Qu went through her briefing in the same platitudinous manner as any other regular update. Emotionless in delivery, she provided the results of data capture and targets successfully penetrated for the week, using it to segue into her encounter with Carver, and his arrival in Shanghai. There were no questions at that point. She left out the specifics pertaining to the PLA and Zhao.

"Gentlemen, I fear we have reached a juncture that may permanently affect our operational effectiveness." There was no video with this call, and she wasn't sure how many members were in conference. With her on the line, members' names were never used, and the total number of members to the assembly never revealed.

"We're listening," was the only response.

With dispassion, she began. "Mr. Hodges has gone missing. His last communication was with Professor Parsons, and upon departing, he cleared his system. All the tracking devices we had in place in the clothing he was wearing had been removed. He left his mobile phone, laptop, wristwatch, and credit card. The items he did take: passports and money."

The line went dead for several seconds. Then, "When you said he cleared his system, what does that mean?"

"He also took his hard drives."

"Madame Qu, as you are, I'm sure, painfully aware, those hard drives are the operation. Every transaction and target are recorded on those drives. His method of operation, along with the programs, algorithms, and

TOR network he developed—including the locations of his intrusions—are on those hard drives. Considering how resourceful Mr. Hodges is, there is the possibility he may also have a client list." The voice crescendoed to a shout.

Another man smoothly, and calmly interposed. "Miss Qu, please tell us what you're doing to find Mr. Hodges."

Qu went through the search process without providing details on the men down, or the fact they'd missed their first chance at apprehending him.

"Gentlemen, it will take time to locate Mr. Hodges. Shanghai is a big city but he's limited to the places he can hide. We have a broad, source network and we will find him. Since he hasn't attempted to enter the U.S. Consulate I believe it is an option he is not yet comfortable in exploring."

"Please be aware that time is of the essence. There are a number of parties who have invested heavily in our project, and will not take lightly to a drop in production."

"Once we have recovered the hard drives, do you have a replacement for Hodges?"

It was clear to all that Randall Ian Hodges had run his course, and while they appreciated his effort, he was not part of what had become another salvage operation.

"We'll start looking immediately. We do have a few relievers in the bullpen we can start warming up. What about Carver?"

The analogy was lost on Qu but she got the riff. "Under the circumstances, Carver is now a major player in this scenario."

"How do you mean?"

"Based on Hodges' correspondence with the professor, along with what I view as his thought process, he will attempt to contact Carver. If he's got a new cell phone or laptop, he may have done so already. While we continue the search, our monitoring of Carver's activity will be important. The two men will come together, given enough time. It would, in fact, be a fortuitous eventuality." Qu was careful not to evince any personal interest in the NCIS Special Agent.

"Yes, well...you already know The Board's concern in getting too close to that man. We are, unfortunately, not positioned to provide you more support in your decision-making. However, we will keep you posted on information we obtain from the embassy and consulate, relevant to your situation. Helen Parsons, unless otherwise useful to your pursuit of Hodges, will be removed from further consideration."

I wonder how soon I'll be removed from further consideration...

"Miss Qu, please be aware that while The Board recognizes your past, excellent record of delivery, this current state of affairs has a few members questioning your overall effectiveness. You must resolve this fully and with haste. Do you understand?"

"Yes."

After the call terminated, she remained seated, feet flat on the floor, and began the exercise. As she touched her *Qi* she lighted on another issue that immediately brought her fully forward: Sonny Xú and the active contract.

She dialed his number and sent a text message, but, unlike their recent exchange, Xú failed to respond.

Sonny hated being stepped on when he was trying to get a job done. He felt his phone vibrating on his side, and recognized the number. The text message, as usual, came seconds later but he was in no mood to talk to the xiǎomì. He assumed there'd be interference but not to this extent. Hemmed in by a couple of Qu's men and what felt like a regiment of PLA, he had no way of executing the smash and grab.

Carver appeared oblivious to what was going on. Probably because he was confused by all the trees in the forest. The players were practically tripping over each other, and so caught up in checking each other out, they almost missed him as he moved through the airport. If it hadn't been for the PLA trigger they would have.

When they got to the Great World, Sonny witnessed the encounter between Carver and the PLA officer. He didn't know who she was, and felt compelled to ring Qu, but let it slide. If it weren't for Carver's reaction to the woman, he would have thought it was a prearranged meet. He sent one of his men in close to listen to the conversation, and what came back to him, at first, made little sense. Talk of an admiral's visit, and a security check meant nothing to him, however, as soon as his man mentioned the dead American Xú perked up.

While Sonny wanted to get paid on this contract, he couldn't afford to run afoul of the People's Liberation Army. The cops were one thing, but the PLA had too many resources, and a long memory. If he was going to make a move on Carver, it had to be done quickly. Based on the conversation, his window would close in the next eight to twelve hours. After pulling his men back, he sent only one man to tail Carver to his hotel.

Sonny took the time to insure the PLA had no more interest in the gwailoh that night, and verified the photos he'd taken of the woman. The news she was related to Qu was interesting, but how he could exploit the information hadn't come to him yet.

Qu's men didn't make it out of the parking lot. Their bodies were stripped and dumped, later, in the river. It was unlikely the tramp would find out who was responsible. To a great extent, his decision to "pull" her surveillance team was as much a reaction to her threat on him, as it was removing them from his playing field.

The man he sent after Carver had already been designated for this part of the set-up. He was in a conservative business suit and had a suitcase. Hustling in true Chinese fashion, he made sure he was checking in at the same time as the dabizi, and within an hour, Sonny had the information necessary to initiate the next part of his plan.

Embarrassed by Major Zhao's conspicuous display, and his own realization he'd fallen asleep at the wheel, Carver was hyper alert as he walked out of the arcade. As much as he wanted to look at everyone within fifty feet, there were too many bodies. He focused on motion, and people heading for taxis. He didn't spot Zhao, but there were a number of men, moving to vehicles, he'd noticed in the arcade while he and the major were engaged in their bandied repartee.

When he arrived at the Portman Ritz-Carlton there was only one person he was certain had been with him at the old portico: a Chinese "businessman" who elbowed his way to the check-in counter next to Ruben. Considering how he'd just gotten burned, he was a little surprised by this jackass's lack of subtlety.

After he threw his bag on the bed he called room service and ordered a pot of coffee. He anticipated a sleepless night. The dirtbag at check-in wasn't one of Zhao's, he was fairly certain. Military "bearing" can't be cloaked by civilian clothes—it wafts like cheap cologne. The guy in the lobby smelled like wise guy.

Sister-in-law? Man, what kinda shit have I landed in?

"Feng, it's me." Zhao was pissed beyond words.

"Bao-Yu, what's the matter? Is there another mistake on your pay voucher?"

"Feng...are you mixed up with your sister again?"

"What...how...I mean, what's this about?"

"*I knew it!* Didn't you learn your lesson the last time?"

"You don't understand. It was a mistake...I didn't mean to but...she's family. Why does it matter to you, anyway? He's just a yangguizi in Japan."

"*No*, he's just a yangguizi in Shanghai, and I have been assigned as his liaison. Your bitch of a sister is after him. If you really cared about me—your wife, the woman you said you couldn't live without—you would have disowned that criminal. *Damn it, Feng! You stupid shit!* If she comes after him I will take her down, and then swear to Buddha I had no idea she was your family. You understand? It won't be like last time."

"Okay, okay... But there's nothing I can do. If you have to put her in jail, I'll stand with you and testify against her, but my mother won't be happy."

"*Your mother?*"

"You know her influence—how she is. She won't like it if you try to take her daughter to jail."

"I'm not talking about jail, Feng."

CHAPTER EIGHTEEN

Qu

After pulling off her boots and jumpsuit, she slipped on a pair of tan slacks, a sleeveless yellow-flower print blouse with a low ruffled neckline, and a pair of Jack Rogers Hampton Navajo flats. Fluffing her hair, she was feeling girly.

Qu leaned forward and told her driver, "It was a bit messy tonight. Make sure you give everything a good scrub. Use the Fluorescein after you're finished to check for bloodstains. The knife felt a little stiff as well. The pivot pin needs to be brushed and oiled."

"Yes, Madame. Are you going back to your apartment?"

"That's right, but we're in no hurry." She couldn't remember the last time she lost control of an operation. The problems had stacked so quickly, even in her *Qi*, she found no easy solutions. It seemed to boil down to kill everyone and start over.

The nuisance Carver embodied, if dealt with individually, would have been a toothsome diversion. However, with Hodges on the run, his girlfriend in hiding, and the advent of Feng's busybody wife, she had a careening predicament.

The priority was the hard drives. She had too much

on her plate to punish Hodges with the spanking he deserved. A quick slice and dice, then sweep him under the carpet. She didn't need to be personally involved. The Board had accepted the professor's disposal.

The fabric was beginning to stick to her inner thighs as she turned her thoughts to the Carver issue. *This is becoming annoying.* She stretched the inseam away from her skin. If Bao-Yu got in the way, Feng would just have to understand. It was business, after all. She'd set him up with a nice replacement.

Life had always had its complications. After the siege on the monastery and the subsequent culinary taste Qiu Hu developed, she was kindly asked to shove off. For a fifteen-year-old girl with shaved head, a jiasha, and woven straw sandals, there was only one place she could go.

Her mother, a resourceful and winsome woman, had packed up and moved to Shanghai just prior to the Red Guard attack. It required a series of sleepovers with the Jiujiang city Communist Party hacks to obtain travel documents, but, in her mind, it was a cheap price to pay. She'd managed to save enough for train fare, and, once again, took only what she could carry on her back. Dragging her son by his earlobe, she headed south.

It wasn't difficult finding work. Her party connections, administrative skills, and looks, got her an apartment, income, and suitors. She sent her new address to the monks at the Donglin monastery, who, in turn, graciously provided it to Qiu Hu as they kicked her out the gate.

Unlike her mother's difficulties as she escaped the purge of 1957, Qiu Hu found her hike to Shanghai both enlightening and entertaining. Her meditation staved off hunger pangs, and her martial abilities yielded the means to put clothes on her back, decent shoes on her feet, and coin in her pocket.

The progressive Buddhist teachings, along with the socialist indoctrination, had endowed her with a flexible morality, with regard to property ownership. If she found herself in need, she simply helped herself to whatever was available. It generally involved overcoming some resistance from those unwillingly to part with the items. She delighted in the practical application of years in the arts, and she savored those moments watching the lights go out.

By the time she reached her mother's abode, her hair had sprouted in a thick, tangled mass. While she did her best to keep herself clean, especially during her monthly bleed, the clothes she'd acquired on the road, and her lack of socialization, made her appear feral. Mom embraced her for a time, but the maternal instincts lavished on Qiu Hu's little brother didn't necessarily extend to her.

After making her presentable, and recognizing Qiu Hu's natural bent toward the illicit, Mom turned her over to another cloistered sphere—the Sun Yee On. How her mother became associated with the organization was never quite clear to Qiu Hu, but the Hong Kong-based Triad accepted her, no questions asked. While their first inclination was to break the beauty in, before inserting her in one of their top-shelf brothels in Macau or Kowloon, two dead and three hospitalized hastened a change in plans.

Qiu Hu was shipped off to London, and under instruction by the Hong Kong leadership, she was sent to boarding school. Within a few months she was speaking Queen's English, with a near native, received pronunciation. She adapted to the new environment so well, she not only excelled in her studies, but also developed a dandy little extortion racket, and contraband business on the side. After a degree in economics and an MBA from Oxford, she was nearly ready for the Triad's mainstream operations.

What she asked for, and what she got, was an opportunity in enforcement. She roamed the remnants of old Chinatown, in the East End, and made a home in the City of Westminster, a borough in the center of Greater London. Chinatown in that area, off of Shaftesbury Road, was developing fast, and the protection rackets, loan sharking, drug trade, gambling, and prostitution were enjoying the same robust growth.

Qiu Hu was not only gifted in collection, but showed an exceptional talent in eliminating competition and expanding the Triad's area of influence. On a few occasions homegrown posses tried to discourage her, much to their regret. However, it wasn't until a local IRA chapter, known as the Balcombe Street Gang, discovered three of their members dressed out like slaughtered hogs, that they got the message and gave her a wide berth. Not wanting to miss an opportunity for a bit of free press, the IRA turned their frown upside down, taking credit for a bomb Qiu Hu left in place of one of their mate's liver.

She spent the next twenty years bouncing back and forth between the Far East and Europe, with a few stopovers in San Francisco and New York. The Triad bosses came to rely on her as their chief trouble-shooter, handling difficult negotiations with competing interests. She was allowed her own crew, paid a handsome compensation, and they even turned a blind eye to her gastronomy. Yet, as her reputation grew, so did her efforts in maintaining anonymity. In the files of most international law enforcement, and intelligence organizations, she remained an enigma known only as Qu.

For Qu, it wasn't merely about murder and mayhem, although a girl did need to have a reason to get up in the morning. The money for her education had been well spent. The Triad bosses were always pleased with the ending balance on a business she was sent in to turn around. Her gift was vision, the ability to navigate the Triad's interests in the most treacherous environments. The end results were going concerns, with sustainable earnings.

Through the many years of faithful service she'd earned a seat at the table with the other bosses, but was always denied. The drawback was her gender. A bone of contention, with major implications among the leadership. If she sat among them, there would always be the possibility, no matter how remote, a woman could become the boss of bosses.

The provincialism around this debate had a ripple effect that caught the interest of The Board. A multinational, postmodernist organization with members, who, in their own rights individually, held positions of power and influence. They included captains of industry, politicians, old money socialists, and nouveau riche capitalists espousing static rhetoric, that together controlled the flow of trillions of dollars worth of assets worldwide.

While uninterested in the arcane trappings and semi-religious vestiges of other secret societies, The Board exercised significant sway in global politics and policy. Their goal being autocracy in directing sociopolitical and cultural evolution, as well as the balance of power, masked by a thin veneer of democratic process.

Always looking for new talent, The Board saw in Qu the type of program manager unaffected by social norms. Never burdened with the naive constraints of a belief in right or wrong, her training and upbringing had made her utterly ingenuous, remorseless and merciless. The Board wooed her with promises of an autonomous role in a new world order, and while she didn't believe a word of it, the money and independence sucked her in. Neither did they complain about her comestible predilection, as one member sagely opined: environmentally, you can't argue with a hunter who eats her own kill.

Carver was out of the shower and in a pair of briefs covered by a hotel bathrobe when the coffee came. The young man pushing the cart had a number-one cut, and spotty, thin mustache. The white waiter's jacket was too small in the chest and shoulders, and the muscles in his arms bulged under the fabric, spreading the cotton weave. The black pants fit better, but his shoes had scuffed toes, and the soles were run down. *I know exactly what's wrong with this picture.*

Tip in hand, Carver handed the tough ten yuan, and as he reached out to take it, Carver spotted the edge of familiar ink. With a short, chopping right hook on the chin, he dropped the phony waiter on his ass. The kid was stunned but not out, and as he looked up at Ruben, eyes clear, he rubbed his jaw.

Here comes trouble...

Ruben didn't want to kill the delinquent, he needed information. He didn't want to beat him into submission, either—he'd just gotten out of the shower. As Carver backed away, he felt the cart handle against his keister. As the gangbanger got his feet under him, still in a crouch, his hand went to a back pocket. Not a particularly crafty move. When he lunged, knife up, Carver had the quart-sized, metal coffee carafe in hand.

He hit the kid's wrist while parrying the knife outside, and jarred the blade loose, sending it sailing onto the bed. Carver then countered, stepping in with his right foot, and with a tennis backhand, nailed the jerk in the face with the jug. The turd hit the wall. With a hole where his two front teeth belonged, and his nose broken, he slid once again to a sitting position.

It's all about the follow-through.

After picking the knife off a pillow, Carver grabbed the chair from the desk and used it to straddle numbskull's thighs. It was time for answers, but the youngster was bleeding heavily from his nose, and the blood running down his throat was choking him. Seated with his feet on the prick's hands, Ruben twisted and reached behind, feeling around on the top of the cart until he found the linen napkin. He folded it into a thick, small square, and after pulling the kid's head forward, used it to apply pressure to the superior labial artery below the nostrils.

Within two or three minutes the hemorrhaging subsided to a dribble and Carver pushed the dude's head back against the wall.

In Mandarin he said, "Okay, let's get started." The banger's eyes widened slightly, and Ruben was satisfied he understood what was said. "What's your name?"

No response other than an angry expression, which turned to agony when Carver cupped his crotch and started to squeeze. The air he exhaled whistled through the toothless space.

"Now don't be that way. What's your name?"

He remained mum until Carver used the knife the kid brought to the party to slice his belt open.

"What are you doing?" The phony waiter squirmed, and beads of sweat broke out on his now-worried brow. The dental work gave him a lisp.

"If you don't answer my questions, beginning with your name," Carver held the blade in front of his eyes,

"I'm going to operate." Not that he actually would. The noise and exsanguination would be difficult to explain to hotel management, but the little shit wasn't in a position to call his bluff. As soon as he flicked off the top button of the trousers, Charlie Chan's #1 son started to sing.

"My name is Li...*Li*!"

"Good...good start. So, Li, who do you work for?"

"I work for the hotel. I deliver room service."

Carver started unzipping the trousers.

"Ja, wait...stop! I work for Xú Bao-Zhi, but honest, I was just to bring your roomservice order. That's it!"

"Then what's this?" Ruben waved the knife.

"You hit me. What did you expect?"

The honesty in that return had Carver thinking. "Xú Bao-Zhi? You mean Sonny Xú?"

"Yeah, I've heard him called that."

"How'd you know I'd want room service?"

"I don't know. He guessed, I guess. I paid a guy in the kitchen to tell me if you ordered anything, then paid him for the jacket and pants."

"What's in my coffee?"

"Nothing."

Carver leaned forward, hand on the zipper.

"It's true. It's not in the coffee.It's in the baozi." Li nodded in the direction of the cart. In a small wicker basket sat four doughy buns filled with spiced beef.

"I didn't order the baozi." Caver spoke to himself.

"Duh...they're 'complimentary'. I brought them with me. Sonny put something in them to make you sleep."

"What?" *This is gettin' good.*

"Yeah, you go to sleep, and we come back and get you. Roll you out on a gurney like you're sick or something. Sonny wants you alive."

Again waving the knife, he said, "You musta forgot about that."

Li shrugged and Ruben let it slide. The kid already explained himself.

"Was Sonny supposed to come for the pick-up?"

"Nah, he don't come outta the office much."

Ruben ruminated for three or four beats before continuing. "This is the deal, Li. I'm not gonna kill you. In fact, I'm gonna let you go. You go back to Xú Bao-Zhi, and you tell him I want a parley."

"What about?"

"You tell him I want to talk about a good lookin' fifty-something Han Chinese woman with a creepy vibe."

"What if he doesn't know who that is?"

"You just tell him."

"Yeah, okay. Can I go?"

"You can go." Carver got up and moved the chair.

After Li picked himself up, he moved toward the door and stopped. "Can I have my knife back?"

"*No!* Now get the fuck out. If I ever see you again I'll use it on you."

Fuck, what is it with the youth today? It's always about them...

CHAPTER NINETEEN

June 6, 2005

Once again, Ruben was out of bed and getting ready before the wake-up call. After Li stumbled out the night before, Ruben rolled the food cart into the hallway, turned the bolt, and threw the doorstop, then propped the desk chair under the knob. He didn't expect any late night visitors, but that ounce of prevention thing was always scratching around in his frontal lobe.

He hadn't talked to Junior Prosser all weekend, and updates were due. Johnson would expect a report on investigative activity and headquarters was sure to be demanding. Fortunately, in DC it was still Sunday, and the suits at HQ rarely bothered with work on the Lord's Day, unless SecNav was giving the Director a poke.

The phone rang at 07:00, with an automated message to rise and shine. Tokyo was an hour ahead, and Ruben figured Junior would be parked in front of the JWICS terminal, looking for any messages. He had sent an Investigative Activity Report from the Defense Attaché's Office after his meeting with Williams, detailing the results of the country team meeting. He anticipated a call from Prosser while he was slamming down some poached eggs and coffee. He didn't have to wait that long.

While picking off one of Li's central incisors stuck to the bottom of his foot, his cell phone buzzed.

"Ruben Carver."

"It's Junior."

"Hey, I was expecting your call. How was your weekend?"

"Quiet. No cops pounding on my door. I read your IA. I'll put out some paper today. There was somethin' else that came in through my SIPRNet email."

Ruben could hear Junior slurping something between words.

"We got a message from the SA in Boston. She passed a cell phone number that's supposed to be Ryan Henderson's."

"What? No way."

"No shit, dude. For real. Apparently, that professor what's-her-name passed it along with specific instructions to give it to you."

"Anything else?"

"Nope. Short and sweet. You want me to read it to you?"

"Yeah."

As Carver waited for Junior to find the number, he cogitated about the implications. He already knew Henderson was looking for a way out. Seemed pretty obvious he was using his main squeeze as his conduit. It certainly made Ruben's job easier, but he wasn't sure he wanted to put the grabs on him yet. He wanted a sit-down with Sonny first; and then he had to determine if the consulate would cooperate.

After Junior gave him the number, Carver asked to check on another name—Qiu Hu.

"What's her connection?" Junior was writing as he spoke.

"She approached me in Beijing. She said her name

177

was Lisa Chin but my PLA contact says she goes by Qiu Hu." Ruben wasn't sure how much he wanted to add, but continued. "Get in touch with the RSO in Beijing, he's got a photo from the hotel security camera. It's not much, but I want you to reach out to the FBI, CIA , and Justice. Also, give it to whoever we're using as the Hong Kong referent, to talk to the cops there; and go through HQ to touch base with Interpol."

"What's her connection with Henderson?" Junior asked again.

"She works for the same 'philanthropic' organization. I have a feeling I'm gonna run into her again. I'm meeting the PLA liaison this afternoon and will try to sweet talk some more info outta her. See what you can find out. It's probably gonna be important."

"Is she good lookin'?"

"Oh, yeah, and she's definitely your type."

"Uh-huh...and what exactly is my type?"

"What, are you kiddin'? Your type's anyone who doesn't say 'no'."

Carver rang off, and finished dressing. Before going out the door, he picked out a tie he rolled and tucked in a coat pocket, slipped the Recon 1 in his right front pants pocket, and put the ASP in his attaché case. He expected the room to be searched that day, and his conversation with Junior reviewed. Carver always assumed his hotel rooms in China would make decent recording studios.

On the elevator, he thought about Ryan Henderson, and whether or not to call him then, or wait until after his meeting at the consulate. The lobby was busy, but he immediately spotted three of Zhao's people, along with the rude fuck that pushed his way to the check-in counter the night before. He still wasn't sure who that character worked for, although he was confident the guy didn't belong to the lady Major.

When he walked into the lobby restaurant the crew followed him in, making any attempt at reaching out to Ryan a public event. He cruised through the buffet for the poached eggs, bacon, and his cheese staple, and after finishing his coffee, he signed for the meal and headed to the entrance.

The Portman Ritz-Carlton was a huge and lavish—but dated—structure with restaurants, boutiques, fountains, high arching ceilings, and winding staircases. Although it had good service and was clean, it was past its prime and in dire need of a face-lift. Ruben continued to stay there because the bar on the mezzanine level shook an acceptable martini, and imported its olives from Greece.

I've got needs just like everybody else.

The driveway at the main entrance was about the size of a soccer field. It was covered in its entirety, with a roof supported by ten or twelve red pillars, at least five feet in diameter. The taxi queue was fast, and within three minutes he was on his way. He spoke to the driver in English, and when he got the I-don't-know-what-the-fuck-you're-trying-to-say hand signs, he figured it was time to see what Ryan was up to.

"Hello?" His voice came out a hesitant whisper. Ruben could hear Chinese pop music in the background. Maybe a bar or coffee shop, but not a department store—aside from the cat-scratch the place was quiet.

"Hello, Ryan. This is Ruben Carver."

"Where are you?"

"I'm in a taxi. Where are you?"

"I don't want to say right now. Not 'til we agree on a few things."

"Hey, man...I got a call this morning from my office in Japan with nothing but your name and a Shanghai phone number. You want to tell me what this is about?"

"Listen, Carver, don't jerk me around. I know I'm the reason you're in Shanghai, and right now I'm in a real fix. There are people after me who will *kill* me if I'm found. I need help." Henderson was whisper-screaming at this point.

"Well, let's say that's the case. Let's say you've been engaging in some serious cyber trespass the last several months. The United States Government's got nothing that actually links you to wrongdoing. There's nothin' I can do to help you unless you've got the goods to show for it. You know what I mean?" While it was clear in Ruben's mind this was the hacker, there was no solid, or even circumstantial, evidence that pointed directly at Ryan. An American in Shanghai, with a history of felonious computer intrusion, would definitely put him at the top of a suspects list. Without proof, however, he couldn't be charged.

"I've got names, IP addresses, target lists..."

"That's a start, but I need the names of the people you've been workin' with, where the data's been going, who it was sold to, shit like that. I also want to know about that multinational philanthropic organization you've been providing your services to. You give that up and I may be able to arrange protection." Ruben could hear him breathing while he mulled it over.

"Okay. I've got your number, I'll call you back."

Ruben heard him click off. *I hope this computer queer isn't more trouble than he's worth.*

The U.S. Consulate in Shanghai provided all the normal consular services, but its offices were scattered around the city. Public Affairs was located in the Portman Ritz-Carlton complex, visa and citizen services were at the Westgate Mall, and the Consul General's building, where Ruben was going, was on Huaihai Middle Road. It was three acres of prime Shanghai real estate, a ten-minute taxi ride from the hotel.

Housed in a highrise, within a multi-structure compound known as the Qihua Mansion, it was also home to the consulates of Austria, Mexico, Slovakia, and Turkey. Not particularly attractive—architecturally, it was about as interesting as a drainpipe.

Captain Fairbanks, dressed in Navy khakis, with silver eagles on his a collar and brown Corfams on his feet, was waiting for Ruben at the gate. A former Naval Aviator, his gold wings sat proudly above his five rows of ribbons. The guy looked to be in good shape, with a swimmer's build—broad shoulders and slim in the hips. Maybe five-seven or -eight, at a hundred and forty pounds of mostly muscle, his hair was salt and pepper, short cropped, and thick. In his mid-forties, he a had slight resemblance to George Clooney, and the pencil-thin mustache was doubtless a nod to his call-sign: Zorro.

The walls of his office were covered in pictures of Navy fighter planes from the last century, and the centerpiece was a twelve-by-sixteen-inch black-framed photo of a younger Zorro in the front seat of an F-14 Tomcat. Ruben figured he'd probably seen action in the first Gulf war.

As Fairbanks moved behind his desk, Ruben parked himself in one of the two brown leatherback chairs in front. The conversation to that point was innocuous chatter about the weather, life in Shanghai, and the tired quips concerning Chinese eavesdropping and the affects of microwave radiation.

"I was thinkin' of wrappin' my balls in tinfoil." Fairbanks guffawed at his overused sally.

Ruben, not laughing, queried, "You ever see what happens when you put metal in a microwave oven?"

Fairbanks stopped chortling long enough to think

about what Ruben said, and again burst into bellowing laughter. "Boy, the ol' lady would have fun puttin' butter on that!"

Carver had business to discuss with this joker but couldn't help but wonder what his meeting with the Admiral was going to be like.

"So, tell me, Zorro, have you ever met Seventh Fleet?"

"Nah...we'll be okay, though. We got our shit wired pretty tight." He leaned back in the chair, talking out of the side of his mouth.

"Glad to hear it, 'cause if the Chinese don't bake your balls with the microwaves, the Admiral will definitely use 'em for shish kebab."

Zorro sat quietly for a few seconds, surveying Carver. "I hear you're going to meet Major Zhao this afternoon."

"I've already had the pleasure. She bagged me last night."

Fairbanks said nothing, not quite sure what Carver meant. When Ruben saw the question mark, he clarified. "Her crew followed me from the airport, and when I had the driver stop at the Great World for some sticky rice, she introduced herself. There was more to it than showing off for her troops, though. She was lettin' me know my shit would be weak if I stepped outta line."

Zorro nodded. "The woman is a class-A bitch. Ya might say the Major has a major hard-on for the U.S.. I don't understand why the PLA continues to use her for liaison."

"I'd guess that's exactly the type of person the PLA leadership wants on the job. She could have better bedside manner, that's true, but they don't have to worry about her sympathizing with U.S. concerns over China policies or getting too friendly with embassy staff. From the quickie last night, she strikes me as someone who gets the job done. I'll bet she fields requests for assistance pretty well."

The Captain's smile was bona fide as he nodded. "Yeah, but she's such a pain in the ass I always think twice about whether or not it's worth the effort." He then added, "You come to China a lot?"

"Not for the last couple of years, but crap like this is always the same. The city may change daily, but the political pissing contests are an inevitable constant."

"Ain't that the truth. So...what can I do for you?"

"As you've already been briefed, my primary mission is to find a hacker in Shanghai that's been givin' the Department of Defense a bad case of ass rash. At first, I thought the task was a ridiculous waste of time and money. But the Army had a man down, and the folks at the NSA and DIA are convinced the guy who keeps cracking the safe is an American."

"Yeah, we all know about it around here. What made you change your mind?"

"Well, as luck would have it, the guy's been identified. I talked to him this morning. He walked away from whomever he's been workin' for, and is currently on the run. He's ready to come in but wants us to agree to some things."

Captain Fairbanks sat forward, hands on his desk with fingers interlaced. "What kinda things?"

"I don't know. We didn't get that far in the conversation but it's sure to involve protection for cooperation. What I need from you is a way to get him out of the country and back to the U.S., without stirring up an international incident. As far as I know, he's got no wants or warrants here, and may only require getting his passport and visa status in order to get him on an airplane."

Fairbanks stared past Ruben to a spot on the wall as

he thought. "Maybe the Admiral could give him a ride. He's coming in on a P3. It would avoid the hassle of putting him on a commercial flight."

"That would mean providing him hospitality on consulate property for a couple weeks. If you put him up in a hotel, you'd more than likely be shipping a corpse. I've had some recent experience with the kinda people he's mixed up with."

"It'll require a boatload of coordination and approvals, but I'll get to work on it. Is the Embassy aware of this guy?"

"Yeah, but not about the conversation today. If the plan is tight, we'll get the Station Chief's support, and after that, the Ambassador and the General Consul here should be agreeable."

"I'll need to get the Regional Security Officer involved, as well as the Legal Attaché. You wanna talk to them personally?"

"It would probably be a good idea to touch base with them, but for now, have them talk to their Embassy counterparts." Ruben didn't feel like spending another three hours rehashing everything with those dudes.

"Anything else?"

"Let's go over the Admiral's itinerary I received from Williams, so I can compare it with the one Zhao will be bringing this afternoon." Thinking of Major Pain-in-the-Ass, Ruben suddenly flashed on Sonny Xú. Without getting into it with Zorro, he asked, "Can you put me in touch with the NCO in charge of the Marine detachment? I need a favor."

CHAPTER TWENTY
Taxi Fare

Another night in a massage parlor. Ryan had plenty of money, but all-nighters, even in the cheap joints like the Yuandian Health Club, could add up. He was also feeling a tad overused. There hadn't been so much attention paid to his crotch and rectum since he was in diapers. The place was in Pudong, on a side street called Lao Shan Road, not far from the bar he escaped to. He was sitting in the lounge area when Carver called.

Helen had obviously passed the phone number along, however, the email he'd sent earlier with the encrypted message meant for Carver apparently wasn't forwarded—either that, or the special agent was playing dumb. Ryan had plenty of information to trade for his freedom, and given the opportunity for a fresh start, falling off the grid was no biggie. The key was getting out of Shanghai, and Carver was his best bet.

Calls that morning to Helen had gone unanswered. It was 8:00pm in Boston, Sunday night, and while she may have unloaded her cell phone, she wasn't the type to go completely incommunicado. A laptop would come in handy now, and he knew where to buy a good one, but it meant going back into center city. Qu wouldn't quit looking for him, even with Carver in town, and her punks would still be roaming the streets.

A metro station was about a half-kilometer away on Century Avenue—a ten-minute walk. From there it was a straight shot to Xujiahui station, forty minutes away. He wanted to get to Metro City, the largest electronics and computer market in Shanghai, consisting of nine or ten stories packed with small shops and eateries.

It was geek heaven. There was even a movie theatre on the top floor. If he could get in there without being spotted, he could hide out for several hours. The place offered free Wi-Fi and on a clean system he could move around the Internet with some anonymity—at least for a while.

One thing the big guy said that sounded good to Ryan —and something he'd been worried about—was how much of what he'd been doing could actually be proved in court. The hard drives represented a double-edged sword. They were his ticket out of town, but also all the evidence a hard-ass prosecutor would need to slam the door on him and throw away the key. He'd cooperate and give everything up, but only for ironclad immunity.

As he paid up and got ready to head out, Ryan tried calling Helen once more. The phone rang a half-dozen times, and just when he was ready to hang up, the line opened. No answer, but there was someone on the other end. Ryan could hear breathing. Stifling the urge to say something, he remained quiet. He stared at the device in his hand, thumb hesitating over the disconnect, when he heard a man's voice.

"Who's calling?"

Who's calling? "Sorry, I must have dialed the wrong number."

"Are you trying to reach Helen Parsons?"

Ryan froze. Beset with a sudden impulse to throw the phone, he forced himself to take a breath. With strained nonchalance he responded, "Yeah, I've been tryin' to reach Professor Parsons for a couple of hours. Who's this?"

"What's your relationship with Miss Parsons?"

This guy sounds like a cop. "What kinda question is that? Who the fuck *are* you?"

"No need to get irate, sir. I'm Detective Burkhart with the BPD. What's your name and relationship with Miss Parsons?"

Oh, shit! "I'm her boyfriend."

"Your name?"

"Ryan Henderson...what happened?"

"Why do you ask that, Mr. Henderson?"

Is this guy stupid? "There's a cop answering my girlfriend's phone. Of course I'm gonna ask what happened."

"At approximately 18:00 this evening, Professor Helen Parsons appears to have been struck and killed by an automobile while crossing a street near MIT. I'm sorry for you loss. Right now we're treating it as a hit and run."

"A what? A hit and run?"

"That's correct. Where were you this evening Mr., ah, Mr. Henderson?"

"Me? I was no where. I mean..." Ryan felt like he'd grabbed a live wire. He was shaking.

"I'd like you to come down to the South End Precinct this evening to provide a statement."

"Yeah, sure." Ryan terminated the call. *I killed her...*

Reclined in her chair, Qu had been in a deep meditative state for more than four hours. Based on the report of multiple surveillance teams following Carver the night before, she was quick to discern the most likely culprit in the disappearance of her two men. Their bodies hadn't, as yet, been found, but she sensed with certainty they were dead.

She learned early in her career the inadvertent loss of personnel was a normal cost of doing business. The perturbation in this instance, however, had to do with the reason behind their removal and what it meant to her relationship with the vendor. Reliance on Xú Bao-Zhi to handle an assist with Ruben Carver was not yet out of the realm of possibility, but she would have to bring him back in line.

How that would be managed was the objective of her extended exercise. In her mind, Qu believed she could manipulate any man within her sphere. It was simply a matter of touching his baser instincts. What she discovered as she circled this riddle came from the revelation her ability to manipulate, direct, entice and incite through willpower and the focus of her *Qi*, was more a matter of brute force than any real understanding of the masculine.

The sound of her own laughter brought her forward as she came out of her cruise through the cosmos. The cachinnating continued, resonating from a spot just below her navel, making her eyes water. A simple and yet profound epiphany rolled over her: when it came to understanding men she'd probably get more insight out of one issue of a *Cosmopolitan* magazine than twenty years of meditation.

Xú Bao-Zhi—Sonny Xú—had let her know he wouldn't be bullied. How to suture the wound she was responsible for required counsel, and since she wasn't going to a newsstand for help, she called the only man she trusted for advice: her driver.

When it came to the two yángguǐzi, Carver and Hodges, she didn't need any special insight. To acquire the hard drives, all she had to do was stay on Carver. Eventually, the hacker would seek him out and she'd wrap them up together. The Board's directive placing Carver off-limits had become irrelevant under the circumstances.

Qu was inclined to give The Board her notice anyway, once she made good on their latest priority. She wasn't necessarily ready for retirement, and getting back into the rackets while she looked for other opportunities suited her current frame of mind.

Baby sister Zhao was the wild card. Qu's initial predilection was to kill her if she got in the way. On reflection, she didn't need the heat something like that would bring her way, particularly since she was resigned to stay in China.

As she pondered, once again dipping into her *Qi*, a simple workaround began to form. She touched a few buttons on the armrest console, and when a voice came on she said, "Do we have people on Carver now?"

"Yes."

"Are there other parties involved?"

"Only one that we're sure about. The woman he met last night."

"Perfect. This is what I want you to do…"

Up early to catch Carver leaving the hotel, Zhao sat behind the wheel of a Polo she'd signed out from the motor pool the night before. The three men she had inside the hotel lobby spotted Carver having breakfast, and while they were ready to follow him out, she told them to stand down. In all likelihood they'd already been made and she followed Carver solo to the consulate.

A half-empty soft-pack of Hongmei was stuck in one of the cup holders on the dash, and an empty venti-sized Starbucks paper cup in the other. She'd been going through the smokes fast as she waited on a side street near the U.S. Consulate. It had been an hour since she'd finished the coffee.

Alone, she was more keen in spotting other surveillance teams on Carver' rather than Carver himself. Her watch showed 11:30, and she began to wonder if she shouldn't drive back to the hotel and wait for him there. She hadn't observed anyone else, and they had an appointment to meet after lunch. It seemed as though his stop at the U.S. compound was legitimate, and besides, she had to pee in the worst way.

The engine cranked a few seconds before it came to life. A puff of dark gray smoke popped from the exhaust pipe as she pumped the accelerator three or four times. As she put the Volkswagen in drive and released the brake, Carver came through the gate. Not wanting to miss the opportunity to fuck with the guizi, she pulled to the intersection and gunned the car into a left turn across traffic to pick him up.

Too late. She could see him crouching into a taxi, and ready to follow, she was cut off by a large van with a picture of a pizza on the side. Blasting the horn, she decided to go around on the left and nearly sideswiped a sedan that appeared next to her. She pulled back in her lane, but didn't notice the van hitting its brakes. The Polo rear-ended the pizza delivery at thirty miles an hour.

The shoulder harness held and the airbag deployed, saving her life, but she was hurting. Besides the pain below the base of her skull, her face felt like she'd been hit with a giant fist. She was bleeding from her nose and right ear. Before she passed out, she turned her head left. The car that had hemmed her in had stopped, and squinting, she could see the driver looking at her.

He was smiling.

The meeting with Zorro accomplished what Carver had

hoped for: he'd gotten the synergy he needed from the Navy in making Henderson feel welcome. He hadn't killed anybody yet, and figured he still had some juice with the station chief to keep the other services at bay. Once he confirmed what the repining dweeb wanted in exchange for cooperation—immunity from everything, he assumed—Carver would push for witness protection and a ticket home.

The Naval Attaché also introduced Ruben to the Staff Sergeant in charge of the Marine detachment. As usual he had to drop a few names as references before the jarhead would even consider the request. He'd know by suppertime if the troop received favorable recommendations.

As he walked through the consulate gate, a taxi was at the curb dropping off a passenger. In a hurry, Ruben bent over, and still moving forward, got the driver's attention. The cabbie nodded, and Ruben slumped in the backseat headfirst.

The meet with Zhao occupied his thoughts, and was five minutes into the ride before he realized the scenery looked wrong. Now alert, he spoke in Mandarin, and when that didn't seem to register switched to Cantonese. When they made eye contact in the rearview mirror, Carver got the message.

His cognitive ability allowed him to remember everything he saw and heard, which, when pressure was applied, turned into a state of intense clarity. He not only remembered, he understood—or more precisely, could instantly place meaning to circumstance. He knew what was happening and why, and for that reason, and at that moment, he relaxed and let the situation unfold.

The driver jerked the wheel hard right until the car bounced over the curb, and a hard left to get the wheels in the gutter before he slammed on the brakes. The technique was get to Carver off balance as he rolled around on the backseat. It would have been effective, but Ruben, anticipating the motion, braced himself for impact with his feet and hands.

At the instant the car came to a stop, the front passenger side and right rear doors flew open, and two men with drawn pistols hopped in. Had the cab not been so small Ruben would have been at a distinct disadvantage, but he was ready for them. Both men were right-handed, which meant the desperado in the front was on his knees facing Ruben with the pistol hanging over the seat back. The highwayman jumping in the rear had his left knee on the seat, right foot on the floorboard, also facing Ruben. The pistols, only a few inches from his nose, were shaking as both men were fueled by adrenaline.

The driver, also excited, didn't wait for the two hijackers to close the doors before he punched it, and not ready for the sudden forward motion, the two lurched backward. At that instant, Carver grabbed the barrels and pushed them away, one high and one low. The firearms went off simultaneously, with the slides pinching the flesh on his palms as they retracted to eject the casings.

The bullet from the guy in the front struck his partner in the neck and the arterial spray was landing on everyone in the vehicle. The driver, pedal to the metal, was going nuts, screaming in a dialect Ruben didn't understand, while he whipped erratically around cars and between lanes.

The pistoleer next to the driver was now seated, gripping his groin and also screaming. The round from the stooge in the back blew through the front seat back, laying waste to the dude's progeny producer. The motion of the taxi slammed the front passenger side door closed, but the door in the back was now banging on the dead man's ankle. Ruben, doing his best to hold on, pushed the body out the door with the heel of his right foot.

He could hear horns blaring, tires squealing, and the dull, metallic thuds of cars smashing against each other. Miraculously, his taxi continued barreling down the boulevard with both men in the front still howling.

Ruben had had just about enough of that nonsense. He retrieved the dead man's pistol from the floorboard, cleared the spent casing stove-piped in the chamber, and placing the muzzle at the wounded man's crown, pulled the trigger. While he suffered with the ringing in his ears, the solution had the desired affect—both men went quiet.

Me and that asshole, Sonny, got plenty to discuss... And where's that fuckin' bitch Zhao? I know she was followin' me...

Perched on the edge of the bench seat, Carver leaned close to the driver's ear while scanning the area where they were driving. Still on Huaihai Middle Road, traveling northeast, they passed a hospital on the left. The ringing in his ears had subsided, and glancing right and rear, he told the cabbie to move into the right lane. When he failed to comply, Ruben put the barrel against his temple with a twisting motion and repeated the order.

"Slow down and make a right at the next corner." Carver wasn't shouting but there was enough emphasis in each word to convince the man behind the wheel to do as he was told.

The street was narrow and lined with trees, parked cars, and small shops painted mostly in primary colors.

"Pull in up there." Carver pointed to a spot right-front that looked like a bus stop. The tires rubbed against the curb as he steered into the space. "Put the car in park." He waited a few seconds. "Now open that door and push your dead partner out."

The body fell onto the sidewalk in a crumpled heap. The bullet went in the skull clean, but exited through the chin leaving a gaping one-inch hole.

"Drive!"

"Where...where do you want to go?" The first words out of the driver's mouth since Ruben got in the taxi.

"Go to the next main intersection and turn right. How much gas do you have?"

"Almost a full tank."

"Then go. I'll give you directions. You're gonna answer a few questions."

As the cabbie drove down the street, Ruben examined the pistol—another QSZ-92. While he initially surmised his unwanted traveling companions belonged to Sonny Xú, he didn't think it too rude to ask, "Are you PLA or do you work for someone else?"

"What? No, no, I drive this taxi...that's all!" He firmed his grip on the steering wheel and turned his head to look at Ruben.

"Keep your eyes on the road, comrade. You may be driving this cab now, but you were working with those two guys. So, unless you want to wind up like them, you better tell me the truth." Ruben nudged him with the pistol.

"I'm a taxi driver, honest. I do—did—some side jobs with those other two, mostly to rob foreigners. This time we got paid to pick you up."

"By who?"

"I don't know his name. He made the arrangement with those other guys. I'm just the driver."

"What's your name?"

"Huh? Why?"

Ruben tapped his temple with the barrel.

"Cheng's my name."

"How much were you gettin' paid for this?" Carver,

always interested in the business end of these arrangements, liked to know what his life was worth to those inclined to take it.

"I was getting two-thousand."

"Dollars?"

"I wish...2000 yuan."

The calculation at the current exchange rate brought the price to about two hundred and forty dollars.

Typical. Bad guys are price point sensitive, too.

"Do you know where you're supposed to take me?"

"Guang Fu Road, to a warehouse."

"Okay, let's go."

"You want to go *there*?"

"You wanna get paid, dontcha?"

CHAPTER TWENTY-ONE

Traffic Jam

"Did you make the pick-up?"

"Yes, madam. That went as planned."

Qu could sense a contra coming.

The building process in establishing a solid, reliable team in modern Shanghai, or anywhere in China for that matter, left much to be desired. There were plenty of disenfranchised youth, but finding smart, trainable personnel presented a number of problems. Most of which were related to time and money.

When she returned to China as a program manager for The Board, she began the process of recruiting candidates. She certainly understood the lamentation of Xú Bao-Zhi regarding the loss of good men. It was a considerable investment to put together a cadre of loyal and effective pirates willing to do her bidding without question. The benefit of The Board was the financing, and the ability to leverage its considerable connections internationally for cross-border operations. It functioned in much the same manner as the Triads, but with better hardware, and the advantages of multi-ethnic and multi-cultural facility.

Her current team on its own was too small to make a substantial power grab in a city the size of Shanghai, and establishing a niche with monthly tribute to the larger organized crime families, while distasteful, was expected. With a plan to proselyte personnel, as well as absorb smaller, unaffiliated groups, she still calculated her rise in power in terms of months. She'd already begun the subtle but systematic removal of the leadership of those autonomous crews, providing a home for new ronin.

What she couldn't afford, at least for the time being, was an outright war with a major organization. Again, with a view of Xú Bao-Zhi and his operation, she had to be satisfied with reliance on vendors and subcontractors.

"What happened?"

"The taxi pick-up went as planned—"

"You've already stated that. What's the problem?"

"He killed the two men we hired to ensure his cooperation."

"So...it didn't go as planned." The ire began to swell.

"In that respect, it did not, but he stayed in the taxi and seems to have continued on to the construction site."

"How do you know that?"

"The taxi has a tracker we've been able to follow."

Amazing. This nosey yánggǔizi is a curious sort.

"How many men do we have at the warehouse?"

"Ten."

"Where are you?"

After a few seconds of dead air, he responded, "There was an accident. We're on foot going for alternative transportation."

"Give me the name and number of the team leader at the drop site."

Within seconds she had it, and terminated the call. When she tried the site, there was no answer. One more call—this time to her driver. "Pull the car around. We're going to the warehouse."

* * *

Rage replaced fear as Ryan found Carver's number and pushed the dial key.

"This is not a good time."

Speechless for an instant, some of Henderson's indignation was put on hold. "Carver?"

"Ryan, I'd love to have a chat with ya, buddy but I'm a little busy."

"But...but...we need to meet. I'm ready to make a deal." Ryan's umbrage turned to frustration.

"That's great, pal, but it's gonna have to wait for a while. Can you give me a day or two?"

"Can I give *you* a day or two? They wanna kill me and they already killed my best friend! I don't know if I have a day or two." Henderson was squeaking every word.

"Yeah, well, that makes two of us. Tell you what. Maybe...maybe you can help me. Do you have something to write with?"

To Ryan it sounded as if Carver was running or walking fast. Not panting, but breathing hard. Then several loud, sharp resonate notes sounded, like the kind that large, flat steel rods make when they fall on a concrete floor.

"Hey, man, are you all right?"

"Peachy. You ready to copy?"

"Huh? Oh...oh, yeah." Henderson jammed his hand in a side pocket, searching for a pen. "Okay, go ahead."

Carver relayed two phone numbers, repeating each twice. "You got those?"

Carver was running again and Ryan could hear the same sharp bangs, now realizing it was gunfire, and that Carver was shooting back.

"Yeah, I got 'em!" Ryan said.

"The first number is an agent in Japan. His name is Junior Prosser. The second is to a PLA major by the name of Zhao. Tell 'em I'm in a warehouse on Guang Fu Road trying to sort out a misunderstanding."

"Where's Guang Fu Road?"

"*Fuck if I know*. It's a district just east of the Bund along some river. I'll leave my Blackberry on. Maybe they can locate me by..."

Ryan lost the signal.

The buzzing of the phone on her hip brought her around, but she couldn't move. She'd been strapped down to a gurney, and while she could hear the siren, the brace used to stabilize her neck made it impossible for her to turn her head. Also, the mask on her face, blowing air up her nose, hampered her ability to make enough noise to be heard over the vehicle's blare.

Emergency medical response in Shanghai didn't have a great reputation. Even if a call could get through on often-jammed lines, the amount of time to reach an accident scene in city traffic could be measured in hours rather than minutes. Shanghai drivers didn't like to be inconvenienced, and the Chinese in general never felt the rules of the road actually applied to them individually. It was every man and woman for themselves, and that included the nuisance of the police, fire trucks and ambulances.

With that in mind, Zhao figured she could have been out anywhere from thirty minutes to three or four hours. The good news: she could feel pain. The bad news: she could feel a lot of it. She tried moving her arms and found they were restrained by only a blanket—no straps. The agony around her left shoulder made it too difficult to move her arm, but the right seemed fine. The struggle to wriggle it free, however, was torturous.

The attendant noticed her jostling, stood, and looked down into her eyes.

"Rest easy, lady. We're taking you to the hospital." Satisfied with his succor he sat back down on the bulkhead bench.

He doesn't sound completely stupid. Against the pain and the restraints, Zhao pulled her right hand free and pushed the mask up to her forehead. "Hey, you!"

"Lady, you need to lie still. You've been injured."

"I know I'm injured. I can feel it. Don't you have anything for pain?"

"Sorry, no. I'm not allowed to dispense medication. You have to wait 'til we get to the hospital."

"How long will that be?"

"I'm not sure—maybe five or ten minutes."

For Zhao that translated to forty-five or fifty minutes.

"I need you to pull my mobile phone from its holder on my right side and put it my hand."

"Lady, you need to rest!"

"Quit saying that, you moron, and hand me my phone. Do it! *Do it now!*" White-hot pain erupted from her shoulder and left side, causing her to shriek the last syllable.

I must've cracked a rib.

With exaggerated reluctance, replete with pursed lips, he lifted the blanket at the waist, felt around until he found the device, and after yanking it loose put it in her hand.

Zhao didn't recognize the number of the last call. It wasn't Carver's, or the office. It was almost three pm, and hitting a quick dial number, she reached out to her senior NCO. Thankfully, he picked up quick. He advised her the police had called to confirm her identity and authorization to operate a government vehicle.

Apparently, the cops arrived about the same time as the so-called EMT. They looked for witnesses and other cars involved—there were neither. Since she wasn't dead and didn't appear to have any life-threatening injuries they took down what personal information they could find, made the arrangement to have her car towed to impound, scratched out a citation for reckless driving, and left. Ignoring the front-end damage, they wrote it up as single car accident. They assumed, as they normally did—Zhao being a woman—it was operator error.

It was tough to concentrate as she listened, but she maintained her cool. When it was her turn to share she detailed the nature of the incident, emphasizing it wasn't an accident. Her own natural bias made her suspect Carver, but she instructed her man to contact the police to review any available traffic cams. When the NCO heard Carver's name, he remembered to tell Zhao about the two dead ex-cons that had been shot and dumped along Huaihai Middle Road. One of them had caused a pile-up, and the drivers who could respond to questions said they thought the body had been pushed from a taxi.

What the hell has that gwailoh got himself into?

Unable to continue the conversation, she handed the phone to the attendant to provide the name of the hospital they were going to. Forty minutes later they pulled into the emergency room driveway.

Meatloaf and mashed potatoes, the Monday lunch special at the Chief Petty Officer's Club. Junior didn't go every week but today he felt like comfort food. Strolling across the main drag of the Yokosuka Naval Station with his belly full, he kibitzed with Brandouski, a fellow counterintelligence case officer, about who was badder: Batman or Captain America. They both agreed earlier Jethro Gibbs was a pussy. As he grabbed the door handle into the lobby entrance, his Blackberry chirped. He recognized the number.

"Hello, Ryan, this is Junior Prosser."

"How...yeah, hi. What is it with you NCIS agents, anyway?"

"I don't know what you mean." Prosser really didn't know what Henderson meant, but he sure as hell wanted to know how he got his number and why he was calling.

"It doesn't matter. Ruben Carver got himself in some kinda jam in a warehouse on Guang Fu Road, somewhere east of the Bund. Anyway, he wanted me to call you 'cause his Blackberry is on and I'm assuming he thinks you can triangulate his position."

"Uh-huh yeah, well, that sounds great on TV, but I'm not sure I can do that. Is that all he said?"

"Yep, but it sounded like he was in a gun fight or somethin' and wanted me to tell you."

Junior was beginning to believe the computer genius didn't have a clue what message Carver wanted him to deliver. That was confirmed with what he blurted next.

"Actually, I'm not sure what he needs you to do. All he said was he was tryin' to resolve a misunderstanding. Does that mean anything to you?"

"You said it sounded like he was in a firefight?"

"Yep. That's right. It was automatic weapons— machine guns."

"Okay, I got it, but I don't know what I can do to help."

"Then I don't know what to tell ya, except he also had me call some PLA major by the name of Zhao with the same info."

"Give me her number."

Prosser tugged a ballpoint pen from his breast pocket and jotted the number on the back of his hand.

"By the way, how you doin', Ryan? Where are you?"

Those few words were enough to set Henderson off, and as Prosser buzzed himself into the section of the building where he shared an office with Brandouski, he listened to Ryan rant. Junior hadn't yet heard about Helen Parsons. He'd have to confirm her death through the agent in Boston.

The rest of his disjointed fulmination made no sense to Junior. Apparently, Ryan, the guy who had bugged the PLA and robbed the DoD of its crown jewels, had been held prisoner in Shanghai by the female version of Doctor No, while doing it all for some omniscient organization called The Board. It wasn't until Henderson said he had proof of his activities on an encrypted hard drive that he had Junior's full attention.

Not one to stand on formality, Junior crashed Henderson's monologue with a Carverism: "Shut the fuck up for a second, dickhead, I'm thinkin'."

Five minutes later, after formulating a simple plan—not even a plan, really, more of an errand for the computer genius—Ryan was instructed to continue to lay low until he was contacted again.

After signing off, Junior didn't know who to contact first. He was aware, however, that if he ever wanted to be considered for promotion, he'd better fill in Johnson and Benson on the new developments.

CHAPTER TWENTY-TWO

The Warehouse

Located northeast of the consulate, Guang Fu Road ran along the Wusong River for several kilometers. Cheng drove about thirty-five minutes with a pistol barrel in his ear before he pointed at an old, abandoned wood and brick building. Carver's head was on a swivel during the ride, trying to detect unwanted company. Unless the bad guys had several cars in play tag-teaming him, there didn't seem to be anyone behind or in front of him—paralleling along the route was impossible.

Carver had the driver slow down, but continue past the aged warehouse so he could get a gander at its size, ingress, and possible inhabitants. After another hundred meters, they pulled off the road. Carver had Cheng turn off the engine and sit tight while he grabbed the ASP from the attaché case, and then crawled over the seat back next to him.

The pistol on the floorboard under the dash slid and bounced against his feet. As he retrieved the shooter, he realized the weapon he was holding was M1911A1, or at least the Norinco version of the classic. A high-capacity .45 with a three-dot sight, a curved back-strap grip with rubber plates, a skeleton trigger, and speed hammer. The magazine had eleven semi-jacketed hollow-points and a round was chambered.

Where do golden goombas like these get such bitchin' guns?

The ASP had a holder with belt clip he fastened over his right hip pocket. The 9mm, with the safety off, went into his waistband an inch west of his belt buckle. Carver then tugged the key from the ignition, and with .45 leveled, ordered Cheng out, following him through the driver-side door.

With the taxi driver in front of him they walked back to the warehouse, a three-story structure that must have been close to a hundred years old, based on its style and overall condition. Most of the windows had been boarded up, and much of the red brick looked loose and timeworn. Dry rot crumbled the wood around the doorframes, and the paved driveway was buckled and cracked.

As they circled to the rear of the building, he found a large steel scaffolding erected along the back wall, and nine or ten piles of new brick, sacks of concrete, wood planking, and other construction material covered in plastic sheeting. There was also a 200-kilowatt diesel-powered generator and lift truck. It was clear someone had renovation in mind, but nothing appeared to have been done yet.

Carver nudged Cheng along with the barrel, being mindful of cover as he examined the exterior for points of entry. In a half-whisper he asked Cheng, "Are you sure this is the right place?"

"Yes. I'm sure." It was a definitive reply that convinced Carver whoever was inside knew about the two dead delivery boys and were now waiting.

Spotting a portal ajar between two closed bay doors—*how convenient*—he crossed to the wooden stairs going up to the loading platform, which was three meters wide and close to thirty meters long. The stringers creaked as they moved up the steps, but the platform was solid and their shoes made little noise. When they approached the entry, Carver stood with his back against the wall, left of the doorframe.

He switched the pistol to his left hand, and with his right pushed the door open. Nothing. He did a quick peek and saw ceiling lights on, more scaffolding, piled boxes, more construction material, and equipment that looked like band and table saws, all scattered around a three-hundred-square-meter space.

Cheng, watching Caver, had crossed his arms with his shoulders hunched. His ankles were together and he rocked on the balls of his feet breaking eye contact to stare at the tips of his shoes.

The boy knows someone's home.

"Hey."

Cheng didn't bother to respond.

Once again, this time with quiet emphasis, he said, *"Hey."*

Cheng glanced up.

Carver cocked his head to the right. "After you."

The cabbie's eyes popped wide and he grimaced, tight-lipped, as he shook his head violently side to side.

Carver didn't bother using the muzzle motivator. "Don't worry...they want me, not you. Remember, your money's inside. It's time to collect."

Not entirely persuaded, Cheng shifted his posture but before he could bolt, Carver had him by the scruff of the neck, jerking him toward the opening. As he stood on the threshold with toes up and heels digging in, leaning against Carver's arm, the welcoming party announced themselves. A barrage of bullets pelted poor Mr. Cheng from head to foot.

The explosion of gunfire lasted until they ran through their magazines. Ruben couldn't tell how many men he was facing but some of them had automatic weapons and he was sure he heard shotguns. Cheng had rag-dolled when the first thirty rounds or so aired him out. The rest of the bullets were going through the empty door or slamming into the brick barrier that provided Carver with cover.

Damn...maybe I shoulda knocked.

Having lost any interest in pursuing further communication, Carver turned toward the stairs. He had the car key in his pocket and decided it was time to beat feet. He negotiated the steps two at a time, and was jogging toward the end of the building when three men cleared the corner. They were coming at a sprint, apparently with the intention of flanking him on the loading platform.

The area at the rear of the building was covered in fine gravel, and as Carver put on the brakes, left foot forward, dragging his right big toe, he went into a controlled slide. His training took over, and with the pistol coming up in a two-hand grip, he fired six rounds, double-tapping each silhouette.

He scored a kill shot on the first man, but while he landed hits on the other two, they returned fire as they went down. The three shooters were doing the dance——firing, moving, and looking for cover. Ruben wasn't sure where he'd hit the two, and with any luck, they'd bleed out. He'd rolled behind a stack of bagged concrete mix he couldn't see around. If they witnessed where he went when he tumbled out of the way, they could rush him.

They were armed with what appeared to be Bullpups, with thirty-round magazines. Scanning behind him, there was a four-foot by four-foot stack of red brick. Three meters to the left of that was a five-foot high pile of four-by-eight plywood. Without waiting to pinpoint their positions, he bobbed up, head and shoulders above the heavy sacks. Unless they'd already started to flank him, he reckoned he'd be able to pick up movement before they started pulling triggers.

He was right about one of them, wrong about the other.

They were spread out in front. The guy he spotted to his ten-o'clock had to pop out from behind the generator to get a shot. Carver pinned him back with two rounds. The guy he didn't see was in a prone position somewhere to his right, and opened up with a four-round burst—one bullet carved a groove out of Carver's right trapezius.

The small, high-velocity round knocked him on his ass.

Motherfucker...gotta move...

His adrenaline was pumping and was able to get his feet under him. In a crouched sprint he headed behind the stacked bricks. The shootout had been going for almost a minute and he knew if he didn't take these pricks down quick, their friends would be joining them. About that time his phone buzzed. It was Ryan in a snit ready to give himself up, and as much as Ruben wanted to hang on the line and shoot the shit, his two new friends decided to make their move.

Fortunately, they thought he was still behind the concrete. With weapons on auto, they used cover fire to approach. Then, as they came over the top of the sacks, emptied their magazines in the dirt. Ruben didn't wait for them to complete their reloads. He drew the 9mm from his waistband, and standing, he took one man down with a headshot, and put six in the torso of the other who was doing his best to evade.

Back in a crouch, he scooted to the sacks of concrete. Ryan was still on the phone and Ruben gave him instructions on who to call before he lost the signal. He snatched the bodies behind the pile of cement just as the rest of the fraternity started to appear. His shoulder hurt like hell and he could feel the blood running down his back. He couldn't ignore it, but considering its location, he wanted to assume it was a flesh wound.

The weapon systems these cretins were carrying were not Bullpups as he originally surmised. They were short-barreled QBZ-95s. More than likely the "B" series, a Chinese-built assault rifle made for the military. The gun fired a 5.8mm bullet, which was roughly the same size the 5.56mm NATO round. For the plinkers back home it was slightly bigger than a .22 magnum. Each man had an extra thirty-round magazine and a couple of extra 9mm pistol mags. Ruben was feelin' flush.

Pistols tucked at the waist, magazines in all his pockets, and an assault rife in the ready position, Carver stayed low as he moved behind the bricks, and then to the plywood. He had to find a place where he could see what the mob was doing without being immediately spotted. Twenty meters to his four o'clock was the lift truck. It had an enclosed cabin, and the windshield would be reflective enough to give him some concealment, but getting to it would be tricky. With the firepower these jaggoffs were packing, the forklift might be just what he needed to get off site.

There was enough crap scattered around the yard to get within ten meters, but after that it was an open field run. Staying as low as possible without going to his hands and knees, he covered the distance in about five seconds. The cabin sat high enough for him to slide easily under the carriage and then low-crawl with one arm to other side. The vehicle was parked at an angle, and from that side the lift mechanism hid his entry as he opened the cabin door.

It was as he hoped. The bastards didn't see him. He counted seven, and sure enough, two of them had shotguns. Nice ones, too: 12 gauge semi-autos with drooping ten-round tactical magazines.

Jesus...I musta really pissed somebody off.

Still bleeding, with the pain radiating up his neck and down his arm, Carver had some range of motion in his right appendage, but he wasn't sure how well his shoulder would handle even the light recoil of the long gun. The gangsters had scattered, using cover as they searched. These troops had been well trained. He wouldn't be able to get past them without more lead flying.

Now completely on the defensive, he inspected the cockpit. It seemed fairly simple: a gas pedal, brake, a three-position gear lever, and fork controls. No key in the ignition, but no real hitch in the giddy up. He eased the tactical knife out of his right front pants pocket, snapped the blade open, and used it to pry the ignition lock cylinder loose.

There were three wires: two red and a brown. The serrated edge at the base of the tanto blade sliced the lines with little effort. He stripped a quarter-inch of the thin insulation off the red power wires and twisted their bare copper ends together. He glanced up to survey the progress of the squad, checked the rounds in the QBZ-95 magazine, and confirmed a round in the chamber.

Safety off, he laid the rifle in his lap, put the gear lever in neutral, released the brake, and after taking a breath, stripped the insulation off the brown ignition wire. As he touched the copper end to the power wires, the engine coughed once and turned over. Right side door open, he had the lift truck in drive mode, and throwing the gear lever in forward, he punched the accelerator.

He drove five or six yards to get it headed in the right direction, and jumped from the cab. With a fullback fake up the middle, he was trying an end sweep to get back to the warehouse. It seemed like a good idea, but when he hit the ground the lesion that had started to coagulate erupted with a stabbing pain that nearly caused him to pass out.

No, no, no...don't do this...

Up on one knee, light-headed, and with slightly blurred vision, he watched the lift truck take fire. It worked better than he thought. It reminded him of the ride-alongs with the cops in Los Angeles and the old rule of thumb: if one person shoots, everybody shoots. They were smokin' the cab of the big machine, but, like Mr. Natural, it kept on truckin'. *Oh, yeah.*

In a crouch, he ran laterally to the action, maintaining cover until he could redirect to his right, getting behind three gunmen. He only had a few more seconds before they'd discover the ruse, and shifting the rifle to his left shoulder, he lit them up with three-round bursts. Blood and dust plumed off each as they dropped straight down.

He didn't care much if they were dead or not. They were out of play and that's all that mattered. He sprinted for the warehouse door and was on the loading platform before the others caught on. He was through the opening moving to his left when they started shooting his direction.

With the exception of the wood load-bearing columns on a twenty-foot spacing, and an office loft at one end, the room was open, floor to ceiling. Stacks of lumber and quarter-inch four-by-eight plywood pallets, laden with cans of adhesive and flooring, and a half-built metal scaffolding erected in a strategic pattern, suggested an urban plan.

No one blasted at him from inside the building, and by

his count, four dickheads remained outside. It had only been about ten minutes, maybe less, since the first shots were fired, but Carver had no interest in extending this brouhaha. He peered around for an exit. The three turds he surprised in the beginning must have come out a side entrance.

The muscles in his back tried to compensate for the loss of strength in his shoulders. While his legs were in good shape, his back was cramping all the way to his waist. He took a firing position with good cover behind a mound of flooring material. No one could get behind him and he had visibility on his flanks. He needed to leave but he also needed the rest and the ability to assess his situation in general.

His cell phone had no signal. He couldn't dial out, and wasn't sure if the GPS tracker he had installed would pick up his location. The information he gave to Henderson would be enough to rally the cavalry, but it also meant he had to trust Henderson to spread the word.

As he sat poking around his wound under his shirt, he glimpsed motion at the open door. They dragged Cheng's body away.

This is it.

For the next twenty minutes he waited for the assault. As usual, under such circumstances, Carver got bored and decided it was time to force them into action. He moved from one cover spot to the next, keeping the wall with the door he came through to his right. It took the better part of another five minutes to find the exit he presumed was there.

The door made no noise as he inched it open. What's more, there was no sound coming from outside. He wondered if he was about to receive the same treatment as the late Mr. Cheng. Maintaining cover behind the frame, he pushed the door hard enough to crash it against the wall. *No need to be too subtle.*

Still no response from the firing squad. After a quick peek, he risked a longer look, and while he wasn't altogether satisfied with what his senses were telling him, he knew the bad guys were gone.

He did a magazine exchange prior to stepping out, and with barrel up, walked to the driveway. No one was shooting. The lift truck, with its cab full of holes, had been shut down. He was alone.

What the fuck?

Qu could hear the gunfire from a half a kilometer away. *What are those idiots thinking?* She'd tried to reach the team leader for the last ten minutes, but no answer. When she arrived on site, what was left of her men were blowing holes in a very expensive piece of equipment. She watched as one man suddenly signaled, and they turned and started firing toward the rear of the structure.

She bought the warehouse, considered an historical property, with the promise of renovation. She intended to convert it into a swanky restaurant and upscale nightclub. While a bit cliché, it was to be the perfect cover for her new role in China's burgeoning organized crime trade. She didn't need her crew turning it into another Golden Dragon massacre, and from what she could discern, her men were on the losing end.

Upon seeing Qu they ceased fire and fell in a line. Four men. The man she relied on to take charge of this rabble was down, along with five other better-trained soldiers. Qu had been clear the intent of the operation was to capture, not kill.

She pointed at the first man on the right. "Where's the foreigner?"

"Inside." He moved his head a centimeter in the

direction of the warehouse.

"Is he dead?"

"I don't think so, but he might be hit. We were going in after him." His words were spoken with confidence to curry favor.

"Are you stupid? He's already put six down and he apparently got you to shoot up an empty—and very expensive—forklift. Are you going to pay for that?"

He smiled and shrugged, only to have Qu knock him down with a backhand he didn't see coming. She would have killed him, but couldn't afford to lose anymore more personnel. Besides, if today were any indication of what was on the horizon, Carver would save her the trouble. She gave instructions to pick up the dead and wounded and go back to Pudong for disposal.

The fact that Carver survived played better into her hands anyway. She turned to her driver and asked, "How many men do we have left?"

He took a second to do the arithmetic. "Twenty-two."

"We still need to locate Hodges and retrieve the hard drives. Carver is our best option for both. I want you to supervise his surveillance. You understand?"

The man nodded.

CHAPTER TWENTY-THREE

The Rescue

She hated the place. Pushed around for three hours in the People's Liberation Army Hospital No. 411 in Hongkou, Major Zhao was ready to shove off. Every year she had to come to this shithole for a duty physical. The salacious groping and probing of the staff physicians was exacerbated by the likelihood of walking out with a drug-resistant infection. When she ordered the ambulance driver to take her someplace else, she was told No. 411 was the only facility that would accept her. It's where her records were located.

An X-ray showed two cracked ribs on her right side, along with a dislocated left clavicle. She had bruising around her pelvis, a broken nose, and two periorbital hematomas; shiners, for the uneducated, and real beauts, too. Not burdened with what she considered feminine vanity, she was nonetheless relieved her teeth were still intact.

Halfway through the ordeal, as she sat for observation with her ribs wrapped, collarbone set, nose bandaged, and left arm in a sling, she started returning her calls. Her boss was more concerned about the vehicle than her condition. It was easy to get another body, with an estimated two-million members in the PLA and another four-million in the paramilitary police. Replacing the car, however, required a purchase request, and his budget had already been drained for the year by his boss, who was building a retirement home.

She disconnected in the middle of his querulous droning to punch up the next number in the stack. She ignored one local number she didn't recognize, but the next call was international.

Japanese country code, what's this about?

Upon dialing, it rang a few a times, and a man answered with an American accent. "NCIS, Prosser."

"This is Major Zhao. I'm returning your call."

"Yeah, thanks. I received a request through a third party that a special agent by the name of Ruben Carver—someone I believe you've met—is in need of your assistance."

"Who are you again?"

"My name is Junior Prosser. I'm also a special agent with the U.S. Naval Criminal Investigative Service. I'm stationed in Yokosuka, Japan."

At that, Zhao launched into a tirade regarding the traffic accident, followed by accusations of a conniving foreign devil with no respect for sovereignty, the law of the land, illicit tradecraft, and spying. A well-rehearsed, three-minute litany of perceived imperialistic abuses levied by one Ruben Carver.

"Whoa, whoa... Major... Please, I don't know what kind of bug you've got up your butt, but I've got a partner in dire need of assistance. I'm sorry to hear about your accident, however, I can assure you Carver had nothing to with that. I mean, for real, if the man wished you harm, it wouldn't involve anything near that elaborate."

"Bug? Butt? I don't know what you're talking about. Anyway, how exactly am I supposed to help?"

"I don't know but since he specifically requested you by name, I've been authorized to tell you that it seems he's been in an altercation involving firearms."

"What? Where?" *First the car, and now a trigger-happy gwailoh. Could it get any worse? If this has anything to do with Feng's sister, I will pin his fucking ears back!*

"We, ah...aren't sure, exactly. His last known position was at a warehouse on Guang Fu Road. I'll text you the coordinates."

She could tell Junior was hedging, maybe because he didn't know who shot first. The bigger problem for her was not about who instigated what. Regaining some composure, and in a chilly, matter-of-fact tone, she asked, "Do you know if he's been taken captive or killed?"

"Major, I can only tell you that with Carver it won't be that simple. I want to give you the number of a Captain Fairbanks at the U.S. Consulate in Shanghai."

"I know who he is. I have his number." *It just got worse.* "I'll call him now."

"One more thing, Major."

"What is it?"

"You'll probably need a lot of body bags."

They didn't bother to police-up the brass. Considering the condition of the lift truck, the blood trails and spatter, Ruben agreed they were doing good just to get rid of the bodies. He hated to dump the assault rifle, but he didn't have a way to conceal it, and couldn't haul it around.

The Chinese bein' the way they were and all.

The Wusong River was flowing only fifty meters beyond the gravel pavement behind the warehouse. The weeds were thigh-high and prickly as he pushed his way to the embankment. Using his left arm, he tossed the rifle, along with the extra magazines, as far out into the water as he could.

Back at the taxi he dropped the .45 in his attaché case. The 9mm stayed in his waistband. His shoulder ached like a son of a bitch, and it didn't take any special perception to deduce the wound needed attention. The gunshot trauma and blood loss was taking its toll on his whole system. Even his legs were starting to give out. Leaning against the left rear fender, he considered his odds of getting treatment at a hospital in Shanghai without the paramilitary police being called were exactly zero.

How am I s'pose to s'plain somethin' like this?

With Zhao now on his mind he decided to pull chocks and motor toward his hotel. He still couldn't understand why she didn't appear during this latest dust-up. He was her responsibility after all. Ruben discovered rags and cleaning supplies in the trunk he'd use to swab down the taxi before he abandoned it. He was mostly interested in smearing fingerprints. There was nothing he could do about the gore.

As he opened the driver-side door, he felt the oncoming vehicle before he heard it—like a slight vibration in the asphalt under his feet. He moved to the front of the car, kneeling against the bumper, pistol out but against his hip. What he saw was heartening but surprising.

Ordinarily, Ruben didn't like surprises, but there are exceptions to most everything. Behind the wheel of a Honda Civic sat the Staff Sergeant in charge of the Marine detachment at the consulate. On the passenger side rested Zorro. As Carver straightened, the muscles in his lower back seized and his knees buckled. The pain made his ears ring, and while he tried to act cool breeze, Zorro was out of the car bracing him with an arm around his waist.

"Special Agent Carver, you have definitely been in some kinda shit."

"Yeah, you could say that. You got someplace I can go to get patched up?"

"It depends on what kinda patchin' you need. Bullet holes?"

"Yeah, my right trap. A thru-n-thru, I think. I don't know how much blood I lost." The woozy head told him it was probably more than was good for him. "Some antibiotics, stitches, and painkillers will prob'ly do the trick."

Zorro started moving him toward the rear door of the Civic, but Carver stopped him. "I need to wipe this thing down," he said, pointing to the taxi.

"Never mind that. One of Art Sheppard's boys will be around shortly. Somehow he figured you'd need an assist. You're gonna have to tell me the story between you two."

"Yeah, sure." Ruben jammed his hand in his pocket and presented the ignition key to the former flyboy. "He'll want this." As Zorro accepted the offering, Ruben queried, "Weren't you guys followed?"

"You'd think. Apparently, your man back in Yokosuka was in touch with Major Zhao. After she talked to him, she called me. That woman can really pitch a bitch. Long story short, she's cut a few corners for us."

"Sorry, Captain, I must've missed something. What are you talkin' about?"

"She got suckered into a traffic squeeze-play out in front of the consulate around lunch time. She got fucked up a little, but she's mostly pissed. She thought you set her up until your guy Junior—I love that name, by the way—talked her down."

Satisfied Ryan did as he was told, Carver wondered what instruction he received from Junior. Then, refocusing on Captain Fairbanks, asked, "How'd you find me?"

"The GPS tracker on your cell phone. Your cyber specialist at the Naval Station was able to plot your last know position."

Ruben nodded. He'd had some success with the same GPS locater application on an FBI agent's cell phone in Malaysia earlier in the year. He had it installed on his BlackBerry after he was reinstated.

"We gotta to go. Zhao is giving us an hour before she has her people on site. Since you're alive, I got to assume they're gonna find locals strewn around in there." Fairbanks jerked his head in the direction of the warehouse.

"Nah, the survivors cleaned up after themselves. Lots of shell casings and blood pools is all. My bag is in the backseat—I'll need that."

"I'll get it, but let's get you situated. Ya, know...I had no idea what we'd find, comin' here like this. I brought the only other person I knew at the consulate with combat experience." He pointed at the Staff Sergeant.

"So, this was a rescue?"

"We try to do as much as we can without getting the Chinese involved—at least initially. Anyway, firefights may be your everyday kinda thing, but not ours."

Carver plopped in the back of the Civic, wincing from the torment in his traps, lats, and lumbar. He made eye contact with the staff sergeant, who was looking at him through the review mirror.

"Thanks for the lift, Staff Sergeant. I hope I didn't ruin your day." Carver forced a smile.

"Call me Jerry, and no problem. I live for this shit."

"Hello."

"Ryan?"

"Yeah..."

"This is Junior Prosser. Are you okay?"

"What do you think? I'm a dead man walking—or least a dead man sitting—in a crappy coffee shop sipping a chai latte. What happened to Carver?"

"He's okay. He's at the consulate getting some bumps and bruises tended to. Did you do what I told you to?"

"Nah, too risky. Besides, I been thinkin'...you don't need the drives."

"Whaddya mean? I thought you said they were your proof."

"To be honest, the reason I yanked them in the first place wasn't so I could use them in the future. I wanted to keep them away from Madam Qu and The Board. Not that they could do anything with them. They'd need the mythical quantum computer to crack the encryption I have on those babies."

"Sorry, you're losing me."

"The system I built had the hard drives in a RAID 5 set-up. I could have reassembled the drives to pull the info on the hacking activity fairly easily, with the USB flash drive in my pocket. It's got the necessary metadata stored in a boot partition. But I didn't wanna."

"Okay, sorry...what's a RAID?"

"If you want the text book explanation, it's a data storage virtualization technology that combines multiple disk drive components into a logical unit for the purposes of data redundancy or performance improvement. RAID is an acronym for 'Redundant Array of Independent Disks'. Do you understand?"

"Ah...no."

"Listen, it doesn't matter, and I don't want to waste my cell phone battery on something that'll take me ten minutes to explain. You can ask your computer guy about it. We don't need the hard drives. I have everything you and I need on the flash drive. It's not the actual data I pirated but I have lists of targets, the systems I infected, data files acquired, and where I transferred them. I have the URL destinations. I also have the algorithms I wrote for my rootkits."

"So what are we talkin' about?"

"I'll tell you what I'm talkin' about...I didn't take the job to be a traitor. I like the good ol' U.S. of A. and I want to go back, just not to jail. I'll cooperate and provide evidence only for immunity." Ryan took a breath. "I destroyed the hard drives. I took 'em apart and scattered the platters from here to the Bund—mostly down sewer drains. Nobody gets 'em. You understand? I want to be brought in, but not until you guys agree to cuttin' me a deal. Is Carver's phone workin'?"

"Yeah, you can give it a try, but before you hang up there's something else."

"What?"

"I tried confirming the death of Helen Parsons. I talked to a Detective Burkhart."

"That's the guy I talked to."

"Yeah, well, he remembers you, too. Fortunately I guess, depending on how you look at it, the information he gave you was premature."

"Huh?"

"There was a woman killed and the ID they found on her was Helen's, but dental records showed it wasn't Helen. It was her assistant. Basically the same build, hair color, and complexion. Anyway, we're makin' an assumption Helen's still alive. The cops have issued a BOLO classifying her as a person of interest."

CHAPTER TWENTY-FOUR

Patched Up

The medical provider stationed at the consulate was a former Navy SEAL who'd been certified as a family nurse practitioner. Zorro called ahead and had him on stand-by. When Ruben walked in the dispensary, the NP had prepped for a gunshot wound and had blood plasma on hand, along with morphine.

A number two cut with a matching beard, he had a clear, mocha complexion, and quick smile. At six-feet, the baggy green scrubs couldn't hide the physique. When this flesh sculpture wasn't handing out aspirin he was in the gym. Twenty-seven or twenty-eight years old, he moved with confidence, and gave Ruben a once-over with a competent eye.

Carver's clothes were caked in red stuff, and as the NP helped him peel off the layers, indicated he wanted to put Ruben on a plasma drip.

"Looks like you've lost a lot of blood."

"Some of that's not mine."

"Uh-huh...well, you don't seem be to exhibiting any severe signs of shock. How's the pain?"

"It hurts. My back is killing me."

"You have a wound here that doesn't look too bad," he said, probing the hole in the trapezius front and back with a gloved forefinger. "But your back hurts? Were you shot in the back?" The NP stepped behind Ruben to get a look.

"No, it's muscle spasms."

"All right, sit on the table over there, and I'll check you out and see what I can do for you."

After a local anesthetic, the NP went to work on the shoulder. It wasn't a gutter wound as Ruben thought when he got hit. While the NP considered it superficial, the bullet did penetrate, causing a tunnel effect in the muscle. He excised it by dragging a disinfectant-saturated gauze through the track using a pair of forceps—not unlike pulling a patch through a gun barrel.

When the NP was satisfied he'd cleaned it well enough, he stood up from the tall stool he'd been perched on, and took two steps to a stainless steel cabinet with glass doors. While pulling out a more gauze strips and items for the suturing job, he detailed the options.

"You've got a thru-n-thru, but it looks clean. The exit wound is about the same size as the entry. Without X-rays I can't be sure, but it doesn't look like any fragmenting took place. You've got very little necrotic tissue surrounding the wound—at least from what I can see. The muscle still looks viable. You were lucky.

"There are a couple things we can do. I can pack the wound with an antiseptic gauze and bandage the epidermis. If we do that the gauze has to be changed at least once a day, but it depends on the amount of serosanguineous discharge."

"Would I have to come in here every day to replace it?"

"I can show you how, and you can do it yourself. This method lets your body heal and close the wound on its own." The NP rolled a small surgical table next to

Carver with a fresh pair of forceps, gauze, a bottle of saline solution, a scalpel, small retractor, and suture material with curved needles.

"This must be for option two." Carver pointed at the table.

"Yeah. Option two is I sew you up. I prefer doing the gauze pack but I've got a feeling you're not finished causing trouble. So, I've got absorbable suture that will maintain its tensile strength for about two weeks. You've got about a quarter-inch cavitation but the entry hole is small. I'm gonna have to make an incision vertically with the scalpel, and use this small retractor to open it. I'll try to use a running stitch to close the wound from the inside out."

"Sounds like you've done this before."

"I've had to deal with worse. Like I said, you were lucky. Where did you get this one?" The NP pointed at a fading scare just below Ruben's left collarbone.

"I picked that one up in Vietnam about thirty years ago. When were you in the shit?"

The NP's eyes narrowed and a couple of wrinkles formed on his forehead. "I was with Team 3 operating in Afghanistan, after 9/11."

Carver just nodded. He wasn't above a little hero worship and he couldn't help but wonder what this snake-eater was doing testing reflexes on disagreeable diplomats. "Okay, Doc...do your worst."

There wasn't much conversation for the next hour as the NP concentrated on the task. He'd put on a surgical mask and pair of loupes attached to a plastic headband. At one point Carver could feel the local starting to wear off and the corpsman gave him another poke of Novocain.

He completed the treatment with a large compress front and back, covered by gauze bandages. Sitting back, he stripped off his gloves and tossed them in a plastic bag inside a metal garbage can.

"There's a lot of bacteria transfer in a bullet wound and the risk of a staphylococcal infection is pretty high. Around here the pathogenic staphylococci can be penicillin resistant. So, along with the penicillin I'm going to shoot you up with, I'll give you a course of flucloxacillin you can take orally."

"Is that it? I'm good to go?"

"Yeah, but sit tight for a minute. Larry is out in the hallway with something for you to wear. You clothes are messed up."

Ruben pulled his wallet and badge out of the breast pockets, slipped the belt off the pants, along with the ASP, and grabbed his money, Blackberry, and knife; putting it all in the attaché case. He couldn't help test the shoulder by rotating his arm. The Novocain was still active, but he could feel a twinge.

"Can you give me something for the pain?"

"I've got oxycodone in the cabinet. It's strong stuff and will get you through the night. Any intense pain should abate by tomorrow, but I'll give you enough for a couple of days. Be sure to take the antibiotics."

"Thanks for the service. If you ever consider changing your line of work, I'd like to hear from you. My name is Ruben Carver. I'm a special agent with NCIS." Ruben extended his hand.

The NP reciprocated, and as they shook, said, "Yeah, I know. I got the low down from Captain Fairbanks. My name is Clarence Johnson."

The Staff Sergeant had Ruben in a red Marine Corps sweat suit, with the eagle, globe, and anchor conspicuously displayed in gold on the chest of the hoodie and the left thigh of the trousers. This stuff was never loaned lightly, so Ruben kept his mouth shut. Jerry insisted on giving him a ride back to the hotel, and considering what he had in his hand, Ruben understood.

They drove through the south gate of the Shanghai Centre to the underground parking. Jerry didn't want to get out, but instead handed Ruben the firearm case and a small zippered bag.

"Go ahead and open them. There's a few things we need to go over with this weapon."

After opening the case and zippered bag, it took a few seconds for Ruben to register what he was looking at. Jerry smiled as he reached over and hefted the pistol from its molded container. He also grabbed an empty magazine and slipped it into the slot below the grip. He then locked the slide back and glanced inside the chamber.

"This bad boy is the FN Five-Seven made in Belgium. It chambers a 5.7 by 28mm cartridge. It resembles a .223 with a shorter casing."

"Like the round I took at the warehouse." Ruben rolled his shoulder.

"Yeah, that's right, about the same size. Anyway, the pistol was originally designed for military use, but the manufacturer, Fabrique Nationale, has been producing it recently for civilian consumption. I think the U.S. Secret Service has this gun in its arsenal."

To Ruben it sounded like Jerry had given this particular weapon briefing a few times.

"This was shipped to me a few years ago for testing. The Corps is always interested in checking out new weapon systems, and at the time I was a firearms instructor—among other things. It's made with a lightweight polymer, has a large magazine capacity, ambidextrous controls, low recoil, and the ability to penetrate body armor when using certain high velocity rounds." He handed it back to Carver.

"Any issues I need to know about?"

"It's loud, but hey, I wouldn't pass you a gun I didn't have confidence in. This ain't no .22 magnum like some people claim. It's a small bore, I'll give you that, but with the rounds you've got in that bag, it'll take down anything short of a grizzly. No shit.

"Take a look at the magazine."

Carver pushed the magazine release and it dropped smoothly into his hand.

"That'll seat twenty rounds. If you load that one plus the two extras, you'll be carrying more than a box of ammo. If you can't get the job done with sixty rounds, then you're definitely in the wrong place at the wrong time—if you know what I mean."

"Yeah, I know exactly what you mean."

"Okay, so before I show you how to break it down, there are a few other features you need to see. It's got a Trijicon red dot reflex sight with adjustable LED. The MOA is 3.25, if that means anything to you."

Ruben shrugged. "I know what it means." MOA meant minute-of-angle; with an understanding of trigonometry and a slide rule, a gun queer could calculate the anticipated size of a shot group at any give distance. Sweet if you're shooting at paper. Ruben liked the reflex because he could get a good sight picture with both eyes open.

"You'll note the barrel is extended and threaded." Jerry tugged a suppressor from the bag on Ruben's lap. "This is a Sparrow 22. It's lightweight, about six-and-half ounces, and will give you some noise reduction—maybe forty db. You know, just enough to take the edge off. The holster is a polymer clip-on. With that wound I didn't think a shoulder holster would be very comfortable."

"This is excellent, Jerry. Do you want it back?"

"If you use it, you own it. Otherwise, I'd like to have it back."

"I can't promise anything, pal. Whaddya say you keep the .45 and that China nine. We'll call it a swap. I can attest to their shootability."

"Yeah, I guess, since you put it that way. Pull out a box of ammo."

Ruben reached in the zipper bag and retrieved one of three boxes of something called SS198LF.

"These rounds were supplied by the FNH. They're rated with a muzzle velocity of 2500 feet per second and are hollow points. According to the manufacturer they'll breach level 3A body armor but I haven't confirmed that. They're also supposed to be lead-free."

"I guess I can feel good about punchin' holes in people with that bullet. Kinda like I'm doin' 'em a favor."

Jerry put on his best poker face. "Well, that's right. Nobody can say you ain't humane. Once the bullet stops tumblin' and tearin' a fuckin' huge wound channel, you can always assure folks the bastard did not die of lead poisoning. Now, let me show you how to break it down. I put a cleanin' kit in the bag as well."

From where he left the Staff Sergeant, it was a five-minute walk to the hotel. He got a few curious looks as he cruised through the lobby. A couple of Zhao's men were hanging around, and he contemplated an evening session with the Major once she heard he was back from the dead.

There was one more person he recognized—a stab from the recent past—having a cocktail in the lobby bar. Self-conscious in his attire, Carver elected to go to his room. He'd brought enough clothes, and wouldn't miss the suit, but he did like the tie he ruined in the mayhem.

The shower was equipped with a hand sprayer, and he was able to scrub the remnants of the afternoon off without getting the dressings too wet. Taking a dump was a problem. His lower back was still giving him grief, which made getting on and off the toilet torture. Fortunately, the stool had a bidet attachment. A person never realizes, until times like this, how many muscles are utilized in the simple act of wiping one's ass.

The door was barred with the chair again. Ruben hadn't bothered with the tape routine that morning. Maid service had been in, as were the PLA. The cock-up around Zhao's accident and the unpleasantness at the warehouse brought them around. He could tell by the condition of the clothes in his suitcase that they'd tossed his room. They'd taken particular interest in his photographer's vest.

The closet appeared to be the one place not subject to a video feed. After getting dressed in a light brown, short-sleeved knit shirt, khaki slacks, and the Geox he'd rinsed in the shower, he opened the closet doors and set the zippered bag on a waist-high shelf. He blocked the view of what he did next from anyone manning a monitor in the security office.

He pulled a pair of black Nighthawk Nitrile gloves from a hip pocket, popped them on and opened a box of ammo. After getting a firm grip on a magazine, he thumbed in the green-tip hollow points. The springs were stiff and it took a few minutes to seat the rounds in all three. When he finished he gave each a tamp, then jammed one in the magazine well. He tapped the butt plate with his palm to ensure it snapped in.

He'd hung the photographer's vest in the closet and after pulling it off the hanger, he draped it over his shoulders. He never paid much attention to how much it weighed, but it laid directly over his injury. It wouldn't bother the stitches, but over time, as the Novocain wore off, it would get uncomfortable. The oxycodone was in his attaché case, and he put a patch of the plastic-covered pills in his pocket. He wasn't sure it was a good idea to mix it with alcohol, but he'd already determined it was time for a martini with a few of those Greek olives.

The holster he threaded on his belt above his right hip was followed by the FN Five-Seven. The extra magazines, his Recon 1, and the suppressor went into pockets on the vest; the ASP clipped on his belt above his left hip. Moving away from the closet, he unplugged his BlackBerry from its charger, dropped it in his pants pocket, and then checked himself out in the full length mirror. Satisfied with the concealment, he was ready to pay the man in the bar a visit.

I love gettin' dressed to go out.

His lower back continued to speak to him as he rode the elevator to the lobby level. The spasm had him leaning about five degrees off plumb. The walking helped loosen the lumbar, and as Ruben strode into the bar, he could almost ignore it. The fella he came to meet had moved to a curved settee in a back corner. Not standing on formality, Carver advanced.

Sonny was exactly as Ruben remembered him. Not quite six feet tall, he was stick thin—the quintessential inscrutable Han Chinese, with thinning shiny black hair combed straight back. He was dressed to the nines, wearing a lightweight, beige cotton suit, with a lightly starched pink pastel Indian cotton shirt, a pale blue paisley tie crimped by a collar pin, and a matching pocket square.

Man, this guy really plays the part.

The bar was dimly lit, with soft jazz playing in the background. It was busy with about thirty customers, but he and the gentlemen on the short, over-stuffed sofa had made eye contact. As expected, within ten feet, Carver had a goon in his face. The prick matched Ruben's size at over six feet, tipping the scales at probably 220. A shitbird like Sonny Xú didn't leave his rat's nest without at least two or three of his favored companions.

Wanting to be polite and observe the gangsta protocol, Carver came to a halt, but the idiot in front of him made the mistake of putting the flat of his right hand on Carver's chest. In a single motion, Ruben grabbed the little finger with his left hand and the middle finger with his right. Twisting the baby digit out, and the middle back, he broke both phalanges at the metacarpals with a coincident crack. To avoid what would come next Carver used a two-finger jab to the guy's jugular notch.

Sure enough, two more hotheads made their move when the schmuck went into the universal choking pose. Sonny quickly waved them off and had them provide what aid they could to their cretin comrade.

As Carver sat down opposite the lean Chinaman, he noticed the drink he had sitting on the small round table between them—a martini with three olives. *This chump can't be all that bad.* Observant, Sonny signaled a barmaid, who wasted no time in answering the call.

After making his order Ruben focused on Xú Bao-Zhi. "I appreciate you stopping by. I'm, ah...sorry about that thing with your guy. I've had a bad day."

232

CHAPTER TWENTY-FIVE

Cocktail Hour

The BlackBerry buzzed a few times during the hour he spent with Sonny. An enlightening endeavor Ruben wasn't sure would net him the results he was looking for. On the other hand, while it was entirely possible Sonny could complete the contract, a simple cost-benefit analysis based on his history with Carver was all he needed to make a decision. He was a businessman after all, and to appraise the desirability of that option didn't require graphs and charts to illustrate the likely impact on his enterprise.

As Ruben sat alone in the bar nursing his third martini, he scrolled through the call log on his phone. Junior rang twice, Henderson once, one number he recognized coming from the embassy, and a couple of calls from...Major Zhao. *Hmmm.*

He selected the first number and pressed the call button.

A friendly voice answered. "Hey Ruben, how you doin'?"

"I'm fine, Junior. A little banged up, but I still have my cleats on. You called?"

"Yeah, I did. I've been on the phone with Henderson a few times. That boy is wired way too tight, but he's willing to cooperate as long as he gets an immunity deal."

"I figured as much. Who've you talked to about it?"

"Our management, of course. Johnson went to the SAC, who's been on the phone with headquarters. Apparently, it's now with Justice. There's also been some talk about the witness protection program."

"That's good. Stay on it. I'll give Ed a call later tonight. Anything else?"

"Yeah, couple more things."

Ruben could hear Junior tapping on his keyboard.

"I tried running down information on the broad you met in Beijing and got something back from the NCIS regional unit in Marseille."

"Isn't that a one-man office?"

"Yeah. The guy's got the Interpol gig and is responsible for parts of Africa. I thought you said a while back you knew him."

"Yeah, yeah...I know him. He convinced someone years ago he could speak French and he was plugged in. You got to give the guy credit, though. He went from pretending to productive in only a half-dozen years."

"I'm sure he'd appreciate your opinion. Anyway, he couldn't do much without more to go on, but he did pass the picture around to the folks at Interpol involved in China issues. They think its someone called Qu."

"Okay. I'm listening."

"Well, there's not much more. This Qu character was believed to be a Triad enforcer for the old Sun Yee On organization out of Hong Kong. She first emerged on the scene back in the late seventies in London's China Town. They had hints of her involvement in Triad activity all over Europe and even in the U.S. up until five or six years ago."

"What about her passport? What's she been traveling

on?"

"I don't know. Our agent in Marseille got most of the information from an old cop who'd been trying to collect intel on her for years. According to him she's a real nasty piece of work. After he traced her origins back to her street days in London, he gathered she was a Chinese immigrant from Hong Kong. Guess what he said he thinks her real name is?"

"Qiu Hu."

"Bingo."

"Did you ask Henderson about this woman?"

"Nah, I haven't talked to him since this information came in. He did rant about a woman who was holding him prisoner, though."

"It seems to fit."

"Oh, there was something else you'll find interesting. The Interpol cop who provided the info gave up on his inquiries not long after she fell off the grid." Junior stopped talking to take a breath.

This fuckin' guy loves his pregnant pauses. "I'm waiting, Junior."

"All his requests for various documentation, video records, school transcripts, airline passenger lists, anything associated with his investigation of Qu, were either stonewalled, lost, questioned for relevance, or just plan denied. He said she's bein' protected."

"That it?"

"Pretty much. Have you seen Major Zhao since the warehouse?"

"Not yet. I just spent an hour with Sonny Xú, but I'm not ready to have our discussion put out in print. I have to think about it for a while."

"You sure?"

"Yeah, but don't worry, you'll be the first one I tell. Anyway, I gotta go. I have other phone calls to make."

"Hey, wait a minute, there was one more thing. It may not have much relevance to you, but it might help in your further contact with Ryan."

"Okay."

"The professor, Helen Parsons, may not be dead. The body the cops found turned out to be someone else."

"Oh? I wonder if she could be playin' for the visiting team..." Ruben was thinking out loud.

"Huh?"

"Nothin'. Forget it. I gotta go."

Ruben didn't feel like talking to Ryan yet, even though he was the primary reason for his recent torment. Funny how shit like that worked. Procrastination. It didn't matter if he was writing a report or doing the laundry, when it came to the number one priority on the shit-to-do-list, there was always something else you wanted to do first.

Surveillance reported Special Agent Carver had been wounded but to what extent it wasn't clear. Two unidentified Americans showed up and were seen taking him back to the consulate. Another gwailoh Qu believed to be CIA, based on description, took care of the taxi.

The PLA, rather than the paramilitary police, came shortly after. Qu was puzzled by their appearance, having been assured they'd been preempted. The fact they'd been alerted to the location at all, as well as the timing of their arrival, suggested coordination. The Americans and the PLA, meaning Zhao in this instance, were obviously working in concert.

Even more irritating was their directness. Neither the Americans nor the PLA had spent any time searching. They knew exactly where to go. They tracked him to the warehouse and she'd have to keep that in mind when it came time to corral Carver and the pesky Mr. Hodges.

She didn't want to be disturbed while supping.

With regard to the warehouse, she'd purchased the property through a straw man. It would be nearly impossible to trace ownership back to her, even if a thorough investigation was conducted. In her experience, thorough wasn't a term she would use for law enforcement in Shanghai, let alone the PLA, unless it was politically motivated. The planned use of the building continued to be feasible.

As she punched the numbers on her console to begin the scheduled video conference with The Board, Qu continued to ponder how she would announce her resignation. Her *Qi* was of disappointingly little use in the matter, other than the obvious care in which the announcement had to be presented. The Board wouldn't take it well.

Fraternities such as theirs reserved the power to terminate associations. Much like her connection to the Sun Yee On. They tolerated her departure not because of the cost in manpower if they tried to stop her—they could deal with that—it was her mother. A woman who, since the days of the Cultural Revolution, had established a vast network of influence through China's socio-political and underworld strata.

Through the years, the sexual and intellectual prowess of the woman made her a muse to the most dominant figures in China's power structure. She, unlike Qu, did understand men. Her sway came through subtlety, charm, and piercing logic. Not invective. She never burned a bridge, nor did she place herself in the way of political infighting or the onslaught of character assassination. While a practiced apolitical, her opinions of the incredibly obtuse nature of the progressive, and communism as a dehumanizing platform, she kept to herself.

Her wealth came through gifts she then quietly re-gifted as investment in people in which she saw potential. Those who made the mistake of crossing her disappeared—not from her command, but from those who sought to keep her from harm.

She used what was between her ears and her legs with such deftness over the years, even the wives and concubines of those she bewitched never complained. They found their own statuses rise with that of their men. Qu's mother, now no longer bound to the corporeal, was still a force of nature. While Qu hated to admit it, she was the shield that allowed Qu to explore, and ultimately construct, a life outside the mainstream.

At the end of the day, however, her mother's finely balanced life couldn't support the burden of Qu becoming solely dependent on her for sanctuary. If Qu was branching out on her own, she had to take a page from mom's book and avoid any ferment.

"Good evening, gentlemen." Once again, she spoke in a neutral tone.

"We've gotten news from our embassy contact that there was an incident involving Special Agent Carver. Was that your doing?"

"It was not," Qu lied. "I found out about it in time to prevent an unwanted final solution to the Carver problem." The truth, if you squinted at it long enough.

"An interesting choice of words."

"I'm sorry."

"Our man in Malaysia used the same expression when discussing Ruben Carver. Let's hope for your sake it doesn't portend a similar fate as his."

Qu was aware of that fellow's demise. She brushed off the veiled threat and continued. "Pursuant to our last conversation, I believe we all agreed the most efficient way of reacquiring Randall Hodges is to maintain a constant surveillance on Carver. At this point we should come to an understanding: do we capture for interrogation, or kill on sight?"

"You may eliminate Carver, but wait on Hodges until we've confirmed we have the data."

"Do you have a way of confirming? Hodges will have certainly encrypted the hard drives. Are you authorizing aggressive interrogation?"

"That may not be necessary. You have indicated Hodges has affection for Professor Parsons, and proposed using her as leverage with Hodges. Is this not correct?"

"That is correct."

"We have Professor Parsons. When you have Hodges in your control we'll proceed with using her to secure the data."

"Understood. Is that all?" Based on the tenor of the conversation, Qu hesitated in telling her employers she would not be renewing her contract.

"Yes. Keep in touch." The call ended.

Ready to dial the next number on the call log, Ruben felt her approach. She had a vibe that was like a low drum beat—a kind of reverberation. Any other time he might have found this woman's bitchy essence an enticing challenge, but was presently in no mood to put up with the 'tude. Ruben greeted her in a fashion akin to a slap in the face.

Speaking in English, he used her given name. "Bao-Yu, kick your shoes off and sit a spell."

Carver's use of the familiar had its intended effect. She found it wholly offensive. "Special Agent Carver, must you be so churlish?"

The word made him look up. *Churlish? Her English teacher needs to be spanked.* What he saw made him sit back. A huge purple mouse on each eye, a swollen, bandaged nose, and split lips. Her left arm was in a sling and he could tell every breath was painful.

"Damn, Major, you can't be feelin' too hot." Said without a hint of amusement, his comment was a genuine expression of concern.

Her reply came out tempered. "I've felt better."

"Well, you better sit down before you fall down." He pointed at the chair directly in front of him.

The uncertainty she exhibited as she contemplated her next move had Carver standing and helping her take a seat. It didn't take a great deal of discernment to sense she wasn't accustomed to this type of attention. He interrupted her inclination to protest by gently gripping her unencumbered forearm to guide her onto the settee.

"Would you like a drink? It's on me."

Her eye flickered with uncertainty. "I suppose I could have a hot tea."

"Major, that's not a drink. Why don't you join me? It might help."

"I'm not here to indulge in some bourgeois carouse. I want to talk."

"Hey, I'm not askin' you on date. You look like crap and you probably feel like it. I think something a little stronger than hot tea would be in order."

She sat, frustration etched on her face as she stared at Carver. "I'll have a whiskey. Neat."

After walking to the bar and having the 'tender pour a double Jameson, Carver placed it in front of Zhao with a napkin and a coaster. Taking his seat, he lifted his martini. "Cheers." She lifted hers and they lightly touched glasses. Then, without further ceremony, she drained half of it in a single gulp and dabbed her mouth on her sleeve. "Who was the person you were meeting with?"

"I've met a few folks today. Who do you mean?"

"The man you met here...a few minutes ago?"

"You don't know?" Carver feigned surprise.

"There are twenty million people in this city; one point two billion nationwide. It takes a while to get around to everyone." The corners of her mouth turned up almost imperceptibly.

Oh, no. A sense of humor. And I was just gettin' use ta not likin' 'er. "His name is Xú Bao-Zhi, but to the round-eye he goes by Sonny."

"Yes, I've heard of him. A fairly recent arrival from Hong Kong, I believe. What does someone with such an unsavory reputation have to do with you?"

Carver signaled the bartender and waved an index finger at both glasses to order another round.

"Not for me." Her back straightened and her fist clenched in her lap.

"Listen, Major, I'm not tryin' to cop a feel. If this conversation is goin' the direction I think it is, it'll be over drinks. We'll discuss the Admiral's visit someplace 'official'."

"In that case, I believe I should go." The bitch had returned.

"Come on, Major. We went through this last night, remember? Did you even talk to your boss about helping me?"

She sat motionless.

"I'll take that as a no. So once more, let's go over what's happening here. Qiu Hu, also known as Qu, is a Triad enforcer and a person of interest with law enforcement in the U.S. and Interpol, and apparently, your sister-in-law.

"She's using Xú Bao-Zhi, a one-time mob boss, and now owner-operator of a murder-for-hire enterprise to either kill or capture me—at present he's not really sure which. Qu's bein' kinda fickle about it and it's drivin' the poor hitman crazy. I suppose if anyone can appreciate his frustration you can, bein' related to her as you are."

Zhao shifted in her chair and adjusted the sling to relieve the pressure on her neck, but maintained eye contact with Carver.

"Another actor in all this is Ryan Henderson—you may know him as Randall Ian Hodges. A sleazy geek, and hacker extraordinaire, with an Einstein IQ and a junior high school libido. He's been Mizz Qu's vassal for several months, doing her bidding with a computer. He wants me to take him home and I plan on doing so.

"I don't know what to say about the dead U.S. Army counterintelligence officer found floating in the Huangpu a couple weeks ago, except his stake in all this was the same as mine. Honestly, I don't want to be served up as an hors d'oeuvre for your sister-in-law.

"Finally, and something I'm pretty certain you are not aware of, is the existence of a well-funded but secret organization that sits at the top of this mess, involved in stealing military critical technologies and getting the west to believe China is the culprit."

Carver took a breath, and peering at her swollen slits, said, "And then there's a little matter of a shoot-out this afternoon at a warehouse on the Wusong River. Your boss and the local party clowns have got to be goin' apeshit about that."

Zhao sighed. "I think I'll have that drink."

CHAPTER TWENTY-SIX
June 7, 2005

The martinis helped knock him out close to midnight, but by four he was up, and downed a couple of oxycodone. He'd rolled over on his side and was hit with a pain so intense he thought it would elevate him off the bed.

Wide awake, he mused on the day before, and tried to think about what he had to do in the next several hours. The conversation with Zhao hadn't improved much, even with a couple of snorts of who-hit-John. He got some assurance she'd help him retrieve Ryan. Since he wasn't stealing from China, no harm, no foul. Her hatred for Qu sealed the deal there, but in her condition the best she could do was run interference with the police and her employer. Then stay out of the way.

While Ruben felt for the woman, she was still contrary —a natural ball buster. Even her laughter, when it did erupt, was sardonic, as if everything were dripping with irony. Her marriage to Qu's brother was an interesting side story. She had no children, and the way it was described through whiskey-sodden lips, if she wanted to get pregnant it would have to be an in vitro process. Either that or get the mama's boy she was bound to in holy matrimony to agree to a surrogate lover.

* * *

Zhao wasn't Han Chinese—she was Zhuang from Nanning in the Guangxi Zhuang Autonomous Region. Formerly a province, Guangxi was in south central China bordering Vietnam on the Gulf of Tonkin. Born in 1968 to a couple of rutting Red Guard fanatics, she was raised by her grandparents. Her radical progenitors were rounded up by the PLA shortly after her birth and executed.

Part of the pure and innocent generation turned marauding xenophobes, they were gunned down with thousands of their post-pubescent playmates. It was during the Communist Party's attempt to stem the carnage brought on by Mao's last-ditch attempt to forge the unending revolution.

Unhappy with what happened to their children, the grandma and grandpa on both sides of the carnal equation allowed her to grow up questioning everything. She learned early, however, that an inquisitive mind was viewed with suspicion and dealt with harshly, particularly if it went outside the party line.

A graduate of the China University in political science and law, she joined the PLA, and after testing and training was assigned to the General Political Department as an international liaison. Her specialties were counter-espionage and foreign organized crime, which was how she met Feng. He was also in the GPD being groomed for attaché duty.

She liked Feng then, and in fact, still considered him her BFF. He was thirteen years her senior, but fun loving and a great shopper. They'd only tried having sex a few times. He'd been so completely emasculated by an overbearing mother and psycho sister his only release was through masturbation. He was too embarrassed and afraid of the fallout from work to hook up with a man, and by the time homosexuality was legalized, he'd lost interest.

It was pressure from Feng's mother, the Dowager Qiu, that saw them married on Zhao's thirty-fifth birthday. Feng was almost immediately assigned to the embassy in Tokyo, and while it was understood Zhao was free to see whomever she wanted, the mother-in-law, with the strings she pulled, kept any suitors at bay. Zhao might as well have been fitted with a chastity belt. Carver would have been a nice diversion for a few days, but thanks to Qiu Hu, even that now seemed remote.

After accepting two painkillers from Carver, she gave her car keys to one of the senior NCOs on the surveillance team and took a taxi home.

Carver hadn't called Ed Johnson like he said he would, and the embassy number he saw on his BlackBerry was from Art Sheppard—a call that had also gone unreturned. He wasn't sure he wanted to hear what Sheppard had to say. The oxycodone hit him in less than ten minutes, and he went back to sleep until his phone rang at six.

"Yeah, who is it"?

"It's Ryan Henderson."

"Hey, Ryan, you're not dead. Good for you."

"What? You kiddin' or somethin'? I want to come in. Are you gonna help me or not?"

"Buddy, you are my number one priority, aside from me stayin' alive."

"Uh-huh, right. Maybe I picked the wrong guy to get me outta this jam."

Ryan pushed the wrong button with that comment. "There is no other 'guy', my man, and while we're on the subject, when do you think you'll start takin' some responsibility for your situation? The American your benefactress carved into cutlets, and the position you've put me in, is on you. Ya know, it ain't exactly a trail of breadcrumbs you're leavin' on the ground. And what about Helen Parsons?"

"Shut up about her."

"She was an innocent and you put her in the crosshairs. Whatever happened to her is your fault. If you want anyone to consider an immunity deal seriously, you're gonna have to man up."

"I don't have to listen to this."

"Hey, it's not like you can take the football and go home. Without the security of the government you betrayed, you are a dead man—pure and simple. You know it and I know it. Otherwise, we wouldn't be havin' this little tête-à-tête."

Ruben heard him take a deep breath and then sigh.

"Okay, what do you want me to do?"

"I want you to give me the address of your apartment and I want you to tell where I can find Qu."

"Man, are you crazy? You can't get to her."

"Gettin' to her is the easy part. What comes after is tricky. Have you got access to a computer?"

"I picked up a laptop yesterday. Why?"

"I wanna put those hacking skills to work."

Ruben rang off once he detailed the plan, and Henderson assured him he could make it happen. It was a timing issue, but if he was successful, he'd have Hacker Boy cuddling in Uncle Sam's arms the next morning.

After Carver's sit-down with Sonny and the slurry elucidation from Zhao, he didn't need to make any large cognitive leaps to point him in Qu's direction. There was no love lost between the two women, but as much as they wanted to eat each other's lunch, there was a familial barrier compounded by political pressures that prevented their showdown.

With regard to Sonny, Carver saw him as man just trying to earn a dishonest buck. From their conversation, it was apparent switching sides didn't necessarily appeal to him but the word was getting out concerning the mortality rate of his employees. It was beginning to impact business development. Qu was a paying customer, and while not necessarily the cornerstone of Sonny's operation, Carver gathered he had to consider the long-term effect on his enterprise by keeping her on his books.

Carver took a chance in meeting the Chinaman. Their encounter would certainly give Sonny some ideas about completing the contract. Especially now that Sonny was able to get up close and personal. The problem, however, was bigger than that. Sonny had to decide if the money he made on the contract was worth the shit storm he'd bring down from every U.S. intelligence and federal law enforcement agency after the deed was done. It only seemed like a quandary. Ruben didn't get the impression this gangster enjoyed turmoil, and appeared savvy enough to recognize its source. Carver made certain Sonny's decision was an easy one.

For his next two calls Ruben grabbed a cab to the consulate. He'd gotten Zorro out of bed to meet him there because he needed a secure line in the SCIF. The conversation with Ed took longer than he hoped. The Justice Department was initially willing to cooperate, but within hours of notification, headquarters was receiving unexpected blow-back. Someone, somewhere, wasn't happy with putting Henderson in witness protection.

It wasn't the Department of Defense—the pressure was coming from the Hill. Johnson didn't want to hear about The Board and what that could mean. He wanted to make it to retirement. As far as what Carver outlined as an action item taking place over the next several hours, Johnson needed plausible deniability if everything went tits-up and NCIS had to disavow the special agent.

Before he terminated the call with Ed, Ruben posited one other possibility. The NSA was always on the lookout for talent. The type of ingenuity Henderson had exhibited, along with his lengthy and successful track record, moral flexibility, and willingness to travel made him a perfect candidate. Johnson liked the idea, especially after hearing from Junior Prosser that Henderson had the ideal bona fides on a thumb drive in his pocket.

The conversation with Sheppard went better than expected. At first, the COS was a bit testy, but when Carver told him of the developments in the investigation, notwithstanding the skirmish at the warehouse, Art smoothed out. What blew his skirt up was the intel on Qiu Feng. It wasn't something Carver would be associated with, but he got the idea Art had a honey pot in mind for the gender-confused gentleman.

The other actionable intel involved Sonny Xú. In 2002, Carver had reasonable success in introducing two of Stanley Ho's underbosses in Macau to an agency case officer stationed in Hong Kong. Stanley, also known as Ho Hung Sun, had a monopoly on the gaming industry throughout the Wanshan archipelago, which included Hong Kong and Macau.

While he enjoyed denying it, Stanley was ostensibly the Triad godfather in the region. The information his two protégés provided over the last three years put the agency out in front on much of the ongoing illicit activity in the South China Sea. The Agency raked in intel on not only the Chinese, but Russian, Israeli, Iranian, Korean, and various African organized crime as well. With that in mind, the information Sonny could provide on China's interior made Art go tingly all over.

Apparently, all was forgiven as they signed off.

There was one more aspect to the scenario Ruben didn't mention. It was feasible, but he didn't have, as yet, the confidence it would happen. He'd have confirmation before bedtime.

On his way back to the hotel Carver contemplated room service for breakfast, but wanted to make sure he had everyone's attention before he left the hotel again. Back in his room, he changed the dressing on the wound, dry-swallowed two antibiotic tablets, then went through the rest of his morning routine. The shower was quick. He wanted to spend some time working over his teeth and gums.

No shave, although he did fuss with a silver dollar-sized bald spot that was forming on his crown. He'd have never been aware of it if a woman he'd started seeing during his suspension hadn't mentioned it a few times. She'd gone to the trouble of buying him a hair treatment gel he now used everyday. She made it sound like it was important to her, and he found if he answered in the affirmative when she asked about it, a tiresome conversation was abated. *The things I do for a little lovin'...*

He plucked the polo out of the suitcase, along with the tactical trousers and the Timberlands. After getting dressed, he went through the same closet procedure he did the night before to load up. As he walked into the lobby restaurant he waved at all the familiar faces, many with the unmistakable all-nighter look.

Finishing a plate of soupy scrambled eggs and limp bacon, he lifted his BlackBerry from a vest pocket and dialed a number.

"Yes?"

"I'll be out in five minutes. Are you ready?"

"Yes."

He punched the disconnect, signed the tab to his

room, and dropped it at the register. The lobby was busy on a Tuesday morning, and as the sliding doors opened to the taxi stand, he couldn't determine how many were behind him, if any at all.

The hotel attendant at the stand tried to put him in the first taxi in the queue, but Ruben handed him fifty yuan and told the youngster in Mandarin he was waiting for a ride. Two cabs later Ruben signaled the attendant, who opened the rear door for him. As he slid in the back, the door slammed and the driver hit the gas.

"I said five minutes."

Zhao adjusted the rearview mirror to peruse him and shrugged a shoulder. "Traffic."

"How long to get there?"

"It's rush hour. Probably forty to fifty minutes."

"Any idea how many are behind us?"

"I won't know for a while. I'll make a few turns as we go and should have an idea in twenty minutes or so."

Ruben tugged his pistol free and felt a twinge in his trap. The post-surgery agony was over but he needed his arm and didn't want to be bothered with the residual soreness. He took a single oxycodone pill, figuring it'd knock down some of the discomfort without doping him out.

"How you doin', Major?"

"I'm fine. Please don't talk to me right now. I don't want you to say anything that will make me rethink this ridiculous plan."

As requested, Ruben shut his mouth, but his acquiescence was like squirting gasoline on a fire. Zhao couldn't keep her mouth shut. "Fortunately for you, I've gotten—I believe your expression is—the green light. I briefed my boss on what you will try to do and he was surprisingly agreeable."

"Is that good or bad?" *Why do I even bother to ask?*

"I suppose it depends on your point of view. If you get killed, your body will be turned over to the U.S. Embassy, with a letter of condemnation and the appropriate media attention decrying your criminal conduct. If you live, which I'm assuming means your plan was successful, you'll be arrested and tried accordingly. Again, with a letter of condemnation and the appropriate media attention decrying your criminal conduct. Either way it's good for China, bad for you."

"Very tidy..."

"So, it's important you keep your side of the bargain. You do that and I'll make sure any corpus delicti can not be produced."

First she tells me I'm screwed no matter what. Then she gives me an ultimatum. Corpus delicti? Where the fuck did that come from? Women...I fuckin' hate workin' with women...

Ruben tapped the suppressor from a vertical pocket on his vest and carefully rolled it onto the threaded barrel. He dropped the magazine to check the seated bullets and drew the slide back a fraction to confirm a round in the chamber.

Zhao peered at him through the mirror. "Well, don't you have anything to say?"

"You told me not to speak."

"*Men!* You are all alike." Her one hand on the steering wheel kneaded it as she huffed in exasperation.

"Whoa, lady...please. If I get through this I'll hold up my end. I have no interest in seeing the inside of a Chinese jail. I don't do well on fish heads and rice."

Her mood suddenly changed. "I count four cars. You won't have much time once I drop you off. Are you sure you want to go back to the warehouse?"

"Yes."

CHAPTER TWENTY-SEVEN
Another Taxi Ride

"Where is he going?" She'd been waiting for a call.

Qu's driver had been coordinating the surveillance as instructed, and had four cars with two men in each picking up the tail from the hotel. Not an easy task considering the layout of the taxi stand and direction Carver went out of the driveway. The taxi he was in turned left across traffic on Nanjing West Road heading northeast toward the Bund.

"I don't know yet. What are your orders?"

Qu had been meditating, and bounced the possibilities against her *Qi*. "This may be what we've been waiting for. He's meeting Hodges. What about Zhao?"

"I didn't see her this morning, and none of her men followed him out of the hotel."

This bit of news pinged against her center. She hadn't yet orchestrated a way to separate Carver from the other players and wondered why they weren't in the mix. With Xú Bao-Zhi now incommunicado, she felt like the only person at the Mahjong table. *Maybe he arranged this somehow.*

"Call me when you've determined the location."

"Are you sure you want to go back to the warehouse?"

Zhao was obsessing over Ruben's plan. "I think we should find a better spot."

Jesus, you'd think we were goin' steady. "Just stick with the plan."

She continued to pick at the proverbial scab. "How do you know they'll follow you in?"

"I thought we weren't talking."

"I think this is *stupid*." She had reverted to the national lingua franca: Mandarin. "I want to find a better place."

"*No*. I know the layout. I have the cover spots already formed in my head. I don't wanna be drivin' around for an hour waitin' for you to come up with a better spot. We're in a taxi...remember?"

"You don't have to yell at me. I'm only trying to help." Her words were crisp and a half-octave higher than usual.

"I'm not yelling, and you are helping me and I appreciate it. All you have to do is drop me off, go find a place to have a coffee or whatever, and I'll call you when I need you to pick me up. Simple."

"You won't call...you'll be dead, and to tell you the truth, I won't care."

And the guys in the office wonder why I never got married... "Please, stick with the plan."

They made eye contact again through the mirror. A channel formed between her purple orbs, and the straight black brows were tilted at forty-five degrees. "*You never listen to me!*"

Oh, for Christ's sake! I've know the woman for...what...two days, maybe...and we're already at the "you never do" stage? Aren't we supposed to have, like, sex or somethin' before this shit starts?

What came out of Ruben's mouth next was pure reflex, or depending on the point of view, reflux. "Bao-Yu, it'll be okay. I like you. Honest. If you do this for me I promise I'll take care of you."

She broke eye contact, hunched forward three inches with her hand at twelve o'clock on the steering wheel, and pressed down on the accelerator.

"He wen' ter da warehouse." Qu's driver had reverted to his native Cockney.

Qu tried to press the receiver closer to her ear, as if not quite certain she'd heard correctly. "The warehouse? And he's alone?" *Why go back there?*

"Yes. There's no one else wiv 'im."

She was now out of her chair pacing, wishing she'd gone with her driver that morning. Again she filtered the possibilities through her *Qi*. The warehouse was not a place Carver would meet Hodges—certainty regarding that prospect was immediate.

He was looking for something, and she ruminated about what that could be. Zhao's men had swept the entire space the previous day and none of Qu's sources indicated they'd found anything of substance. Then a spark of intuition ignited the logical.

"Do we have anyone in the building now?"

"No. The rest ov da blokes 'ave been pulled back ter Pudong. What do yew know?" Her driver had learned long ago to trust the presentiment his mistress possessed.

"He's waiting for you."

Three seconds of dead air, then, "What are yew instructions?"

Her priority was the same as Carver's: the acquisition of Randall Hodges. She had no interest in allowing this *yángguǐzi* to cull her staff. If he was going to do what she'd visualized, he was coming after her anyway. This ruse was nothing more than an attempt to level the playing field.

"How many men are with you?"

"Eight in faaahr vehicles."

Qu learned how to play chess at Oxford, having enjoyed a similar game in China growing up called xiangqi. Carver's strategy was a dangerous but effective move. He was forcing her to withdraw her pawns or lose them.

He went to the warehouse because he'd been there before and knew how to move around in the dim light. If they entered in force he'd pick them off within minutes. In the event she had them wait Carver out, he'd come for them. Leaving would allow Carver to set up his meet with Hodges, and she'd be forced to intercept them on their way to either the consulate—the most obvious destination—or the various other departure ports in the city.

Another palpable option would be to try to kill Carver now, leaving Hodges stranded. She would eventually have him cornered, but it would take more time than The Board would be comfortable with. Hodges was smart and she was aware he may also be able to find a way to disappear permanently.

"Madam...are yew there?"

"Yes, yes, I'm thinking." She took a few more seconds to scoop out a strategy and said, "Split your team. I want two cars east of the warehouse a half-kilometer and two set up a half-kilometer west. Do not engage him unless it can be done without losing any men. Conceal your teams as much as you can along the road, but be ready to follow him. If he can't shake the surveillance there is only one place I believe he'll go."

"Where's that?"

"Here. He'll come for me." Qu heard her driver laugh.

"He's a fool har'ee gen'ulman. I see why yew like 'im."

"He's an American...and who says I like him?"

* * *

255

Before stepping out of the cab, Carver tucked the FN Five-Seven in his vest under his left armpit. He didn't want the suppressor dangling visibly at his thigh. The traveling companions, exhibiting patience and discipline, set up a few hundred yards from his position. They'd funneled along Guangfu Road and had done their best to conceal themselves in the driveways of other buildings along the thoroughfare.

As he stood outside the taxi looking in at Zhao, he held his right hand up to his cheek. With the thumb and little finger extended, he mouthed the words "I'll call you". She rolled her eyes, curled her mouth up on one side, turned her attention to the road in front of her, and jammed the accelerator to the floor. *Oh, yeah...she wants me.*

Carver wasn't necessarily convinced this snippet of the scheme would work. In fact, he wasn't sure he could pull off any part of the plan. The shoot-out the day before didn't strike him as something Qu's crew had expected. It had the sensation of spontaneous combustion. Had the first two characters gotten into the cab without the hardware, Ruben wouldn't have made such a fuss. He'd have gone along for the ride and the blowout by the river would have had a significantly different tenor.

Today, however, the tigers in the tall grass were biding their time. Ruben was certain he wasn't the primary target. That honor fell to Ryan Henderson. Although Carver would get around to collecting the geek, he wanted more information—the kind of intel the lithe cougar could provide.

Sonny had nothing on the organization called The Board, except they likely financed the operation Ruben spoiled in Malaysia and Singapore earlier in the year. He also suspected they were the people bankrolling Qu. Zhao, in her apparent zeal to undermine her sister-in-law, didn't have a clue regarding the woman's true iniquitous aims. Ruben had to find Qu and squeeze her.

Had it not been for that objective, he would have enlisted Zhao's aid in putting the grabs on Ryan and run a protective service drill with her squad to the consulate. He'd have his man, and she could make a show of cooperating in the preparation of Seventh Fleet's visit to Shanghai. Her part in a little Sino-U.S. glasnost action.

It was fifty yards from the point where Zhao dropped him off to the side door he'd exited the day before. He could see it had been propped open with what looked like a foot-long piece of lumber. He walked with an unhurried but steady pace, wanting to make sure he was spotted heading for the building. With any luck, the liúmáng would be craving payback, or at least be a little curious why he came back to this place.

Carver didn't enter immediately. He hugged the frame for cover as he pushed the door hard enough for it swing in and hit the wall. A quick peek first, then another longer scan before he crossed diagonally into the space—pistol up.

He didn't have the time to explore, but was fairly certain there were only two accessible points of entry. He didn't include windows in his assessment; however, they were seven or eight feet off the ground. Not impossible, but improbable, at least for an initial breach.

Sweeping left and right, he moved around stacks of building material for about sixty or seventy feet until he came to a four-foot cube of piled powdered concrete. It had good coverage of the door to the loading platform and his entry portal from three minutes earlier.

He'd give the outlaws outside a half-hour. Whether or not he'd go looking for them if they didn't show he'd decide then. Even though they'd probably see him coming, he figured his chances at the clubhouse in

Pudong would improve without these bandits on his six.

It almost worked as planned.

After splitting the team and giving them their orders, the driver sat reflecting on his conversation with his long-time employer and cohort. He'd been with her since their early days in London. His Christian name was Bentley, but everybody called him Turtle. His parents owned a small restaurant in Soho's Chinatown. The type of establishment that catered to the local Han community, with roast duck and pork in the window and dim sum for lunch on the weekends.

His father was a classic Chinese businessman. An entrepreneur with a keen sense of how to make money and how to keep it. He'd fought alongside the communists against the Japanese, sharing all he had in a common effort, against a common enemy.

In doing so he was inundated with communist dogma that decried capitalism and preached servitude to a benevolent leadership that would, in turn, care for their every need. He recognized a lie when he heard it, and couldn't understand why his comrades choose to believe slavery was the true freedom.

When the civil war resumed in 1946 between the U.S.-backed Kuomintang, also known as the Chinese Nationalist Party and the Communist Party of China, the pony the Soviet Union was spurring to the finish line, Dad packed his wagon. He'd accepted refugee status and headed south to Vietnam. As far as he was concerned, Chiang Kai-shek and Mao Zedong were two apples off the same tree—rotten to the core and bad for business.

By 1952, Turtle's dad was in Hong Kong after reconnecting with an old war buddy named Heung Chin. Heung shared Dad's dislike for the commies, and with sincere predilection formed the New Righteousness and Peace Commercial and Industrial Guild. Dad helped relocate the organization, known to many as Sun Yee On, to the British dependent territory. He got himself a British passport and a pretty new wife, and at the direction of Heung, sailed for England.

Conceived on the way, Turtle was born in London's East End in 1954. He was a smart kid, but had no interest in the bean counting his father was noted for. Turtle enjoyed the muscle aspect of the business and was good at it. Arrested several times for aggravated assault, none of the charges stuck because witnesses and victims alike developed memory gaps or simply refused to cooperate.

When Qiu Hu arrived in the late sixties, Turtle was smitten. In the summers when Qiu Hu was released from boarding school, she and Turtle practiced a form of Kung Fu his father taught during the day, and ran the streets at night. The bond grew tighter through her years at Oxford, and after graduation, they were nearly inseparable.

While her grooming by the Triad bosses was a deviation from their basic tenet of no women in the organization, it didn't dispel Turtle's father's concern she was tainted—a bad influence. Notwithstanding her circumstances, Qiu Hu was considered a "broken shoe". He saw a demon in the soiled, unbridled young woman.

The hope within the London enterprise was that Turtle would grow into the business. He was expected to take his father's place, but even then Qiu Hu had her own plans. Dad's concerns about the relationship between the youngsters was indeed justified. Initially through sex, then through ideas, she captured Turtle's mind, body, and soul. He was her training ground for developing her *Qi* to manipulate and motivate.

What Qu never realized through those many years

was the hold she had on Turtle was a mutual union. The more he allowed himself to be used, the more she relied on him and confided in him. He became a part of her, which is what he wanted. He saw his future in her.

Turtle would always have her back and that's why, after following her instruction to reposition the team, he left his car where it was parked and walked to the warehouse, a short barrel QBZ-95 in his right hand.

CHAPTER TWENTY-EIGHT

The Driver

His footfalls made no noise until he stepped on the gravel paving at the back of the warehouse. He had no idea how far the sound carried, but assumed Carver was now aware of his presence. With that in mind he ran toward the service door on the loading platform.

Turtle prided himself on his martial skills. Open hand, knife, sword, stave, and a variety of firearms—he practiced regularly and stayed in shape. Never a soldier, but always a warrior, he wanted to hasten this gwailoh's end. Carver had not yet made anything personal, and Turtle liked his style.

That may have been a contributing, yet subliminal reason for his sudden contravention. He didn't share his mistress's culinary inclination. Neither did he hunt for her. She only ate what she killed and based on that rationale, this big nose deserved to be buried with his manhood intact.

With a nod to his own preference, he also recognized talent when he saw it, and knew the fuckin' wanker would wreak havoc if he got to the apartment building in Pudong. He wouldn't go down without taking several men with him.

This fuckin' Septic is aboutta getta bitta bovver.

As he got to the entrance he paused. Not allowing himself to be framed in the doorway, he glanced inside. The lights were off but the place was illuminated by sunlight through the windows. Outside looking in, it was murky shadows, but he reckoned he'd see well enough once he made entry.

Carver was waiting, that much was clear, but it was a big building with lots of hidey holes. He thought it best to get a general location before he presented himself. The boys found weapons missing when they tidied up the day before. The crazy wooden plank more than likely had a pistol or two.

"Oy! Căvă...ya fancy a bittova bowla before ya cop it?"

Who the fuck is this? The last time Ruben heard an accent like that was at "Joe Bananas" in Hong Kong's Wan Chai. A British merchant ship was in port and three or four of the crew went belly-up to the bar swilling pig's ear—beer—as fast as the bartenders could pull it.

Ruben picked up languages almost on the fly. He could be conversational in a foreign tongue in an hour or two if the person he was with had the patience to hash out word meaning and pronunciation. With a text and tapes, or teacher, he could be near native in a couple of weeks. It was his memory.

It was different listening to those merchant seamen. They allegedly spoke English but after two hours of chatter, he hadn't a clue what they were talking about. The accents and slang had him so baffled his responses were nothing more than smiles and pretentious nods of comprehension.

This chump's cockney glottal stop sounded like theirs, and it was native. Then he remembered Lisa Chin's—Qu's—accent, a mix of posh and estuary. *This must be her homeboy.*

"Whatsa matta wivya 'obsons? Cookin' fat got yaaahr tongue?"

I still don't get the lingo but he ain't exactly subtle about wantin' to get a fix on me.

"Cum-o-nen, grow a pe'a cobblas why don' cha."

Oh, well...what the hell. There was no use trying to communicate with the toad in English. Ruben went to Mandarin. "The floor is yours, mister. Did you bring any friends to the party?"

"Oh, now me ol' china, don' be a spaz. I reckon me English is goo' 'nuf for the likes o' you."

In English: "Buddy, I have no idea what you're tryin' to say."

"*Capishe dis, mate?*" Turtle came through the door laying down cover fire in the direction of Carver's voice.

Ruben ducked as rounds pelleted the sacks of concrete and sailed overhead. The guy had successfully pinned Ruben down as he moved diagonally to Ruben's right, a flanking move Carver would have to counter. Fortunately, the gint was a lone gunman and it was Carver's turn to try to pinpoint his position.

Once again in Chinese, he asked, "What's your name?"

The disembodied reply came from behind a table saw at Carver's two o'clock. "You may call me Turtle."

The Mandarin was old-fashioned. Ruben heard it spoken this way in Taiwan, and from a few second and third generation Americans who made an effort to hang on to their roots. He could also tell the ethnic Asiatic was still moving right, trying to catch him on his starboard. With Carver slipping left to maintain cover from the direction of the voice, they were now doing the dance.

While maintaining his focus on Turtle's progress, Carver continued to wonder about the other members of the squad. Seconds later he heard the gunfire. Soft pops. If there had only been one or two shots he might have dismissed them, but this sounded like a distant small arms firefight.

The situation in the warehouse with this dude was only a minute old. Nevertheless, until the shootout began outside, the mug acted with deliberation as if he had all the time in the world. That changed instantly. He rose and fired a three-round burst an inch above the barrier protecting Carver, and then continued to move clockwise, dropping behind a table sander.

Ruben matched the movement and discovered the door was now at his six. He was certain this malefactor was alone, but he didn't like the exposure.

An instant later, another three-round burst, but this time Carver returned fire before Turtle regained cover. He wasn't hit, but the bullets landed close and as soon as he ducked, Carver, still in a crouch, bolted for the door.

It was farther than he thought; taking eight or ten seconds. Turtle was now up and blasting, with fire directed at the g-man's last position. Carver angled out the door in a dive and roll onto the loading platform. The prick redirected his fire, and while Carver wasn't in the mood to count bullets, he figured Turtle spent what was left in his magazine chasing him through the opening.

Carver came out of the roll on his feet for two long strides before he went over the edge. It was a five-foot drop to the gravel pavement, and although he landed knees bent, the jarring impact traveled up his spine to the weak spot on his shoulder. A piercing sensation in his upper back caused him to collapse on his ass, but pumping his legs, he pushed himself under the loading platform's eighteen-inch eave.

* * *

The cockney mook leaped the sander and sprinted toward the light. He did a sliding stop at the doorframe and reloaded as he scrutinized the exterior for possible cover spots around the paved expanse. He said nothing, knowing shit-talk wouldn't draw the wanker out a second time. If Turtle wanted to locate him, he'd have to make himself a target. Weapon up and peering down the barrel, he stepped out onto the platform.

Carver could hear shuffling, and as he sat pondering his next move, realized the mongol was now directly above him. Not one to waffle, he pulled his legs in, then stretched out on his right side. It was painful, but as he rolled onto his back, he pushed himself away from the ramp wall, right arm extended with pistol at eye level.

Clearing the eave, he caught sight of the rifle stock and trigger guard, along with Turtle's hands. As he pushed off with his left foot he fired three rounds. The first hit the forestock, severing the ring finger on Turtle's left hand. The second smashed the frame above the trigger guard, an inch in front of the ejection port. As the weapon came out of Turtle's hands, the tip of his nose disappeared from the third bullet.

Stunned, Turtle staggered backward two paces, his hands stinging and face inflamed. Instinct and rage took over, and with a running leap, he catapulted himself off the platform. When he hit the ground four yards to Ruben's eleven-o'clock, he did a shoulder roll to his feet, tugged a 9mm from a holster laced on his belt, and spinning, began to shoot.

Carver rolled right as bullets to his left kicked up gravel. Since he couldn't extend his right arm above his head, he continued the motion until he was able to push himself up with his left hand to a combat kneel. He had the FN Five-Seven pointed in the general direction of the cocksucker and pulled the trigger three more times.

Turtle felt a bullet tear his flesh on his right side just below his bottom rib. His adrenaline was up and he maintained his footing, getting a good site picture on Carver, who was now kneeling fifteen feet to his right front. He punched two primers and the slide locked back. With his thumb on the magazine release, he stuck his wounded hand in his coat pocket for a reload.

The Kevlar did its job on the bastard's last two rounds, but Carver felt them. They damn near knocked the air out of him.

That fuckin' guy...that's gonna leave a mark.

Now standing, he could see the wayward warrior was having trouble getting another magazine in the well. Speaking English, Carver warned, "Yo, Turtle, you don't want to do that."

"Of caaahrse I wan' toh, ya fuckin' geeza. Unless yer ready to pa'k up..."

When the hand came out of the pocket with a full magazine in tow, Ruben tried one more time. "I'm tellin' ya, pal. Give it up."

When Turtle seated the magazine Ruben double-tapped him, with both rounds landing center mass. The cockney kitchen sink dropped to his knees, his arms flaccid. As Ruben approached the man, he saw him drooling pink foam.

I nicked a lung.

Ruben took the pistol from Turtle's hand and tossed it. "Is she gonna be there?"

Turtle's head bobbed up, facing Carver with a blank stare. "She wou'ent miss it fo' the world, mate." He wheezed each word. "Finish it."

Carver stood reflecting on the chump's last request. As

he broke the suppressor loose and unscrewed it from the barrel, he walked to the spot where Turtle's pistol landed. He holstered his Five-Seven, put the suppressor in its pocket, picked the pistol up, and walked back to the dying man.

After racking a round, he dropped the magazine in his hand and punted it. "Ya know, Turtle, ordinarily in a situation like this—and you wouldn't fuckin' believe how many times I been in these types of predicaments... kinda makes me shiver just thinkin' about it—I would finish you. I'm sorta careful in that way, if ya catch my drift. Anyway, I know a DIY kinda guy when I see one." He showed Turtle the firearm—hammer cocked. "Do yourself a favor."

He set the pistol on the ground next to Turtle's right knee, then turned and walked away. At twenty feet the gun went off and he felt the bullet whiz past his right ear.

See what ya get when ya try to be a nice guy...

Ruben didn't bother to turn around as he moseyed to the driveway. With a collapsed lung or two, and what looked like an arterial bleed, the guy would be dead in minutes. Ruben was now more interested in seeing what Zhao was up to.

The shooting had stopped, and while he had mixed feelings about the possible outcomes, he hoped Zhao had prevailed. He needed the ride.

Ten feet from the road his phone buzzed in his pocket. *Speak of the devil.*

"Yallow."

"Carver?"

"That's me. Was that you doin' the shootin' a few minutes ago?"

"The road is clear to the west. The cars on the east side of the warehouse scattered."

Carver took that response as a yes. Her tone suggested

remnants of an adrenaline rush, and he wondered if she'd managed the dissolution solo.

"Don't you ever worry about disturbing the neighbors?"

"These were criminals. The police are on their way." Her voice turned clipped—officious.

"Uh-huh. Well, if you're not too busy, you wanna come pick me up?"

"I'm with my men right now going over the cleanup. I think I should also brief the paramilitary police on the operation. I don't think it wise for you to be here for that."

So I'm supposed to stay here with my thumb up my ass?
"You'll need to send someone down here to take out the garbage."

"How many?"

"One."

"I'll make arrangements in a few minutes."

This conversation was getting Carver nowhere, literally. Still connected, he put Zhao on hold mentally as he surveyed the area in front of the warehouse. In a second he had his answer and his ride.

"Carver? Are you still there?"

"Yeah, standing by." He then flicked the disconnect and put the phone back in his pocket. He considered initiating silent mode but thought better of it. Apparently, he and Zhao now had a thing goin' on, and he knew the grief she'd give him if she couldn't reach him when she wanted to.

Dead as a doornail came to mind as Carver dragged the lifeless lump out of the blood pool. He'd grabbed what he thought might be a car key, along with a cell phone and considered the pistol, but left it lay. Where he was going he figured there'd be plenty on the ground, if he needed one. As he knelt next to the body a question emerged: *who was this guy to Qu?*

The fucker charged into the warehouse alone and with confidence. Absolutely fearless, the sudden departure from his mortal coil came as complete surprise. Carver saw it on his face as he left the dumb bastard to bleed to death. What's more, the guy appeared to be about fifty, moved like he was twenty, was dressed as a chauffeur, but fought like force recon.

Now worried he was going to run into more perps like this one, he began to strip the body. As he crushed and wadded the material in his hands, he emptied pockets and felt for hidden weapons or other items that would give him a clue what he might be up against. The body armor was an appropriate piece of attire—rated a level three. Fortunately, the pointy green-tipped hollow points the Staff Sergeant gave him went through it like gelatin.

There were a few other doodads Carver found interesting. One was a feng shui charm—a dragon carved from jade—that went in his pocket. That little item would have been a gift to a mug like this, and Carver didn't need extraordinary powers of deduction to know who to return it to. He left the knives, brass knuckles, and the garrote wristwatch—something he'd only seen in the movies—along with some currency, for Zhao's boys.

The body revealed very little, other than the man had been exceedingly clean and fit. The musculature was impressive, marred only by excessive scarring. *This idiot never backed down from a fight.*

He did have a small but old cicatrix from a cut on the lower part of his right palm. Shit like that bothered Ruben because more often that not it indicated some kind of blood oath. If there was one thing he fuckin' hated to deal with it was a shit-for-brains fanatic. Other than that, there were no other marks on the body; no tattoos, not even hair...anywhere. *This fuckin' guy is clean as a whistle.*

As Carver stood over the body he noticed one last thing before leaving the scene. The dude was missing his testicles. *Seriously? I'd a thought a dipshit like this would be swingin' a massive pair.*

CHAPTER TWENTY-NINE
Pudong

The BMW 735i had something called a key fob. It's previous owner had locked the sleek, black luxury car and while Ruben hadn't as yet had the pleasure of sitting behind the wheel of the "ultimate driving machine", the mechanics seemed intuitive enough. While no longer a singular visage in Shanghai, it was, nevertheless, a cool set of wheels. *Nice way to get to the prom.*

The fob, a rectangular device maybe one-inch by two-and-a-half-inches, had neat little pictures engraved on silver buttons illustrating function. The middle button, with the BMW emblem, unlocked the doors, the top button with the arrow locked the doors—of course, the word "lock" etched below the arrow was also a hint. The bottom button released the trunk lid, and Ruben couldn't help himself—he had to check.

To his delight he found a small arsenal that nearly gave him a woody. The weapons included an AA-12, a short barrel close combat twelve gauge auto-shotgun with a thirty-two-round drum magazine; another QBZ-95 with a seated thirty-round magazine; and a couple handguns—the stainless Ruger .44 magnum with the seven-and-a-half-inch barrel being the standout.

The half-dozen flash bangs, though, had him a bit

puzzled. Ruben wasn't using earplugs, even though he had a set in a vest pocket, and one of those bad boys would have definitely put a hurt on him. *Why didn't the badass use one for his entry?*

The guns and grenades had been neatly stored with tie-downs, and before Ruben slammed the lid he pulled the shotgun from its mount, along with three flash bangs. He then checked his sidearm. He had twelve rounds remaining, and decided he didn't need a magazine exchange.

When he opened the driver side door, he reached down and pulled the switch to run the seat back, adjusting it for his legs. Another switch next to it lowered the seat for the length of his torso. He propped the shotgun against the passenger side seat with the butt on the floorboard, and stuffed the grenades in the dashboard glove compartment.

Glancing around the interior Carver noted it was as spotless as its former driver. On the rear seat by the right side door was a neatly folded full-length midnight black, soft leather jumpsuit. On top was a rolled black snakeskin belt, with a thick buckle Ruben recognized as a nasty piece of work, and on the floorboard in front of the garb sat a pair of black, lightweight combat boots. *For best results first distract with erect nipples and camel toe...then apply copious amounts of buckle knife...*

He had to get going before Zhao showed up, but he did find one final piece of equipment. A perfect little something for the ride-along he was about to contact, tucked away in the center console storage compartment: a Sig Sauer P290. A 9mm double action only compact death-spitter with an eight-round magazine full of hollow points. *Why do the bad guys always have the best shit?*

Ruben dropped the dead man's cellphone in a cup holder and eased out his BlackBerry. The recently dialed numbers flashed on, and scrolling down to the one he wanted, punched the dial key.

"*What?*"

"I'm sorry, Ryan. Is this a bad time?" *Maybe I caught him on the can.*

"Huh...no...no, it's fine. Are you ready?"

"Yeah, how about you? Are you good to go?"

"I'm ready. I confirmed the remote access capability I installed for the building's systems is still intact."

"That's great. Are there any hotspots around that area?"

"Which area?" The pitch in Ryan's voice went up a quarter step.

Ruben let it slide. He could tell something else was bugging Ryan from the hesitation in his diction. "Do you know a place called The Great World? It's on Middle Xizang Road."

"Uh...no. I, uh, don't know the place."

"What's wrong with you, Ryan? You havin' second thoughts?"

After a few seconds of dead air he responded. "I've been in contact with Helen Parsons." Ryan's speech was once again strained.

"That's good, isn't it?"

"She's been kidnapped. The people who have her want me to give the system hard drives to Qu."

"How do you know she's still alive? Did you talk to her?"

"No, an email, but she used a code she and I developed. No one else knows it. It was kind of a personal thing, ya know?"

"Ryan, you're a smart guy. You already know if you give up the drives..."

"I can't, I destroyed them, but I have a flash drive with the pertinent stuff."

"Same thing. Anyway, if you turn it over you're a goner. The folks who have her sweep up after themselves. If they let her go, then you've got to figure it's not the first time they used her to get to you."

"*Bullshit!*"

"Yeah, okay, listen, we can talk about this after I pick you up. Did you make a copy of the drive?"

"Of course."

"Good. Where are you? Are you on the street?"

"I'm in an Internet cafe on Nanjing Road."

"Go outside where you can flag a cab and call me back. Do it now." Carver rang off.

He slipped the fob in its notch on the dash and pushed the start button next to it. The V8 rumbled to life, and as he dropped the gear lever into drive, the cell phone in the cup holder rang through the Beamer's speakers.

This should be interesting.

The device had been paired with the car's Bluetooth system, and on the left side of the steering wheel he saw the button with a telephone symbol.

He gave it a push and announced, "Ruben Carver, may help you?"

There was an odd tapping sound, like fingers drumming before she responded. "Do you like my car?"

"I *love* this car. I especially liked the toys in the trunk."

"Where's my driver?"

"You mean Mr. Clean? Yeah...he encountered one of those hazards we often hear about in occupational safety and health briefings."

"Are you trying to be funny?"

"No, no. I wouldn't joke about somethin' like that. Just know he ain't comin' to work tomorrow. Anyway, as much as I'd like to hang on to this black beauty, I can't afford the upkeep. I'll come by and drop off the key this afternoon."

"I'll be sure to roll out the welcome mat. Please, do drive safely." The phone went dead.

That went well, I guess.

Carver was two minutes down Guagfu Road when Ryan got back to him. The boy was in a taxi but having difficulty communicating with the cabbie. At Carver's command he handed the mobile to the driver and Carver gave him the address in Chinese. The cabbie said he'd be there in ten minutes, and Ruben calculated his drive to be about the same. With the phone back in Ryan's hand, Carver told him where to stand for the pickup and they signed off.

Turning onto Middle Xizang Road heading south, his BlackBerry vibrated. Two-fingering it out of a pocket, he glanced at the number showing on the LCD. He decided he needed two hands on the wheel for this conversation and thumbed the kill switch. His phone went back in its place and he grabbed the one from the cup holder.

After dialing the digits, it rang several times before he heard her voice in surround sound.

"Wèi."

"Hi, it's me."

It was several more seconds before Zhao replied, and when she did it was icy. "Where did you go?"

"I'm on my way to retrieve Ryan Henderson and take care of that little matter you and I discussed."

"But, how——?"

"I borrowed a car from the guy you found behind the warehouse."

"You did what?"

"It's okay, really. He won't mind."

"We had an agreement."

"And we still do, but I need you do me a favor and

keep the police at bay. Hopefully, by this evening, all you'll have to do is pack a bag. If it doesn't go as planned, you're safe from nothing more than an inquiry about a rogue agent who gave you the slip. Be happy; I'm taking care of you."

"Hmm...I've already told you my boss and his boss have no issue with you disposing of that vexing concern. Just know, however, if the paramilitary police arrive while you are still there, you will be arrested. I don't believe I need to explain what that means."

"Yeah, I get it."

Zhao didn't bother to reply. *Short and sweet 'n' sour.*

Not fretting a tail, Carver checked the clock on the dash. Although not yet lunch time, he was hungry and zongzi wasn't the only dish served at The Great World. One of the stalls on the ground floor made a killer wonton noodle soup. His mouth watered thinking about it. Besides his empty stomach, his bladder needed tending as well.

As luck would have it, Henderson was stepping out of a taxi when Carver arrived. He filled the space the cab had vacated, and after rolling down the window, told Ryan to go inside the arcade and wait. He then feathered the accelerator as he merged back into traffic. He drove through the first intersection, making a right at the next. Fifteen seconds later he was motoring into the parking structure of Golden Bell Plaza.

With the number of luxury sports cars and sedans in the lot, the BMW blended in. The smoked gray tinting on the windows also provided enough concealment to make him comfortable leaving the shotgun in the front seat. After trotting out of the structure, it took him five minutes to get back to the colonnade.

When he saw Ryan he signaled him to find a place to

sit. After going to the head and then ordering, he joined the computer whiz at a cheap card table; plopping into a low-back white resin chair facing him. They'd never met face-to-face before, and as most first encounters go, it modified initial perceptions. Carver was impressed by Ryan's evident physical fitness.

Ryan's impression was evident. "Yo, dad, aren't you a little old for this shit?"

"You tell me, dipshit. It's your fault I'm here."

As they stared at each other Ryan was again first to speak.

"Why do you think Helen is workin' for The Board?"

Ruben didn't need to be Dick Tracy to detect a twitchy note in that question. Professor Parsons was a weird wild card for sure. A factor analogous to dark matter, she was a gravitational lens when it came to Ryan's emotional state. Whatever the psychological hold was, it shown like an Einstein ring arching around an invisible mass. However, in all his anxiety, Ryan was starting to do the math.

She musta been a helluva muse.

Before Ruben could answer the soup arrived. A large, steaming, conical-shaped white bowl with green dragons emblazoned on the inner lip was placed in front of each man. Ruben broke eye contact to snake a pair of wooden chopsticks from a rectangular box in the center of the table. After snapping them apart, he dipped the tips in the amber broth that covered a mound of long, thin egg noodles. A dozen plump dumplings filled with minced pork and bok choy floated in the mix. *Yummy...*

"Did you ever stop and wonder why The Board singled you out? Even ponder a little about why they'd go to all the bother of pluckin' you out of a federal penitentiary, expunging your record, and setting you up in a cushy job? I mean, with all the gray matter bouncing around places like MIT and Caltech, there's gotta be hundreds of guys, maybe thousands, who can do what you do. "

"Actually, I didn't think about it too much. I learned early on in the joint not to ask too many questions. I was just happy gettin' outta that place. Anyway, there's probably only a couple of guys who can do what I do."

When Ruben heard that he dropped the noodles he'd pulled back in the bowl. "Sheeit, the NSA is full o' guys who make you look like a case of trisomy 21."

"I don't get that."

"Mongolism...down syndrome...fuckin' Corky from *Life Goes On...*"

Ryan snorted a giggle as he poked around in his bowl. "Yeah, well, I will tell you this: I still wonder, once in a while, how the feds got onto me in the first place. It wasn't like I left my wallet at the scene of the crime, if ya know what I mean."

"Sure, I know whatcha mean, which brings us back to Professor Parsons. From my limited experience with The Board, it is not an organization that leaves loose ends. If this amalgamation of evil has your girlfriend, no matter what you do, no matter how much you cooperate, they can't afford to have you two wandering around unattended."

Ryan cocked an eyebrow. "So by your logic, if they let her go, she must be one of them. But, ya know, you're forgettin' one thing: she gave me your contact number. If she had anything to do with why I got this target on my back, why would she do that?"

"Maybe it's the only way they could see gettin' you out of China without souring whatever relationship they've got established. Anyway, the folks behind all of this don't view the world the same way you and I do. There's no moral compass involved in setting the direction of their operations. They'd have no more compunction in killing her than you would in deleting an unneeded computer file. If she walks away from this then you've got to figure she represents something of value to the organization and that's a problem for you.

"Now eat up—your soups gettin' cold."

It was true. There was a hole in her *Qi;* a painful emptiness at her core. The yángguǐzi had indeed killed her driver, Turtle. If she had a soul he would have been its mate. While the venereal aspect of their relationship ended not long after it started, he was still the anchor in their somatic kinship. The blood oath of their youth had never been a trifling matter in either of their eyes. They'd been bound in life.

When, in his prime, he acquiesced to her request, allowing her to consume his cullions with a bit of chopped garlic, scallions, and thyme, again, it wasn't from a bond of love. It was reciprocal dependence, reliance—a surety of trust...obsession. He was no longer able to spread his seed and she no longer worried about him straying to the sound of another siren's song. He was her property and the bastard destroyed him.

Enveloped with rage over the loss, her ire was piqued further by Carver's feigned nonchalance. His infuriating insolence. After overcoming years of abuse with the monks, the contempt of the Triads, and the worthless demagoguery of the communists, she now faced being undone by a clown. She broiled with the notion this man could have had such a devastating affect in a mere speck of time. *He's nothing more than a party favor...a fuck toy.*

Desperate to control her fury and give it direction, she punched three numbers on her console.

"Yes, madam."

"We're about to receive a unwanted guest. I want you

to have all the men stationed in the building. He will be armed and inclined to shoot. I would prefer you take him alive, so ensure everyone has a Taser, along with their bulletproof vests."

"As you wish."

"Call me as soon as he arrives."

She then an encoded a message for an emergency session of The Board.

CHAPTER THIRTY

Storming the Gate

Ryan had recognized the car. "Oh, man, does she know you have this?"

Carver didn't bother to answer.

"Where's the driver? Is he dead? Where'd you put him...in the trunk?"

Again no response, but at the parking lot exit Ruben paused, looked at the dweeb, and asked, "Well, which way?"

"Make a left, go to the light, and make a right. We're goin' to Pudong."

The exchange set the mood for the rest of the ride. It was a twenty-minute trip that turned into forty as they crept through jammed traffic. Henderson described the sea of shit they were heading to as a twenty-four-story bunker. Except for water and fiber optics running into the building, it was off the grid, powered by a two-megawatt diesel generator.

The lobby was bare, with a single receptionist on duty for show during the day. At night the front doors were card key and keypad accessible with individual six-digit pins issued to her minions. Ryan had spoofed a card key and pin number in the system to mask his departure and was hoping it still worked to get them inside.

The third floor was where Ryan's workspace was located, and while the directory in the lobby listed dozens of firms throughout the edifice, he believed them to be bogus. The security office was on the sixth floor. The people working there monitored and managed the structure's fully integrated systems, from building and room access, alarms, and fire control systems to air conditioning, lighting, water consumption, elevators, and the power generator. It was also the location of the weapon stores.

Qu's system administrator had, on occasion, come to Ryan for help in solving irksome glitches with the nexus. Granted full administrator rights, the geek used the opportunity to install a wireless network he could join anywhere in the building. It was well designed, however, and while there was always a strong, persistent signal on the interior, it dissipated rapidly on the exterior. He could tap the network remotely, but without a decent hotspot he had to go inside the lion's den.

Ryan didn't know how many guns Ruben would be facing or where they'd set up. To assist in the sweep he'd have to take control of the building's integrated network. He could start cracking the system from the lobby, but he had to find someplace quiet to manage the lights, run the elevators, close off the stairwells, and seal floors as Ruben cleared each one.

The building was situated in a cluster of cloned erections five hundred meters south of Century Park. They had initially decided to use the service entrance, but after making a pass by the front door they adjusted the plan. The driveway was empty and the street surveillance was gone. Since they were indubitably expected, Ruben didn't see any reason to be coy.

He made a cautious U-turn. Then gave the Beamer the gas, and five seconds later, gyrated the wheel left into the driveway, stopping directly in front of the foyer door. The lid on the center console flipped up with a twist of the wrist, and reaching in, he extracted the tiny 9mm, handing it to a reluctant Ryan.

"Buddy, I wish I could tell ya if we get through this you could have any woman you wanted."

"Yeah...but?"

"But your heroic exploits will go into a classified folder with limited distribution, and you...well, you will still be you. Hand me that." Carver pointed at the shotgun propped between Ryan's legs. "And get the flash bangs from the glove compartment."

Out of the car, Carver hung the grenades by their spoons on metal rings attached to his vest. He then pulled out his Blackberry, along with a hands-free earbud and a single earplug. He inserted the earplug in his right ear, the bud in the left, then attached the cable to the phone, which he slipped back in his pocket.

"Keep your cell phone handy. It's the only way we can communicate once we split up."

"You think that's gonna work?"

"I don't know, but it's all we've got to work with." Carver looked toward the entrance. "Okay, they gotta know we're here. Do you know where you want to set up?"

"I can't see the receptionist, but I need to start at his desk. After that, if you can get me to my office I'll control the building from there."

Ryan pulled the pistol's slide back a fraction and checked for a seated round. He then tucked it in his hip pocket. He grabbed his backpack from the backseat and noticed for the first time the leather jumpsuit.

"Hey, that's nice. Is it yours?"

"It belongs to the lady of the house. Hurry up—get a move on."

Ryan spun and took three steps to the sliders. Not surprisingly, the building was in lockdown and the lobby empty. Ryan pulled the access card from his right front pocket, swiped it along the reader, and holding his breath, pushed the four-digit code he'd created for his escape. The doors slid open with a soft hiss.

Muzzle up, Carver went in first. A bank of four elevators were thirty feet directly in front of him and the reception counter was twenty feet to his left against a marble wall. The four CCTV cameras mounted in the ceiling were all pointed at him, with their red lamps blinking. The door to the stairwell was next to the reception area, and Carver positioned himself at the vertex, where he'd have a clear field of fire on the elevators and the stairwell door.

Henderson then hustled in, moving in a straight line to his first objective. Perched on the edge of the receptionist's chair, the counter in front of him obscured the camera's view. Wrestling the laptop out of the backpack, he was able to set up, turn on, and login in less than a minute without being observed by those watching the monitors.

In Carver's mind, what Ryan did next was absolutely fucking brilliant. He issued a blanket denial of access for every door with controlled entry, doing the same for every computer terminal in the building. He turned off the Wi-Fi and telephone service, routed all CCTV monitoring to his computer, and shut down the elevators. With a final flourish, he poked a little fun by turning out the lights.

After telling Carver what he'd done, he took a few more minutes to recode his access card, set the pin number as four ones, and authorized it to open any space in the structure, including Qu's on the twenty-fourth floor. Carver was ready to rub one out. Then he began to worry.

Ol' Rube may have been a Christian, but experience in life suggested some validity to karmic balance. If the solution to one aspect of a problem was too easy, then get ready for Mr. Toad's wild ride on the flipside.

Mr. Hodges. She stood in the dark, with only the luminous glow from the sixty-inch monitor providing visual orientation. Now fully aware Carver had drafted the problem child to give himself an edge, she wondered why.

After Turtle went down, Qu had to face the realization she'd lost more than her driver. Her *Qi* had never failed her before, and on reflection it became apparent she'd been ignoring its warnings about Carver from the beginning. When she touched his spirit in Beijing, she discerned then Carver wasn't the vindictive type. It wasn't his style—his skin was too thick.

The momentum was manifestly in his favor. By all respects, he'd won by doing nothing more than showing up in Shanghai, which made this play difficult to fathom. Why not simply take the trophy and go home? That question alone produced the portal she needed to approach the riddle. Now in her chair and relaxed, she discovered her *Qi* waiting for her.

"If we take the elevator, they'll know. They don't have any control of the cars and the cameras on their end are offline, but any movement on an active shaft will still register on the monitors in the security office."

"So, what's the recommendation? We take the stairs?"

"It's only a couple flights." Ryan looked Ruben up and down with an assessing eye. "You can probably handle that okay."

"Fuck you. Handle this." Carver grabbed his crotch.

The stairwell door was only five feet away, but Henderson wanted to pack his gear. Ruben, thinking they'd jailed the occupants with the geek's sleight of hand, let his guard down. When the door came open the two choads who came through had the drop on them.

Throughout his half-century there had been more than a few times when Ruben thought he'd sucked his last breath. This was definitely one of them. He didn't wait for an invitation to boogie down. Instinct and muscle memory ramped into overdrive as the five-square-feet they all occupied went slo-mo. They fired as he dove left to take cover in front of the reception counter.

One barb burrowed into his right triceps, the other hit the counter. With only one probe in him, the circuit wasn't complete and he could still move, but the bastard kept the juice flowing. The barb was burning his arm.

Ryan wasn't so lucky. Both pins hit his torso—chest and abs. Ruben heard him scream through clenched teeth and felt the reception counter shudder as he crashed sideways against it. Stiff as a four-hour-old corpse, he bounced, spun, and dropped on the chair, sending it smashing into the wall. The floor finally broke his fall as he hit nose first. The pencil-necked prick persisted, however, and with a constant current, Ryan's whole body spasmed.

The electrical burn was excruciating, but the barb that hit Ruben had stopped emanating its sizzling current. He realized why, when the fella who shot him stepped around the counter fitting a fresh cartridge in his Taser. He had a satisfied grin and pinched brow as he peered down at Ruben, getting ready to have another go at the foreign devil.

It wasn't just the cauterized wound on his arm that caused him difficulty in bringing the shotgun into play.

The stitches in his trapezius tore away, and the pain was enervating. As the gangster brought the Taser up to fire Ruben tensed. He'd been tased before and knew the Kevlar in his vest provided almost no protection.

There was only one thing he could do to survive this, as in any close-quarters shootout: he had to move. The tension in the hands and expression on the face telegraphed the trigger pull, and as the dickhead's finger came back Ruben rolled right. He didn't feel like he was going to pass out, but the agony he was in had a debilitating effect. Twisting over the shotgun, which lay on the floor, propped sideways because of the drum magazine, was like trying to run in hip deep mud. No impetus. When he did finish the rotation, the AA-12 lay wobbling on his left side.

After the probes struck the floor, Qu's henchman dropped the Taser and went to the pistol holstered on his belt. Ruben, still flat on his back and now in a panic, slapped the floor, trying to find the shotgun. The adrenalin rush tunneled his vision, but as soon as he touched the familiar texture of the pistol grip, he took hold of the weapon and brought the barrel up.

His assailant, watching the old man flop on the floor like a landed fish, began to laugh as he cleared his holster. That changed when he saw the black hole staring him in the face. Ruben, likewise, spotted the pistol and used his legs to shove himself away from the business end of the semi-auto. The meathead got two rounds off before Ruben returned fire.

The AA-12 had a cycle rate of 300 rounds of pure double-ought ugliness a minute—forty .36 caliber lead balls per second—with a recoil as light as the M-3A1 submachine gun. With the buttstock tucked into his side, he squeezed off two rounds. Before the face exploded, Carver became conscious of the fact the man standing in front of him couldn't have been more than nineteen or twenty years old.

Ruben hadn't forgotten about the second miscreant, but as a reminder the curious cat stood up from behind the reception desk. Seeing the crumpled form of what used to be his friend, he howled and tugged at the firearm snagged on his belt.

With the use of his right arm returning, Ruben did a sit-up while twisting his legs to get to a knee. Light recoil notwithstanding, he held the alley-sweep in tight to his ribcage and fired three more rounds. Fist-sized chunks of oak flew off the counter and pellets that didn't hit their mark dug quarter-sized holes in the marble wall.

When he stood and took a step, he discovered the Taser wire was wrapped around him and the probe still lodged in his arm. Yanking it free, he pulled the wire away as he shuffle-stepped behind the desk. Ruben found the guy he hit, still alive laying across Henderson. Like his compadre, he was a youngster. He was bleeding from several spots, but he took the brunt of the shot in the chest.

Ruben couldn't tell if any of the lead passed through the body armor but his eyes had glazed over and he was fighting to breathe. The three or four pellets that penetrated his trachea and upper esophageal sphincter were what did him in.

Henderson moaned as Carver pulled the dying man out of the way. He then rolled the dweeby genius onto his back, and tracing the wires, located the barbs. He carefully removed them and checked the nasty burns they'd left.

These are gonna take a while to heal.

Ryan's nose had also been bleeding, and from the new angle, Ruben was fairly certain it was broken.

This guy could have used some rhinoplasty anyway.

"Hey, Ryan." Ruben gripped his shoulder and gave it a shake. "Hey, my man...can you hear me?"

Ryan's eyes fluttered open. "Fuck me...what was that? My body feels like rubber."

Even with the pain he was in, Ruben managed a chuckle. "No shit, boy. You just rode the lightenin'."

"Huh?"

"Never mind. We gotta get you on your feet."

"I don't know if..."

"We can't stay here, bud. We gotta go. You'll feel better once you start movin'."

 Carver didn't want to carry the man. He couldn't, but he had to get him on his feet. He gripped Ryan's wrists and pulled him to a sitting position, his legs extended and slightly bent. Henderson was doing his best to help, but his muscles weren't cooperating.

Ten seconds later, Ryan's eyes were focused and he nodded at Carver. "Hey, you're bleeding."

"Yeah, I pulled the stitches."

"Huh? No, dude, your shoulder." Ryan bobbed his head at Carver's left shoulder.

One of the bullets from the first man down grooved a two-inch canoe in his lower deltoids. *Well that's a surprise.* It had begun to coagulate and Carver elected not to mess with it. *Crap. I'm gonna feel that later.*

"Grab the desk and try and pull yourself up. I'll help." Ruben stepped to Ryan's left side, bent, and wrapped an arm around his waist. "Okay, on three...one, two..."

With both men grunting, Ryan managed to pull himself up on shaky shanks.

"I know how you feel there, tiger, but once you get moving and get the blood flowin', you'll shake it off."

The stairwell lights were out, but the emergency signs above the doors had batteries. Their green glow provided enough illumination to keep them from tripping on the risers. It was slow going. Ryan's condition was a contributing factor but Carver was in a penitent mood, taking particular care to clear the stairs as they went. He couldn't kick himself hard enough in the ass over the two bugaboos who caught him napping.

With the fire power he witnessed the day before and the trunk full of goodies he found that morning, he wondered why Team Puberty were carrying Tasers. Qu wanted both gwailoh alive for some reason. Maybe it had to do with the hard drives, but Ryan wasn't with Carver earlier when he and Madam Dragonfly had their chat.

When they reached the third floor, Ruben used the access card. While standing about eighteen inches from the edge of the frame he had Ryan pull the door open, using it as a shield. With the side sole of his left shoe touching the wall, he slid his right foot, which was even with the jamb, back almost two feet. In that position he was able to lean right and peer down the long, dark hallway.

He tugged twice to release the MagTac flashlight from a side pocket. At 320 lumens it was good to about sixty feet. A half-second tap on the recessed button at the end of the five-inch cylinder did the trick. At least two guys opened up with automatic weapons.

I guess they didn't get the memo about non-lethal...

Without sticking his head out, Ruben pointed the shotgun down the hall and pulled the trigger for six or seven shells. He then dropped the gun between his legs, and after resting the muzzle on the floor, pulled a flash bang from a ring and yelled at Ryan. "Get ready to slam the door!"

Yanking the retaining pin, he let the spoon fly and underhanded the ear-splitter through the door.

"Now!"

Ryan had apparently found his legs, putting his shoulder into the door, driving it closed. Within a second there was deafening crack. With the access card in hand, he swiped the door open and went in low.

The hallway was full of smoke and the carpet was on fire where the grenade went off. *Jesus...what do the Chinese put in those things?* With judicious use of the MagTac, he continued down the corridor until he found them. A couple of Tommys: deaf, dumb, and blind. Within seconds they were also dead.

He retraced his steps to the stairwell to retrieve the wunderkind, finding him in relatively good condition.

"What's the chance we're gonna find an unfriendly waitin' for us in your office?"

Ruben got a blank stare for a response. Then, "Don't be throwin' one of those firecrackers in there. How am I supposed to work with all that smoke and shit? I already have a massive fuckin' headache."

Carver peeled off an oxycodone and popped it in his mouth. He then offered the med strip to Ryan. "Here, one of these'll take the edge off."

He accepted it without hesitation.

"Okay, come on. We need to put that fire out first."

CHAPTER THIRTY-ONE

The Penthouse

Ruben pushed the button on the MagTac twice to get a sustained beam. Henderson's office had zero ambient light. The inky blackness was so complete it was as if the radiance from the flashlight was cutting a round hole in a curtain.

The light fluttered and darted around the room as they walked toward Ryan's workstation. While their initial perception upon opening the door was that it was sans bad guys, Ruben's trust in his own sagacity was left in the lobby with members of Qu's boy band. To add to that, absolute dark in any foreign setting was a creep fest.

Ocean night diving, moonless jungle patrols...buildings with their lights out in Shanghai: my least favorite things.

At the desk in ten seconds, Ryan had the cube lit two minutes later. Ruben found the images flashing on the laptop's monitor oddly comforting as he waited for the set-up.

"Okay, I'm ready. What do ya want me to do?"

"Put the lights on in the hallway and give me an elevator that will take me to the lady upstairs. Keep everything else locked down."

"That's easy. She's on the twenty-fourth floor and there's only one elevator that goes there. It's a card-activated express that runs from the lobby straight to the penthouse. When you come out it's the door on your right."

"I have to go back to the lobby?"

"Nah, I'll bring it down to this floor."

"You know anything about her apartment?"

"Not much. She never invited me in. I lived on the same floor so ya gotta figure the living room is straight in from the entryway like mine was. Don't know, really, though, 'cause from what I could see standing outside her door it was pretty sparse. I didn't see any furniture."

"All right, once you get it ready and I walk out the door, you have to haul ass. Here's the whatchamacallit for the Beamer." Ruben held out the fob. "I want you to go straight to the consulate and ask for Captain Doug Fairbanks. He knows who you are and he's a good guy. He'll take care of you."

"Hey, wait a minute. I'm not goin' there…"

"What, you gonna hang out in Internet cafes for the rest of your life? Look, everyone knows what the deal is, and if I don't leave here under my own steam, the consulate is your only safe haven. Make the right fuckin' life choice for a change, knothead."

"Yeah, okay, okay… I'll go to the consulate but I better not get shafted."

"I guess that's somethin' you never really get used to. Unless of course you miss all that jail house romance." Before Ryan could express his contempt, Ruben added: "I almost forgot. In two minutes turn the lights on in Qu's apartment."

"Sure, but at this time of day you probably won't need them. Unless she's got blackout curtains, the sun is gonna be beatin' through a floor-to-ceiling, wall-to-wall picture window."

Carver nodded, *Good tip.* "Let's do this. Oh,

wait...shit."

"*What?*"

Ruben pulled the door open and after stepping into the corridor looked back a Henderson. "Maybe I shoulda brought flowers."

It was time. In the construction of her sanctum sanctorum, she was careful to have access, telecommunications, and computing run through separate and shielded power lines and servers. The lights and air conditioning, however, remained connected to the main building systems. Sitting in the dark, she keyed in the number and security code for the call.

The wall monitor coruscated for a heartbeat before it snapped on, displaying fifteen boxes, each with an animated head. For the first time in the many years she serviced The Board's needs she saw the full membership. A confluence of men and women spanning three generations, and a dozen different time zones peering out at Qu.

The talking head in the center box began. "We're ready. What's your status?"

In a noncommittal tone she began. "Special Agent Carver is paying me a visit."

She could see lips moving but she had no sound. Her audio had been muted while they decided how to respond. Seconds later. "Please clarify."

"I believe in Western parlance you'd have to say our operation in Shanghai has been blown. Whether or not the interloper is successful in leaving here alive, our activity has gained too much attention to consider a salvage attempt."

"Then it is safe for us to assume you have failed to acquire the young American, Hodges...or Henderson...whatever he's going by now."

"Safe is not the word I would use, but yes, your assumption would be correct." Qu was aware Hodges had entered the building but with her men now trapped on each floor, her confidence was high she'd be greeting Carver before they could break out. She elected to keep that to herself.

"If Carver has our programmer, why is he risking certain death coming after you?"

"What makes you think Caver has Mr. Hodges?"

"Please, Madam Qu..."

"Yes, well, I think Carver's intentions should be obvious—he knows about the existence of The Board and believes I can provide information he cannot glean from Hodges."

"Will he?"

"I haven't decided yet. Be assured, however, now that Carver is in my house, I will be having him for dinner."

"Madam Qu, we must secure those hard drives."

"Ladies and gentlemen since this call will, in all likelihood, bring to a close our lengthy association, I wish to be frank. Unless something miraculous occurs, you should initiate what incident management operation you have in place for this contingency. The hard drives are lost to you—at least in Shanghai. Should they fall into the hands of the U.S. military, then you already know where they'll be going." Qu did her best not to be curt.

The gentleman sighed. "Indeed. Unless anyone else would like to say anything, I will on behalf of the organization accept your resignation. Unfortunately, it could not come under more favorable conditions. You will, of course, be adequately compensated for your efforts."

The last comment registered ominously in that spot just below her navel. *I'll get what I deserve.*

Qu bowed her head deferentially and said, "By your

leave," then terminated the call.

The lights came on as she stepped away from her chair, and in that same instant she heard the explosion and automatic weapon fire. Uncontrollable excitement swept over her as she realized he would soon be there. Breathing in through her nose, then slowly exhaling through her mouth, she regained her composure.

I will have him at my leisure...this is my home.

She began to undress.

On the ride up, Carver wriggled a flash bang free. It was an item that came in handy, but the necessity to use both hands to yank the pin always made a one-man scenario a little precarious. He couldn't just cradle the shotgun—it weighed sixteen pounds. He had to prop it in the corner of the car and hope the welcoming party at his last stop wouldn't be waiting in front of the doors.

As they slid open, he couldn't push himself close enough to the bulkhead. Ryan had left the elevator lamps off—a thoughtful touch—but anyone shooting into the car would start in the middle. He tossed the noisemaker left, cupped his ears, and closed his eyes. The bud and plug were in place, but in a confined space the concussion would pop tympanic membranes, and the flare would blind everyone for several seconds. The blast wave rippled his clothing.

In a crouch with his shotgun up, he breached the hallway to the right. The short corridor was full of smoke, but the small conflagration on the carpet gave him sufficient light to navigate. Two turds with Tasers took two rounds a piece. He fired low into their groins. If they didn't bleed out quickly, they'd be more concerned about their dicks than some crumby gwailoh. Ruben turned his back on them and went the direction he threw the flash bang.

He found two more men groveling on the floor in front of what he assumed was Henderson's old pad. Along with the normal discomfort associated with close proximity encounters with a stun grenade, their pant legs were burning. *The damn thing musta landed at their feet.*

Ruben drew his pistol and put a bullet in each head. Quickly stomping out the fire, he looked at Qu's door.

So, do ya think she knows you're here?

The AA-12 was a great companion, but he decided not to schlep it into the apartment. Short barrel notwithstanding, it was heavy and a bit ungainly for the coming courtship. While perceptive enough not to expect a tea ceremony, Carver felt a hand-held howitzer lacked a certain je ne sais quoi. *Like havin' a chaperone on a date.* Before he dropped it, he removed the magazine and cleared the chamber.

FN Five-Seven in hand, he attached the suppressor, performed a magazine exchange, and stepped to what he discovered was a steel door. Before he tried the handle, a thought floated through his frontal lobe. He holstered the pistol and tugged his BlackBerry out. Not exactly his last will and testament, the text message was short but concise. He then took the time to send it to all the current stakeholders. As the door latch released, another mental image suddenly emerged: *the man had no balls.*

He pushed the door hard while maintaining cover, and just as he did a quick peek it slammed in his face. The hinged metal barrier had a fast hydraulic closer attached. *I bet she fuckin' loved that...*

Bracing himself for a blind entry, he grabbed for the handle once more, only to have it move out of reach as the portal swished open. Qu stood before him, her only apparel a pin that held her hair off her shoulders.

"Shall we dispense with the dramatics?" Her voice was the husky tenor he remembered as she stepped back to invite him in.

Oh, man...I hate it when this shit happens...

With the pistol trained on a spot about an inch right of her sternum, roughly on the same latitude as her silver-dollar-sized black areolas, he replied, "I hope I'm not bein' too indelicate in askin' if there's anyone with you."

"Would you believe me if I said no?"

"Only if you pinky swear and cross your heart and hope to die." Ruben stepped across the threshold, glancing right and left.

"Mr. Carver, you are such an odd man."

"That's Special Agent to you, lady. Ya know, you didn't have to go to all the trouble of dressin' up just for me."

"I find clothes confining when I'm at home. Besides, the outfit I prefer at times like this is sitting in the backseat of my car."

"You mean that Catwoman cosplay thing? And you think I'm odd. Anyway, I recognized one of the accessories."

Qu smirked. "Yes, I'm particularly fond of that ingenious little item. I discovered the company that made it when I lived in San Francisco."

The way Qu glided to the center of the bare room struck Ruben as verging on feline. Her muscles tensed and relaxed in a seductive, even hypnotic, fashion. The real allure, however, was the way she smelled, the musky odor.

He noticed something else. In his recent dust-up with Turtle he could put it in context. The woman was hairless. He was used to women with very little hair, especially in Asia, but Qu had no hair...anywhere. As if reading his mind, with her back to him, she stroked her body as her hands slipped to the top of her head and in a slow, luxuriating manner, lifted the wig away from her scalp.

This is about to go surreal. "Does The Board know you've been in chemotherapy?"

Qu turned to face him, going effortlessly into a deep horse stance as she began a rhythmic t'ai chi ch'uan routine Carver couldn't place. "Western sarcasm is a rather boorish concept I've never personally been able to appreciate. However, since it is apparent you may not be equipped to escape the banal, I'll put things in perspective.

"As I told you, I am the product of Chan Buddhism. While I prefer the temporal, there are aspects of the ascetic—the self-discipline and abstention—I rely on. I understand its power, its liberating force, even in the secular. I've never had any interest in the mystical teachings of practitioners trapped in their own perversions. That is not to say, however, the mysticism they vainly pursue doesn't have supreme potency when tapped properly."

What she said didn't lure Carver in. Bullshit is bullshit no matter how it's presented. It was her voice modulation, along with the fluid motion of her smooth body, that corralled his mind. He was so caught up in witnessing the ethereal transformation, not only did he fail to see the spinning sidekick, he didn't actually feel it land, either.

It was his head cracking on the floor that brought him out of the trance. The impact broke his grip on the pistol and it flew out of his hand, skipping across the parquet like a flat stone on a glassy lake. Stunned, he knew she was bringing the fight, but the weakness in his shoulders didn't allow him to move as quickly as he needed to. When she leaped he tried to brace for impact, but the pain she inflicted with her knees as she drove them into him deltoids and upper biceps paralyzed him.

Oh, shit! "What, no dinner and a movie first?"

With his arms pinned she pummeled him with blows to his face, ears, and temple. Perched too far up on his chest to deliver a killing blow on his thick neck, she was content to work on his head until his skull cracked.

"You...took...my...driver." Each word punctuated with a knuckle strike. "Now I'm going to take from you what he so willingly gave to me." She began working him over with forearm smashes. "The essence of a man doesn't swing at the end of that appendage you're so proud of. It resides in those two floating globules behind it."

Carver was fading with every shot, but he wasn't going to simply lie there and let her beat him unconscious. Neither did he cotton to the notion of the psycho chinkerbell helping herself to his "essence". He liked using them once in awhile.

He pumped his knees into her lower back and kidneys, and it started to take some of the sting out of her punches. When she shifted her weight lower on his torso to get more zip on her forearm bashes, Carver's arms came free.

Still almost entirely defensive, he thrust a palm strike to her chin. He slid his head left, moved his hips right, and brought his right leg over, around and down, hooking her head and neck. Carver wanted to execute an arm bar, but as he used his leg to push her off, he lost control of her left wrist and she countered with an elbow to his groin.

The auto response was hands on crotch and knees up. That motion on the floor's slick surface allowed him to spin into a kneeling position, facing her as she came back in on him. Muscle memory made him bring his hands up, and as he blocked a punch with his left, he countered with a right hook that caught her upper mandible below the left ear.

He knew he tagged her by the way it radiated up his forearm to the elbow. A blow that would ordinarily put someone down, he watched her roll with it to a fighting stance and shake it off. *Fuck me. What has this woman been eating?*

Qu's head snapped right and her body followed, doing a shoulder roll that brought her to her feet. The power in the punch surprised her. *Such wonderful energy in this yángguǐzi.* She bounced on her toes, rotated her delts with clenched fists by her cheeks, and flexed the muscles in her jaw, opening and closing her mouth a few times. She then bobbed her head side to side to shake off the effects, all the while maintaining eye contact.

As she directed her *Qi* at the kneeling form in front of her, ready to finish him, he did something utterly unexpected. He was no longer fighting. She was certain he wasn't aware of what he was doing, yet she could feel him feeding on her, draining her power. *Fascinating.*

While she stood gauging him, Carver quickly glanced around the room, spotting the pistol about ten feet to his four o'clock. He had a pretty good idea she'd be on him before he reached it. He had his Recon 1, as well as the ASP, which would definitely do more than just hurt her feelings, but he decided to try something else.

He sat back on his heels and held up a palm. "I don't know about you but I could use a break. You got anything to drink around here?"

CHAPTER THIRTY-TWO

The Conversation

The laugh was more like a snorty giggle. To Ruben's ear it was genuine, but had a self-conscious quality, as if the woman wasn't sure she was doing it correctly. Aside from having his ass handed to him by this tall, curvy, and utterly glabrous femme, he was intrigued.

Fists now on her hips, with her weight on her right leg, she was silhouetted against the massive picture window Ryan described. "Well, what would you like? Hard or soft?"

"A glass of water would be a great starter." Ruben eased himself off the floor and shook each leg a few times to get the circulation going. They kept their eyes on each other and Ruben, sensing the naked babe was about to pounce again, gave her another wave. "Hey, truce...I'm more interested in talking than fighting. Oh, and by the way, you can't have my balls. Not only are they firmly attached, they've got a lot of sentimental value."

The smirk came back as she spun on the ball of her left foot and skimmed across the hardwood toward to what Ruben assumed was the kitchen. As she moved he did as well, taking five steps and bending to retrieve his firearm. He left the safety off and suppressor on as he slipped it in the holster.

He considered swallowing another oxycodone but reminded himself how much he'd already downed. He confirmed that by pulling out the med strip. One pill left.

When she emerged she had a chilled, half-liter bottle of Evian in her left hand and a chromed cleaver in the other. She set the water on a narrow shelf affixed to and running the length of the wall to Ruben's right. With his hand on the pistol grip, he did a cross-step to his left, keeping distance between them.

"Oh, I'm sorry, Special Agent Carver. Would you like me to remove the cap?"

"Yes, please, and call me Ruben."

"Isn't that sweet. As much as I appreciate the gesture, I don't think we should get too cozy. We don't know how this will end."

Carver nodded and applied his best boyish grin. He then drew the one-hole punch and transferred it to his left hand. When she backed away from the shelf, he crossed stepped laterally to the offered agua. He quaffed a quarter of the liquid as he stared at her from the top of the shadowless dome to the tips of the long, painted toes.

I know how I wish this would end.

She twirled the cleaver at the handle. "What shall we talk about?"

"Let's talk about your day job."

"Oh, how predictably mundane."

Carver reset the bottle on the shelf and transferred the pistol to his right hand. With his left, he rubbed his jaw and touched what he discerned was a broken nose. *I gotta stop blockin' punches with my face.* "Hey, lady, this ain't exactly a social call."

A slight, almost imperceptible twitch in her stance made Ruben take two steps back. *I fuckin' flinched...shit.*

The snorty giggle was back, and holding the cleaver

up with her thumb and first two fingers, she cooed, "I can bury this in your chest before you can pull that trigger."

Generally, Ruben never felt compelled to rise to a challenge, but in this case he immediately fired two rounds. Like a lot of guys who'd spent years working with firearms, he had good eye-hand coordination. He never had much trouble hitting what he was looking at, but when both bullets struck the flat of the blade, he had to fight the urge to do his endzone dance or stick his fist out to let the bitch give him a little knuckle love.

He'd been lucky in bad situations more times than he liked to remember. In his experience, however, it wasn't the fortuitous event that made the difference. It was his reaction to it that turned the worm. The ol' do-you-wanna-see-me-do-it-again look.

The cleaver had come out of her hand and wobbled as it stuck a half-inch into the teak parquet. Massaging the sting out of her mitt, she glared a Carver in disbelief.

Without expression he redirected the barrel to one of her erect nipples. "Well?"

With arms limp at her sides, feet shoulder-width apart, she closed her eyes. Breathing in through her nose and exhaling out her mouth, she stood motionless. Ruben's own dabbling in meditation cued him in to what he was witnessing.

He contemplated doing Zhao's bidding with a single bullet, but that thought evaporated as quickly as it came. His brain in overdrive, he reckoned her days were already numbered. That Delphic international philanthropic organization, known to him now as The Board, would see to it.

She only needed a minute or two to sort things out. Qu had no doubt about Carver's designs. An aggravatingly strong-willed man, he wasn't there for the express purpose of killing her. She, on the other hand, at least in the beginning of the engagement, had every intention of carving him up. Now, as she stood studying the bruised and bloodied battler, she had a *Qi*-induced change of mind. *Leave this one alone. This is a man who won't take what is not offered.*

"If you'll excuse me, I need a minute to put something on."

"Gee, I hope it's not something I said. I could get naked if it would make you feel more comfortable."

With what would have been a raised eyebrow if she had one, she responded in a trenchant tone. "Keep your pants on, Ruben. I've lost my appetite."

In a half-dozen fluid strides she fetched the wig, giving it a gentle shake and survey. She then flipped it over her shoulder, shooting Carver a sultry sideways glance, and cat-walked to a door he hadn't noticed on the other side of the room.

In her Zen atelier, Qu used the remote control to open a closet she stored her business attire. Wig in place, she pulled on a sports bra and panties, black silk high-collar blouse, and a charcoal gray pinstripe pant suit. She then slipped her bare feet into a pair of black suede pointed flats.

At her chair she opened a small recessed chamber in the left armrest, exposing a red toggle cover emblazoned with the simplified Chinese characters that read "cāshi". She thumbed it up and pressed the toggle forward. Three words in large white block letters appeared on her monitor: "Are you sure?"

After punching the "y" on the keyboard the screen went blank as the system began wiping her drives. At the same instant timers on incendiary devises were activated that would turn the entire space into a furnace.

Before dialing a number on the cell phone she'd stowed by the chair, she opened a panel in the wall revealing a one-man lift. Stepping in, she made the call.

The mobile phone he'd removed from Turtle's clothes was in his pocket and ringing. He wouldn't have noticed if the earbud he was using with the BlackBerry hadn't been trashed in his brawl with Qu. The thin cable was still dangling from the phone but the earpiece was missing. He looked at the number displayed and shook his head.

Oh, man, I'll bet she's blowin' me off.

"Please tell me you need me to bring you a towel or somethin'."

"Sorry, Ruben. As much as I'd like to stay and get better acquainted, I have to run. Let me give you a telephone number I believe will help you further your inquiry into my former employers." Qu recited a number starting with 41-22. "Good-bye, Ruben. You should hope we never meet again. You have less than fifteen seconds before you feel the heat."

Carver didn't reply. Qu didn't seem the type to use cute euphemisms, and the warning registered. He conducted a five-second scan of the room, checking for anything that may have fallen out of his pockets during the tussle, and hustled to the door. He'd barely stepped into the hallway before the apartment ignited.

Ryan had shut off the fire control system, and although the automatic closer slammed the metal door on his way out, Carver suspected the blaze would spread within minutes. He had no way of getting the men out who were trapped throughout the building. The irony he faced, pondering their plight, was that he would have killed them in a face-off anyway.

He briefly considered the shotgun but left it lay. *I'd like to see ya get a taxi humpin' that thing...*

On the ride down he cogitated about evacuation routes and escape plans, but not his—hers. He closed his eyes as he reconstructed the room from flash images he got during the fight and their all-too-brief confab. It was after she left the room, though, and he found himself staring out the picture widow when he saw them. In the distance, to his ten-o'clock, were the two new iconic expressions of Shanghai: the Oriental Pearl Tower and the Jin Mao Tower.

With those to ostentatious displays of China's modernity in view, he deduced Qu's apartment faced Huamu Road—a major boulevard on the southern border of Century Park. He and Ryan had passed the west side of the building from the south and had entered the lobby through the north entrance. He saw no easy egress from those sides, considering the position of her digs relative to the layout of the rest of the building.

That left the east side as her probable exit. It then dawned on him a building like this would have some parking available, and if it were a part of the structure the entrance would have to be from the east. He now knew where he was going, but it would have to wait a minute or two.

He heard them as soon as the elevator opened. Four, maybe five guys in the lobby, one in particular who seemed to be in charge. Ruben was pretty sure he wasn't lamenting the condition of the reception desk. The elevator bays were out of sight of the lobby's reception area, and with their hubbub, Ruben had gone undetected.

His right ear still had its Peltor plug in place, and shaking its mate from the container, he put the yellow end in his left. Tugging loose the last flash bang, he released the spoon and bowled it in the direction of the reception desk. He barely had time to take cover in the elevator when it went off. Stepping out and into the lobby, Carver began acquiring targets.

He had eighteen green tips in the magazine and he fired until all five were stretched out. Again, as advertised, the twenty-seven grain SS198LF went through their body armor like a hot knife through butter. This time he finished up with headshots.

He hadn't checked his watch, but he calculated it took about a minute-and-a-half. The last full magazine went in the well, and after releasing the slide, he seated a round in the chamber as he went through the lobby sliders.

The only part of his body that seemed fully functional were his legs, and he was stretching them out as he sprinted to the east side of the building. The street was tree-lined between the curb and sidewalk. With the edifice on his right he had the sense of running in a tunnel. He was also self-conscious. A big, bloodied gwailoh running full out with a gun in his hand had a tendency to alarm folks.

When he reached the corner of the building he slowed. As expected he spotted the garage entrance but he was fairly certain she'd be on foot. The dragon lady was definitely pissed about Turtle's demise but she referred to him as her driver. While she may have had more than one car to use, she never sat behind the wheel. She wouldn't even know where he kept the keys. *Pro'bly a Buddhist thing...*

Initially focused on the driveway, he scanned the street and sidewalk. He spotted her about a hundred yards directly in front of him heading south. He'd never mistake that silhouette and gait, and he started running again.

At about fifty-yards, Ruben called her name. *"Qiu*

Hu?"

For whatever reason, possibly because he used her given name, she stopped. It was a rather leisurely turn, facing him with a beaming smile. Ruben halted, and in haste checked behind him, doing a full one-hundred-eighty-degree scan, pistol at the ready. He wasn't sure she was actually gazing at him. He'd recognized the look, having been on the receiving end of that singular expression a few other times in his life. A woman in love. *No fuckin' way.*

Utterly confused, he twisted back her direction. She hadn't moved, continuing to peer into him. *Oh, brother...and I thought I was in trouble in her apartment.*

He took exactly five steps when a recently polished black sedan drove past. The front passenger-side window, and the rear window adjacent to it, came down and with tires screeching, the car braked ten feet from Qu. Carver heard the automatic shotgun fire and watched the woman being shredded. The gunmen held the triggers back for another ten seconds after she'd collapsed.

There was nothing he could do for her, but he couldn't stuff the sudden urge to run to her. He got within twenty yards when the front passenger door opened and out stepped Sonny Xú. A Chief's Special in hand, he walked to the body and put a .38 caliber bullet in what was left of her head. He opened the cylinder on the revolver, removed the spent casing, and dropped it on the remains. Then glancing at Carver bobbed his head and went back to his car.

Sonny's personal touch spoke volumes to Carver. As he broke the suppressor loose, spinning it off the barrel, he thought about their disjointed conversation from the night before. He wondered when it was going to be his turn, and he holstered the pistol and slipped the suppressor in a pocket. He walked across the street, heading toward Century Park. He could hear sirens coming his way, and decided it was time to find someplace else to be.

The battery was low on the BlackBerry and he figured it was only good for one more call. As much as he wanted to have Zorro pick his sorry ass up for more medical attention from the special forces corpsman, he had a promise to keep.

Zhao answered. "Where are you?"

"I'm walking into Century Park. I need a pick-up."

"Go to the Shanghai Science & Technology Museum on the north side. I'll meet you there."

"It's too public."

"What's the matter?"

"Let's just say I'm socially unacceptable. I'll find a place to hunker down. Let me give you another number to call when you're close. You ready to copy?"

"Yes."

Ruben recited Turtle's number, twice.

"I have it. There's a building on fire in the Century Park area. Do you know about that?"

Carver would eventually have to come clean on at least some of his recent activity, but didn't want to get into it over an open line. "I can hear the sirens."

"Hmmm...what about her?"

"Pick me up. We'll talk then."

CHAPTER THIRTY-THREE
The Summation

"Good morning, Professor Parsons." As usual, the voice had an unnatural, almost metallic quality over the secure line.

"Good morning, everyone."

"How are you faring, now that you're back to work? We're pleased your abduction story with the federal authorities resolved satisfactorily."

"I'm fine, thank you, and yes, the case at the federal level as been closed with the subsequent demise of those 'responsible' for my apparent kidnapping. The amusing collateral fallout has been my sudden celebrity with the Boston community. I've had book and movie offers, and letters of support have flooded my department."

"We're happy to say your role in our plan to unwind our position in Shanghai hasn't in any way jeopardized our association." There was a pause as the voice took a breath. "On another topic. Have you had any contact with Ryan Henderson since his repatriation?"

"Not really. He sent me a rather cryptic message a few weeks ago apologizing for not reaching out to me earlier. While he did attach a photo of himself lounging on a beach somewhere, he didn't leave the door open for further contact."

"Ah yes, well, it is our understanding the Naval Criminal Investigative Service was successful in obtaining witness protection for his cooperation. Through our connections at the government level, though, it seems Mr. Henderson's services are now being utilized by the National Security Agency. We're not sure it's in The Board's best interest to pursue the matter further. We'd prefer to avoid the kind scrutiny that could be brought to bear should he fail to make it to work one morning."

"So, on to new business. Our client base for the product he provided has, for the time being, dried up. In addition, our operations in China, while not completely defunct, have required us to trim our expectations with regard to vendored resources."

The professor had no idea what the dissonant voice was referring to, but she was savvy enough to understand the explanation was leading to a new role for her. "Are you looking for his replacement?"

"Yes, but under the circumstances, we believe your responsibilities should be limited to only identification and assessment, possibly vetting. The actual recruitment process will be handled by one of your younger colleagues."

Parsons felt a slight pang of indignation. The aging process for a once attractive woman was difficult enough without it being rubbed in her face. "I understand. I'll begin immediately."

Seventh Fleet's visit to China went without incident. The country team's briefing, held in Shanghai for the Admiral's convenience, highlighted the successful culmination of U.S.-Sino cooperation in uncovering and dismantling a criminal computer intrusion operation.

Based on a number of factors detailed by the country

team, the Admiral showed tasteful restraint in not addressing the incident during his meetings with the Chinese. Apparently, there was some disgruntlement on the part of Shanghai city authorities after their own cost-benefit analysis. The damage to a luxury high-rise in an exclusive part of Pudong, along with an unexplained body count, soured their enthusiasm for the joint operation.

Ruben's name had been left out of much of the reporting that filtered back to CIA headquarters. Army MI, while pleased the culprits responsible for the death and dismemberment of one their own, had gotten the deserved comeuppance, continued to bleat for months that they could have done it better.

NCIS was happy to forgo another 2B on Ruben, considering the mileage it was getting from the Agency on Zhao's defection and the information pouring in on China's organized crime problems. Once Art Sheppard's boys showed Sonny the green, he evidently became quite garrulous. Ruben elected not to implicate the gangster in Qu's death. It may have seemed personal at the time, but Carver had no doubt that some one...some organization, had funded the execution. Professionals don't do anything for free.

The NSA was practically licking itself all over after getting Ryan and his thumb drive. Not only did that agency pinpoint all the buyers of the technology he'd pirated, the bug he planted on Helen Parsons' system provided them with front row seating at The Board meetings. It was popcorn and Jujyfruits all 'round for those sessions.

Notwithstanding a Geneva connection with the phone number Qu so graciously unassed before her inevitable end, many of the members of the secret society they identified were sacrosanct campaign contributors—to both sides of the aisle. Much of the information developed, therefore, was never revealed outside those hallowed walls on Fort Meade. No use getting lawmakers' panties in a twist over anything less than world-ending scenarios.

For Ruben, he was happy to be home playing his harp in the band, drinkin' three olive Tanqueray martinis and tellin' lies with his buddy Barry. Zhao showed up in Tokyo not long afterward to tell Feng to go fuck himself before he got pulled to the motherland for his mother's public purging.

Zhao hung around long enough to present Ruben with a couple of lost weekends before she continued east toward the west. She landed a gig at the Naval Academy teaching modern China studies. It would be almost a year before she and the near-retirement-ready special agent renewed their friends with benefits liaison

Ruben had some trouble with the Special Agent Medical Benefit Association, known as SAMBA. It initially denied coverage of his medical expenses, expressing concern the bullet holes were not somehow law enforcement related. Other than that everything was hunky dory until he got orders from headquarters. One of the suits back there thought he'd make a fabulous NCIS representative to the Counterintelligence Field Activity in Crystal City.

But that's another story...

Made in the USA
Lexington, KY
07 May 2017